FERRYMAN

FERRYMAN

CLAIRE McFALL

WALKER BOOKS

Copyright © 2017 by Claire McFall

First US paperback edition 2022
First published by Floris Books (UK) 2017

Library of Congress Catalog Card Number 2021945654
ISBN 978-1-5362-1845-9 (hardcover)
ISBN 978-1-5362-2821-2 (paperback)

22 23 24 25 26 27 TRC 10 9 8 7 6 5 4 3 2 1

Printed in Eagan, MN, USA

This book was typeset in Adobe Caslon.

Walker Books US
a division of
Candlewick Press
99 Dover Street
Somerville, Massachusetts 02144

www.walkerbooksus.com

For Charlie.

You are my ray of sunshine, my orb in the dark.

PROLOGUE

HE SAT ON THE HILLSIDE AND WAITED.

Another day, another job. Before him, rusting tracks disappeared into the depths of the tunnel mouth. In the gray gloom of the cloudy day, the light barely penetrated beyond the stone arch of the opening. His eyes never left the entrance. He was expectant but jaded.

There was no thrill of excitement or flicker of interest.

He had long since ceased to be curious. Now the only thing that mattered was completing the task. His cold, clinical eyes were lifeless.

The wind stirred, blowing frigid air around him, but he didn't feel the chill. He was focused, watchful.

Any moment now.

ONE

THE FIRST HEAVY DROPS OF RAIN ANNOUNCED THEMSELVES, tapping out a disjointed rhythm on the tin roof over the train platform. Dylan sighed and plunged her face down deeper into her thick winter jacket, trying to warm her freezing nose. She could feel her feet going numb, and she stamped her boots on the cracked concrete to get her circulation going. She glared at the slick black train tracks littered with chip bags, crumpled beer cans, and bits of broken umbrella. The train was fifteen minutes late, and she had arrived ten minutes early in her eagerness. There was nothing to do but stand, stare, and feel her body heat slowly seeping away.

As the rain began to fall more steadily, the stranger beside her tried in vain to read his newspaper, absorbed in a story about a gruesome murder spree in the West End. The roof provided feeble cover, and droplets fell thickly onto the paper, exploding and expanding the ink in a blotchy mess. Grumbling, he folded it up and stuffed it under his arm. The man glanced around, searching for a new distraction, and Dylan immediately looked away. She didn't want to have to make polite conversation.

It had not been a good day. For some reason, her alarm had failed to go off, and really it had all been downhill from there.

~~~~~

"Up! Get up! You're going to be late. Were you on your phone again last night? If you can't organize yourself, you'll find me taking a much more active role in your social life, and you won't like it!"

Her mother's voice rang out, barging in on a dream involving a handsome stranger. Her mother's screech had the ability to cut through glass, so Dylan's subconscious offered little challenge. Her mother continued to complain as she marched back down the long corridor of their apartment, but Dylan had already tuned out. She was trying to remember the dream, to hold on to some of the details for later. Walking slowly . . . a hand, warm around hers . . . the scent of foliage and damp earthiness heady in the air. Dylan smiled, feeling warmth bubble in her chest, but the chill of the morning dissolved the image before she could lock his face into her mind. Sighing, she forced her eyes open and stretched, luxuriating in the cozy warmth of her thick duvet, then squinted left toward her alarm clock.

Oh, God.

She was going to be so late. Scrambling around her room, she tried to pull together enough clean clothes to create a full school uniform. A brush through her brown shoulder-length hair created the usual frizzy mess. Bad hair life. Dylan didn't even glance at her reflection as she hid the frizz in a messy topknot. How other girls managed to create artfully styled, perfect hair was a mystery to her. Even when she made an effort to blow-dry and straighten it, two seconds outside was enough to return her unruly hair to its natural state.

Not having a shower was out of the question, but today she had to make do with a quick twirl under water that was always scalding hot, irrespective of knobs turned or buttons pushed. She scraped a rough towel against her skin and yanked on the black skirt, white shirt, and green tie that made up her uniform. In her haste, she caught a jaggy nail on her last pair of tights and ripped a huge run in them. Grinding her teeth, she lobbed the tights in the garbage and clattered, bare-legged, down the hall to the kitchen.

A glimpse in the fridge revealed nothing that could be eaten on the run. There was no time to dash into a café. She would just have to be hungry. At least she had enough money left on her school lunch card for a decent meal. It was Friday, which usually meant fish and chips—although of course there would be no salt, vinegar, or even ketchup. *Not in our health-freak school,* Dylan thought, rolling her eyes.

"Have you packed?"

Dylan turned to see her mother, Joan, standing in the kitchen doorway. She was already dressed in her uniform for a grueling twelve-hour shift at the hospital.

"No. I'll do it after school. The train isn't till five thirty—there's loads of time." *Interfering as usual,* Dylan thought. Sometimes it seemed like her mum just couldn't help herself.

Joan's eyebrows rose in disapproval, deepening the wrinkles that ran across her forehead despite the expensive lotions and potions she applied each night.

"You are so disorganized," she began. "You should have had it done last night instead of messaging with your friends—"

"All right!" Dylan snapped. "I'll figure it out."

Joan looked as if she had many more things to say, but instead she simply shook her head and turned away. It was easy to guess the reason for her mother's bad mood. She highly disapproved of Dylan's weekend trip to see her father, the man she had once promised to have and to hold until death—or in this case, life— did them part.

Anticipating that her mother had not given up on the matter, Dylan threw her shoes and jacket on, grabbed her bag, and stomped down the hall, trying to ignore the rumbling that was already coming from her stomach. She paused at the door to yell a compulsory goodbye—met with silence—before traipsing out into the rain.

By the time she had walked for fifteen minutes, her cheap winter jacket had given up the fight against the drizzle and she could feel the wet leaking into her shirt.

A sudden, hideous thought made her stop in her tracks, despite the downpour. White shirt. Rain. Wet shirt. She remembered rooting through her underwear drawer for a clean bra and coming up with only one—dark blue.

She hissed a word between her clenched teeth that would have gotten her grounded if her mother had been in the vicinity. There was no time to run home. In fact, despite rushing, she was still going to be late.

Terrific.

Head down, she splashed along the high street, past the thrift stores, boarded-up failed dreams, cafés with cheap furniture and extortionate-priced coffee, and the obligatory liquor shop or two. There was no point trying to avoid the puddles. Her feet were already soaked through; they were now the least of her worries. For a moment she considered crossing the road and hiding in the park until her mother left for work, but she knew herself better than that. She didn't have the nerve. Muttering a stream of complaints interspersed with obscenities, she turned off the high street and through the gates of Kaithshall Academy.

The school was three floors of uniform boxes in various stages of disrepair, and Dylan was sure it had been designed to curb enthusiasm, creativity, and, most importantly, spirit. Homeroom was in Miss Parson's room on the top floor—another tired-looking cube that the teacher had tried to brighten with posters and wall displays. Strangely, her efforts only made the space more depressing—especially now, filled with thirty clones chattering about inconsequential rubbish as if it were life-altering drama.

Dylan's tardy entrance earned her a pointed look. As soon as she sat down, the teacher's high-pitched whine shot over the classroom din. "Dylan. Jacket."

Amazing how students have to be polite to teachers, but it doesn't work in reverse, Dylan thought.

"I'm cold. It's freezing outside." *And in here,* she thought, but didn't add.

"I don't care. Jacket."

Dylan considered resisting but knew it would be futile. Besides, any further complaints would draw attention to her, something she tried to avoid as a rule. Sighing, she battled with the cheap zipper and shrugged the jacket off. A glance down confirmed her fears. The sodden blouse was transparent, and under it her dark blue bra seemed to glare like a beacon. She hunched down in her chair and wondered how long she could hope to remain invisible.

The answer was about forty-five seconds.

It began with the girls, of course. Snickers erupted somewhere to her left.

"What? What is it?" The harsh, snide voice of David "Dove" MacMillan cut across the titters.

Dylan looked resolutely at the front board, but in her mind's eye she constructed a crystal-clear image of Cheryl and her cronies smiling gleefully as they pointed manicured nails in her direction. Dove was so dense it would take him another few seconds to realize they were even pointing at her, and he would never work out the joke without a sledgehammer-size clue. Cheryl would provide that service, mouthing, *"Check out the bra,"* or perhaps a suitably obscene hand gesture.

"Ha!" Again, another mental image of the spittle and soda that would be soaring onto the desk now that Dove had finally gotten the picture. "Ha, Dylan, I can see your tits!"

Dylan cringed and slunk a little farther down in the chair as titters elevated to open hilarity. Even the teacher was laughing. Cow.

Ever since Katie had left, no one at this school even gave the impression of being on the same planet as Dylan, never mind the same species. They were sheep, all of them. The boys wore joggers, listened to hip-hop, and spent their evenings down at the skate park. Not skating, just vandalizing things and drinking any booze they'd managed to get their hands on. The girls were worse. Five layers of makeup and fake tan, and catty, screeching voices picked up from reality shows. They couldn't seem to have a conversation unless it involved tanning, terrible music, or—most disturbing of all—which of the jogger-wearing players was the most appealing.

Of course there were other outsiders, but they tended to be loners, too, just trying to get by and avoid being targeted by the mob.

Katie had been her one companion. They'd known each other since elementary school and spent their time quietly mocking their fellow classmates and plotting a way out of the place. Last year all that had changed. Katie's parents had decided that, since they despised each other, the time had come to split. They'd hated each other as long as Dylan had known Katie, so she couldn't understand why it had to happen now. But Katie had been forced to choose between living with her alcoholic father in Glasgow or moving away with her obsessive mother. Dylan hadn't envied her choices. Caught between a rock and a hard place, Katie had chosen to go with her mother, to a tiny village in Lanarkshire called Lesmahagow. It might as well have been on the other side of the world. Since she'd left, life had been a lot harder and a lot lonelier. Dylan missed her friend. Katie wouldn't have laughed at the see-through shirt for a start.

Although the shirt had dried out by halfway through first period, the damage was done. Everywhere she went, boys from her year—and some she didn't even know—followed her and laughed, making sarcastic comments and attempting to ping her bra strap (just to check that it was still there). By lunchtime, Dylan had had enough. She was sick of boys making fun of her, sick of girls with snide looks, and sick of teachers who pretended to not notice anything. When the bell rang at the end of fourth period, she passed by the cafeteria, ignoring the scent of fish and chips and the pangs from her stomach, and went out of the school gates with the crowd heading to the pizza place or the bakery. When she came to the end of the line of shops, she just kept on walking.

Her heart beat double time as she reached streets that the students never ventured into at lunchtime—unless, of course, they were planning to do exactly what she was doing. She'd never skipped school before, had never even considered it, really. She was the shy, serious student. Quiet, diligent, but not particularly clever. All of her successes had to be earned through hard work, which was easy when you had no friends. But today she was becoming a rebel. When fifth-period attendance was taken, there would be an *A* for *absent* beside her name. Even if they phoned the hospital, there would be nothing her mother could do about it. By the time her shift finished, Dylan would be halfway to Aberdeen. Dylan put the unease she felt out of her mind. Today she had more important things to think about.

At home, the first thing she did was yank off the school shirt that had caused all of today's embarrassment. She dumped it in the laundry basket and stood in front of her closet, examining her clothes. What was an appropriate thing to wear when meeting your dad for the first time in ten years? It had to make the right initial impression. Nothing revealing that would make her look like she was out partying; nothing with cartoon characters to make her look childish. Something pretty and grown-up. She stared. She pulled clothes aside to see what was hidden at the back. Finally she was forced to admit that she did not own anything fitting that description. She grabbed a faded blue T-shirt with the name of her favorite band emblazoned across the front and topped this with a gray zip-up hoodie. She kicked off her school skirt and replaced it with comfortable jeans and put on some old Nike sneakers. She scrutinized herself in the full-length mirror in her mum's bedroom. It would have to do.

Next she grabbed an old bag from the hall cupboard and dumped it on her bed. She shoved in another pair of jeans and a couple of T-shirts, some underwear, and then her black school shoes and a green skirt, just in case he wanted to take her out to dinner or something. Her phone and wallet she stuffed into the front pocket along with some toiletries.

Then she grabbed one last, important item from the bed. Egbert, her teddy. He was graying with age and fairly battered, with one eye missing and a slight tear along the back seam leaking stuffing. He'd never win a beauty contest, but he'd been with her since she was a baby and having him nearby made her feel safe and comforted. She wanted to take him, but her dad might think she was childish. She hugged the teddy to her chest, undecided, then put him on the bed and looked at him. He seemed to stare back, unwanted and abandoned. Instantly feeling guilty, Dylan grabbed him and placed him gently on top of her clothes. She zipped up the bag, then unzipped it and chucked him back out. This time he fell facedown and couldn't gaze forlornly at her with his one accusing eye. She zipped up the bag again and walked determinedly out of the room.

Exactly twenty seconds later, she dashed back in and grabbed him.

"Sorry, Egbert," she whispered, kissing him quickly before stuffing him into the bag as she ran out the door.

If she hurried, she might be able to catch the earlier train and surprise her dad. This thought carried her down the stairs and along the damp street. There was a café en route to the train station; maybe she could duck in and grab a burger to sustain her till dinner. Dylan picked up the pace, mouth already watering in anticipation, then as she passed the high metal gates of the park, something stopped her dead. She stared through the bars at the melee of greenery, not quite sure what she was looking at.

Déjà vu.

She squinted, trying to work out what had triggered the feeling. A glimpse of tousled blond peeked out beneath the branches of a wide oak. For a second, Dylan had a flash of that same halo of hair, wrapped round a face, featureless but for eyes of shocking cobalt blue.

The dream.

She sucked in a breath, her pulse suddenly pounding, but a cackle of boyish laughter shattered the illusion. The head turned to reveal a smirking mouth pouting out a stream of smoke, cigarette dangling from his lips. Dove MacMillan, with his pals. Dylan wrinkled her nose in disgust and stepped back before he could see her.

Shaking her head to chase the last tendrils of the dream away, she crossed the road, eyes fixed on the hand-painted sign above the greasy-spoon café.

TWO

"IT'S OUTRAGEOUS. SCANDALOUS." THE STRANGER ON THE platform had clearly decided that, since reading the paper in the dripping rain was out, he would concentrate on the next best thing: complaining.

Dylan glanced at him dubiously. She did not really want to get into a discussion with this tweed-covered, middle-aged man and end up being drawn into awkward conversation all the way to Aberdeen. She shrugged, a gesture almost lost under her heavy parka.

He carried on, unfazed by her lack of enthusiasm. "I mean, the prices they're charging, you'd think they could be on time. But oh no. Outrageous. I've been waiting here for twenty minutes, and you know when it comes in there won't be a seat left. Terrible service."

Dylan looked around. The platform was not crowded enough for her to melt away and disappear.

The tweed man turned to look at her. "Don't you think?"

Forced into a direct response, Dylan tried to be as noncommittal as possible. "Mmmm."

He seemed to take this as an invitation to continue the diatribe. "Better when it was National Rail. Knew where you were with them. Good, honest men working the trains then. It's all gone downhill now. Run by a bunch of charlatans. Outrageous."

Where is *the train*, Dylan thought, desperate to be relieved of this social charade. And then there it was, rolling in like a knight in rusting armor. One glimmer of hope in a day full of embarrassment and torment.

She reached down for the bag at her feet. Like most things she owned, it was faded and showing signs of wear and tear. As she heaved the bag over her shoulder, a faint ripping sound made her grimace. It would be in keeping with the pattern of today for the seam to tear open and scatter her underwear across the station. Mercifully it held, and Dylan shuffled forward with the rest of the weary passengers as the train coasted slowly to a standstill. She quickly eyed the direction in which the tweed stranger was headed and dashed toward a different door.

Once in the carriage, she glanced left and right, trying to identify the red flags—drunks, weirdos, people who wanted to tell you their life stories and philosophize on the meaning of life—who seemed inexplicably drawn to her whenever she took public transportation. She was anxious to avoid them today when she had so many other things on her mind. She scanned the carriage for free seats: one next to a mother with her screaming baby, its red face puckered up and angry. Another opposite a pair of drunken teenagers in blue Rangers tops. They were drinking from an inexpertly hidden bottle of what looked suspiciously like beer and singing loudly and very out of tune.

The only other option was in the middle of the carriage, squashed in beside a large woman who had arranged her shopping bags on the seats beside and across from her in a manner that made it blatantly clear she did not welcome company. However, glaring or not, she was the most appealing option.

"Excuse me," Dylan muttered, shuffling over to her.

The woman sighed loudly, her displeasure obvious, but she moved the bags, nonetheless. After shrugging out of her jacket, extracting her phone and headphones, and chucking her bag up onto the overhead shelf, Dylan settled herself down. She closed her eyes, stuck her headphones in her ears, and turned the volume up high, letting the heavy drumbeats of her favorite band drown out the world around her. She imagined the rude lady glaring at her and her awful music, and the image made her smile. Too quiet for Dylan to hear, the train groaned and strained, picking up speed as it raced on toward Aberdeen.

Keeping her eyes closed, she thought about the coming weekend. Nerves and excitement fought for control of the butterflies in her stomach as she contemplated stepping off the train and searching for the man who was all but a stranger to her. It had taken months of persuasion and wheedling for her mother to relinquish the phone number of one James Miller, her father. Dylan remembered how her hand had shaken as she'd called, hung up, called again, and then hung up. What if he didn't want to talk to her? What if he had his own family now? What if, worst of all, he turned out to be a huge disappointment? A drunk or a criminal? Her mother had been unable to give her any more details. They didn't talk, ever. He'd left when she'd asked him to and never bothered either of them again, like she'd asked him to. Dylan had been five years old at the time, and in the decade that had passed, his face had become less than a memory.

After two days of inner turmoil, Dylan had called in the middle of the day, finding a quiet spot on the school grounds that wasn't already claimed by the smokers, amorous couples, or gangs. Her hope was that he'd be busy and no one would answer. It worked. After six heart-stopping rings, the voice mail kicked in, and she suddenly realized that she hadn't thought about what to say. Panicking, she left a hesitant, rambling message.

"Hi, this is for James Miller. It's Dylan. Your daughter." What else to say? "I, um . . . I got your number from Mum. I mean, Joan. I thought, maybe, we could meet up, maybe. And talk. If you want to." Breathe. "This is my number . . ."

As soon as she'd hung up, she'd cringed. What was wrong with her? She couldn't believe that she hadn't planned a message. She'd sounded like a bumbling mess.

Well, there was nothing to do but wait. And she had waited. All afternoon she'd felt sick to her stomach. Biology and English passed in a blur. At home she'd numbly watched TV, not even changing the channel when the infomercials came on. What if he didn't call? Would he have listened to the message yet? What if he never got the message? Dylan had imagined a female hand answering the phone and listening, then slowly pressing a painted red fingernail on the delete button. Too scared to call again, she'd had no choice but to cross her fingers and stay within easy reach of her phone.

It took a whole day, a day that felt like a month to Dylan, but he did call. At four o'clock, just as she was sloshing home through yet another rainy day of school with wet socks and increasingly wet shoulders, her phone vibrated in her pocket. This was it. Her heart seemed to stop beating as she yanked the phone out of her pocket. A quick glance at the caller ID confirmed it: it was an Aberdeen area code. Pressing her thumb on the screen, she put it to her ear.

"Hello?" Her voice sounded rough and strangled. She tried to clear her throat quietly.

"Dylan? Dylan, this is James. Miller. I mean, your dad."

Silence. *Say something, Dylan,* she thought. *Say something, Dad.* The silence hung between them, but in the stress of the moment, it sounded like screaming.

"Listen." His voice broke through it, melted it away. "I'm so glad you called. I've wanted to get in touch with you for so long. We've got a lot to catch up on."

Dylan closed her eyes and smiled. She took a deep breath and started to speak.

It had been so easy after that. Talking to him felt comfortable, like she'd known him forever. They'd talked until Dylan's phone ran out of charge. He wanted to know everything about her, her school, hobbies, who she hung out with, what movies were her favorites and what books she liked to read. Boys—though there wasn't much to say there, not from the selection on offer at Kaithshall. In return, he told her about his life in Aberdeen, where he lived with Anna, his dog. No wife, no kids. No complications. And he wanted her to visit.

That had been exactly one week ago. For seven days, Dylan had been wrestling with her nerves and excitement about meeting him, and trying not to fight with her mother, who made no secret of the fact that she disapproved of Dylan connecting with her father. Dylan hadn't even spoken to Katie about it yet. Sitting on the train, a pang of nerves made her start a text:

Katie! How are things? New school still suck?

It didn't take long for Katie to reply.

New school, same morons. These ones are just country morons.

So glad that this time next year we'll be starting college, I can't wait to get out of here!

Howz things at glorious Kaithshall?

Sucks. Got some news though!

Ooh, do tell!

I called my dad.

Dylan hit the send button and waited. Her heart was racing. She wanted Katie to say something nice, wanted someone to tell her that she was doing the right thing. There was a pause that seemed to last forever before the little icon popped up that meant she was writing back:

. . .

So . . . how did that go?

A cautious response. Her friend didn't want to stick her foot in it.

Actually, great! He wants to meet me! He sounded really nice on the phone.

Don't know why my mum hates him so much.

Who knows? Parents are weird. Look at mine!

So is he coming down to see you, then?

Nope, I'm going there. Right now.

What?! That was fast! You scared?

No, I'm super excited. What is there to be scared about?

The reply came through instantly.

Liar. You're shitting yourself!

Dylan laughed out loud, then clamped her hand over her mouth when she saw the woman next to her glaring even more fiercely. Typical Katie; she always saw straight through her pretense.

OK, maybe a bit. Trying not to think about it too much . . .

Kind of worried I might chicken out if I actually think about what I'm doing!

It'll be cool. You need to meet him anyway. And if your mum really does hate him, then keeping them in separate cities might be a good idea!

How you getting there? Train?

Yeah, he's bought me a ticket. He says he wants to make up for ten years of lost time.

Dylan held that train ticket in her hand. She was supposed to text her dad to let him know she was on her way.

She opened up a new text.

> Dad, on train. Got an earlier one. Can't wait to meet you ☺ Dylan.

Just as she hit the send button, the window beside her went black. *Fabulous*, she thought, *a tunnel*. The phone—an expensive Christmas gift that her mother had paid for through several extra shifts at work—scrolled one word across the screen:

Sending . . .

It rolled through three times before the alert popped up:

Message failed.

"Dammit," Dylan muttered. Irrationally, she tried holding the phone up above her head, knowing it was useless inside the tunnel; no signal was going to get through that much rock.

She was poised like that, arm in the air like a mini Statue of Liberty, when it happened. Light vanished, sound exploded, and the world ended.

THREE

SILENCE.

There should be screams, cries, something, thought Dylan.

But there was only silence.

The darkness was so heavy, it was like a thick blanket smothering her. For one panic-stricken moment, she thought she was blind. Frantic, she tried waving her hand in front of her face. She saw nothing but managed to poke herself in the eye. The shock of the jabbing pain made her think for a moment. They had been in a tunnel—that was why it was dark.

Her eyes couldn't make out even the tiniest pinprick of light. She tried to push herself up from where she'd been thrown sideways onto the seat next to her, but something was pinning her down. Twisting to the right, she managed to pull herself down onto the floor between the seats. Her left hand landed on something warm and sticky. She yanked her hand away and quickly wiped it on her jeans, trying not to think about what the stickiness might have been. Her right hand curled around a small object— the phone that had been in her hand when the world had turned upside down. Eagerly she picked it up and flipped it over. Relief rolled through her, but it was quickly replaced by disappointment. The screen was blank. Her fingers jabbed at it, hope fading fast. It was dead.

Crawling into the aisle, Dylan got her feet beneath her and stood up, smacking her head hard on something.

"Shit! Ow!" She ducked back down. Her hand reached for her temple, which was throbbing ferociously. It didn't seem to be bleeding, but it hurt like hell. Carefully this time, she straightened up again, using her hands to guide her head to a safe place. It was so dark, she couldn't even see what she'd bumped into.

"Hello?" she called timidly. There was no answering voice, no rustling sounds of other passengers moving about. The carriage had been packed—where the hell was everyone? The pool of liquid on the floor by her seat flashed back into her mind, but she pushed it away.

"Hello?" Stronger this time. "Can anybody hear me? Hello!" Her voice cracked a little on the final word as panic began to rear its ugly head. Her breathing quickened, and she struggled to think through the fear that gripped her. The darkness was claustrophobic, and she clutched at her throat, as if something were strangling her. She was all alone, surrounded by . . .

She didn't want to think about it. All she knew was that she couldn't bear to stay in the carriage a second longer.

Mindlessly she surged forward, tripping and hauling herself over objects that lay in her way. Her foot landed on something soft and slick. The soles of her sneakers found no traction and slipped. Horrified, she tried to jerk her leg up and away from the suspiciously spongy object, but her other shoe couldn't find a safe and level place to land. As if in slow motion, she felt herself falling toward the floor and the fearsome things that lurked there.

No!

Gasping, she threw her hands down to protect herself as she tumbled down. Her flailing arms caught a pole, and her fingers tightened around it, bringing her to an abrupt stop that strained the muscles in her shoulder. Her momentum carried her forward, and she jarred her neck painfully against the cold metal.

Ignoring the throbbing in her neck, Dylan held on to the pole with both hands, feeling like it was her grip on reality. *Pole,* her brain told her. *The pole is next to the door. You must be next to the door.* Relief flooded her system and allowed her to think a little more clearly. That's why she was alone. Everyone else must have made their way out already, and they'd missed her because she'd been buried under that stupid woman's bags. *I should have sat next to the Rangers fans,* she thought, laughing weakly.

Not trusting her feet in the darkness, she reached along the partition connected to the pole, expecting to come into contact with the folded open door. Her fingertips stretched out but found nothing. Shuffling a little farther forward, she touched the door at last. It was shut.

That's weird, she thought. Everyone else must have gone out the door at the other end. That was just typical of her luck. Her logical reasoning calmed her and helped her think clearly. Unwilling to travel back across the carriage and risk stepping on some more worryingly soft things, she felt around for the button to open the door. Her fingers found its raised edges and pushed, but it remained closed.

"Dammit," she murmured. The electricity had probably been

cut off during the crash. She looked back over her shoulder, a pointless exercise since she could see nothing. Her imagination filled in the blanks, packing the route through the carriage with upturned seats, luggage, broken glass from the windows, and squishy, slick things that were solidifying in her mind's eye into limbs and torsos. No, she was not going back that way.

Putting both hands flat against the train doors, she pushed hard. Though the doors held, she felt them buckle a little. With enough effort, she thought she could force them open. She stepped back, took a deep breath, and launched forward, kicking the door as hard as she could with the bottom of her left foot. The bang sounded very loud in the confined space, ringing a little in her ears, and her knee and ankle twinged painfully. Nonetheless, she could feel fresh air against her face and that gave her hope. Her hands confirmed it: one section of the door had been forced off its runner. If she could do the same to the other door, there would be a gap big enough for her to squeeze through. She took two steps back this time and threw herself against the door with as much strength as she could muster. The door screeched as metal rasped against metal, before finally giving way.

The gap was not large, but luckily neither was Dylan. Turning sideways, she squeezed her body through the opening. There was a ripping sound as her zipper caught between her body and the door, but suddenly she was free and falling toward the track. She felt a moment of fear thrill through her, but her sneakers crunched on gravel after just a short distance, and the feeling of claustrophobia lifted like a chain that had been cut free from around her throat.

The tunnel was as dark as the train. The crash must have happened right at the center. Dylan looked first one way, then the other. It didn't help. She could see no light, and apart from the gentle sound of air rushing through the enclosed space, there was silence.

Left or right? she thought. Sighing, she turned right and trudged forward. It had to lead somewhere.

Without a light to guide her, she tripped often, so it was slow progress. Every now and then, something by her feet would scurry quickly away. She hoped there weren't rats in the tunnel. Anything smaller than a rabbit caused outbursts of irrational fear in her. A spider in the bathroom could trigger half an hour of hysteria until her mum was persuaded to come and rescue her. If anything ran over her shoe in here, she knew her flight instinct would kick in. In the dark, though, with the uneven ground, she'd probably fall flat on her face.

The tunnel went on and on. She was on the verge of turning back and trying the other way when she saw what she thought was a dot of light ahead. Hoping for a way out, or a rescuer equipped with a flashlight, she stumbled faster, desperate to be outside in the brightness again. It took a long time, but slowly the dot turned into an arch. Beyond it she could only see a little daylight, but that was enough.

When at last she exited the tunnel, it was raining softly, and she laughed with delight as she turned her face up to the gentle shower. The dark of the tunnel had made her feel dirty, and the misty droplets felt like they were cleansing some of the horrors away. Taking a deep breath, she put her hands on her hips and surveyed her surroundings.

The landscape was empty except for the train track, which wound forward across a wild backdrop. She had clearly left

Glasgow far behind. The horizon was ringed with large, imposing hills. Low-slung clouds blurred their edges as the mist skimmed the highest peaks. It was a muted palette of colors, purple heather fighting for space amongst great swaths of brown bracken. Small copses of trees grew in irregular patterns on the lower gradients of hills dark-hued with evergreen pines. The slopes closer to the tunnel were gentler, undulating mounds coated with long grass. There was not a town or a road in sight, not even an isolated farmhouse. Dylan bit her lip as she studied the scene. It was untamed and unfriendly-looking.

She had expected to see a melee of police cars and ambulances parked at random angles in their haste to get to the scene. There should have been hordes of men and women in brightly colored uniforms ready to rush forward and comfort her, check her for injuries, and ask her questions. The area just outside the tunnel should have been littered with groups of survivors, ashen-faced and huddled in blankets to keep out the cutting wind. In reality, there were none of these things. Her face fell into a mask of confusion and unease. Where was everybody?

Turning round, she looked into the black mouth of the tunnel. There was no other explanation: she must have gone the wrong way. They must all be at the other end. Tears of frustration and exhaustion sprang up in her eyes. The thought of going back into the darkness, of having to walk back past the train filled with the limp, lifeless bodies of the less fortunate, was excruciating. But there was no going round it. Hacked out from the base of a massive line of hills, the bracken-covered ground rose up on either side like a sheer cliff face.

She looked up toward the heavens, as if pleading with God to change things, but all she saw were the steely gray clouds ambling across the sky. With a quiet sob, she turned back to the bleak landscape before her, desperate for some sign of civilization that would save her from having to return to the dark tunnel. Holding her hand to her forehead to protect her eyes from the wind and the rain, she scanned the horizon. And that was when she saw him.

FOUR

HE WAS SITTING ON A HILL TO THE LEFT OF THE TUNNEL entrance, his hands wrapped around his knees, and he was staring at her. From this far away, all she could tell was that he was a boy, probably a teenager, with sandy hair that was being tossed around by the wind. He didn't stand or even smile when he saw her looking at him, just continued to stare.

There was something odd about the way he sat there, a solitary figure in this isolated place. Dylan couldn't imagine how he had come to be there, unless he'd been on the train as well. She waved at him, glad to have someone to share this horror with, but he didn't wave back. She thought she saw him sit up a little straighter, but he was so far away it was hard to tell.

Keeping her eyes firmly on him, just in case he disappeared, she slipped and slid down the gravel bank of the train tracks and hopped over a little ditch filled with water and weeds. There was a barbed-wire fence separating the tracks from the open country-side. Dylan gingerly grabbed the top wire between two of the twisted metal knots and pulled it downward as hard as she could.

It dropped just low enough for her to awkwardly swing her legs over. She caught her foot as she pulled her second leg over and almost fell, but she managed to cling on to the wire and keep her balance. The barbs cut into her palm, piercing the skin and causing little droplets of blood to ooze through. She examined her hand briefly before rubbing it against her leg. A dark stain on her jeans made her take a second look. There was a large red patch on the outside of her thigh. She stared at it for a moment before remembering wiping the sticky stuff from the carriage floor off her hands. Realization made her blanch, and her stomach heaved slightly.

Shaking her head to rid herself of the sick images that were swirling in her brain, she turned from the fence and fixed her eyes back on her target. He was seated on the slope about fifty yards above her. From this distance she could see his face, and so she smiled in greeting.

He didn't respond.

Slightly abashed by this frosty reception, Dylan stared at the ground as she made her way up the hill toward him. It was a hard climb, and before long she was panting. The hillside was steep, and the long grass was wet and difficult to wade through. Looking down, concentrating on her feet, gave her an excuse not to make eye contact—not until she had to.

WITH COLD EYES, THE BOY ON THE HILL APPRAISED THE GIRL approaching him. He had been watching her since she exited the tunnel, emerging from the dark like a frightened rabbit from a burrow. Rather than shouting to get her attention, he had simply waited for her to see him. At one point he had been concerned that she would head back into the tunnel, and he had considered calling out, but she had changed her mind, so he'd contented himself with sitting silently. She would notice him.

He was right. She spotted him, and he saw the relief pool in her eyes as she waved energetically. He did not wave back. He watched her face falter slightly, but then she approached him. She moved clumsily, catching herself on the barbed-wire fence and tripping on clumps of wet grass. When she was close enough to read his expression, he turned his face away, listening to the sound of her drawing nearer.

Contact made.

AT LAST DYLAN REACHED WHERE HE SAT AND WAS ABLE TO get a much better look at him. Her guess at his age had been spot-on; he couldn't have been more than a year older than her, if that. He was wearing jeans, sneakers, and a warm-looking navy sweatshirt with the word *Broncos* written across it in flowing orange letters. Curled up as he was, it was hard to guess at his size, but he didn't look small or weedy. He was quite tanned, with a line of freckles marching across his nose. His face was set in a hard, disinterested mask, and as soon as Dylan got closer to him, he'd begun to stare off into the desolate landscape. Even when she stood right in front of him, he didn't change his expression or the direction of his stare. It was very disconcerting, and Dylan fidgeted where she stood, unsure of what to say.

"Hi, I'm Dylan," she mumbled at last, looking down at the ground. Waiting for a response, she shifted her weight from one foot to the other and stared off in the same direction, wondering what he was looking at.

"Tristan," he eventually replied, glancing at her briefly and then looking away again.

Relieved that he had at least answered, Dylan made another stab at conversation. "I guess you were on the train, too. I'm so glad I'm not the only one here! I must have passed out in the carriage, and when I woke up I was on my own." She said all this very fast, nervous about his frosty welcome. "All of the other passengers had already gotten out, and apparently nobody had noticed me there. There was this horrible woman with all these bags and stuff—I got stuck under them. When I got out, I couldn't tell which way everybody had gone, but we must have come out the wrong side of the tunnel. I bet the firemen and police and everybody else are on the other side."

"Train?" He turned toward her, and she got her first look into his eyes. They were icy blue and cold. Cobalt. She felt like they could freeze her blood if they were angry, but just now they were merely curious. They appraised her for half a second before flickering to the tunnel mouth. "Right. The train."

She looked at him expectantly, but he didn't seem inclined to say anything else. Biting her lip, she cursed her luck that the only other person here was a teenage boy. An adult would've known what to do. Also, although she hated to admit it, boys like this made her nervous. They seemed so cool and confident, and she always ended up getting tongue-tied and feeling like a total freak.

"Maybe we should walk back through the tunnel?" she suggested. It didn't seem like such an awful proposition with someone else. Then they could meet up with all the other passengers and the emergency services, and she might still be able to salvage her weekend with her dad.

The boy turned the force of his gaze back on her, and she had to stop herself from taking an involuntary step backward. His eyes were magnetic, and they seemed to see through to her very core. Dylan felt exposed, almost naked, under his stare. Unconsciously, she folded her arms across her chest.

"No, we can't get through there." His voice was disinterested, as if he wasn't worried at all about their current predicament. As if he could quite happily sit on this hillside forever.

Well, Dylan thought, *I can't.*

After staring at her for another long moment, the boy went back to glaring at the hills. Dylan bit her bottom lip as she tried to think of something else to say.

"Do you have a phone, then, so we can call someone, like the police or something? My phone died in the crash. And I should probably call my mum; when she hears what's happened she'll freak. She's very overprotective, and she'll want to know I'm OK so that she can say, 'I told you so' . . ." Dylan trailed off.

This time he didn't even look at her. "Phones don't work out here."

"Oh." She was getting annoyed now. They were stuck here, on the wrong side of the tunnel, with no adults and no way to contact people, and he was being no help at all. However, he *was* the only person here. "Well, what should we do, then?"

Instead of answering her, he suddenly stood up. Upright, he towered above her, much taller than she would have guessed. He looked down at her, a half smirk playing on his lips, and started to walk away.

Dylan's mouth opened and closed a few times, but no sound

came out. She was motionless and silent, transfixed by this strange boy. Was he just going to leave her here? She got her answer quickly. He went about ten feet, then stopped, turned, and looked back at her.

"You coming?"

"Coming where?" Dylan asked, reluctant to leave the site of the train crash. Surely staying here was the most sensible thing to do? How would anybody find them if they went wandering off? Besides, how did he know where he was going? It was already late afternoon, and it would be dark soon. The wind was getting up, and it was cold; she didn't want to get lost and have to spend the night roughing it.

But his self-assurance had her doubting herself. He seemed to see the indecision in her face. He gave her a patronizing look, his voice dripping with superiority. "Well, I'm not just going to sit and wait. You can stay here if you want."

He watched that comment sink in, gauging her reaction.

Dylan's eyes widened in fear at the thought of being left alone, waiting. What if night fell and nobody came?

"I think we should both stay here," she began, but he was already shaking his head.

Looking as if it was extremely inconvenient, he walked back over and stared at her, so close she could feel his breath on her face. Dylan looked into his eyes and felt her surroundings fade away. His gaze was compelling—she couldn't have looked away if she'd wanted to.

"Come with me," he commanded, his tone leaving no room for negotiation. It was an order, and he expected her to comply.

Her mind strangely blank, it did not occur to Dylan to disobey. Nodding numbly, she stumbled forward toward him.

The boy, Tristan, didn't even wait for her to catch up before he was off again, striding up the hill, away from the tunnel.

HE HAD BEEN SURPRISED AT HER WILLFULNESS; THERE WAS inner strength in this one. Still, one way or another, she would follow him.

FIVE

"WAIT, STOP! WHERE THE HELL ARE WE GOING?" DYLAN HUFFED to a standstill and cemented her feet to the ground, folding her arms across her chest. She'd been blindly following him, but they had been marching for twenty minutes in total silence now, going in who knew which direction, and he hadn't said a word since his curt "Come with me." All of the questions, all of the reasons for staying at the tunnel mouth that had inexplicably vanished from her head when he'd ordered her to follow had now returned with full force.

He continued on for a few strides before turning and looking at her with his eyebrows raised. "What?"

"What?" Dylan's voice rose an octave with incredulity. "We've just come out of a train crash where everybody else seems to have disappeared. I have no idea where we are, and you are marching us halfway across the middle of nowhere, away from the place where they are going to be looking for us!"

"Who do you imagine is looking for us?" That arrogant half smirk snuck back onto his lips.

Dylan frowned for a moment, confused by the strange question, before launching into her argument once more. "Well, the police for one. My *parents*." Dylan felt a little thrill at being able to say that in the plural for the first time. "When the train doesn't arrive at the next station, don't you think the train company might wonder where it is?"

She raised her eyebrows here, secretly pleased with the strength of her line of reasoning, and waited for him to respond.

He laughed. It was almost a musical sound, but underpinned with a hint of mockery. His reaction confounded and infuriated her again. Dylan pursed her lips, waiting for the punch line, but it didn't come. Instead he smiled. It changed his entire face, warming his natural coldness. But there was still something not quite right about it. It looked sincere, but it didn't stretch to his eyes. They remained icy and aloof.

He walked over to Dylan and ducked down slightly so that he could look into her eyes, shocking blue into startled green. His closeness made her a little uncomfortable, but she stood her ground.

"If I told you that you weren't where you thought you were, what would you say?" he asked.

"What?" Dylan was totally confused, and not a little bit intimidated. His arrogance was infuriating: making fun of her at every turn and coming out with nonsense statements like that. What could be the point of his question except to bamboozle her and make her doubt herself?

"Never mind," he chuckled, reading her expression. "Turn around. Could you find the tunnel again if you had to?"

Dylan looked over her shoulder. The landscape was empty and unfamiliar. Everything looked the same. Stark, windswept hills as far as the eye could see, dipping down into gullied valleys where vegetation reveled in the shelter from the constant gales. There was no sign of the tunnel entrance or even the train tracks. That was weird; they hadn't gone very far. She felt a tightening in her chest as she realized that she had no idea what direction they had come from, that she would be completely lost if Tristan left her now.

"No," she whispered, grasping how much trust she had put in this unfriendly stranger.

Tristan laughed as he watched the realization trickle across her face. "Then I guess you're stuck with me." He began marching again.

Dylan stood motionless, torn, but as the distance began to open up between them, her feet seemed to act of their own accord, afraid of being left alone. She scrambled over a small cluster of boulders and jogged through some short grass until she had bridged the gap. He continued to stride out, his long legs and loping gait allowing him to outstrip her easily.

"Do you even know where you're going?" she panted as she hurried to keep up.

Again that irritating smirk. "Yes."

"How?" Matching his pace was reducing her to one-syllable questions.

"Because I've been here before," he replied. He seemed supremely confident and had taken control of the situation—and of her—completely. Though she hated to admit it, she had little option but to trust him.

"Will you *please* slow down?" Dylan's legs, unused to exercise, were already burning.

"Oh, sorry," Tristan said, and despite his frostiness, he seemed to mean it. He slowed to a more moderate speed.

Dylan gratefully matched his pace and continued her questioning. "Is there a town or something nearby? Somewhere where the phones *do* work?"

"There's nothing in this wasteland," Tristan murmured.

Dylan bit her lip, concerned. The later it got, the more worried she knew her mum would be. One of the conditions of Joan allowing her to make the trip had been that she would call as soon as she arrived and met her dad. She wasn't sure how much time had passed—she'd clearly been unconscious for a bit on the train—but she was sure that her mum would have heard about the crash. If she phoned Dylan's mobile and got the voice mail, she'd start to worry.

She also imagined her dad waiting at the station for her. Maybe he'd think she hadn't wanted to come, that she'd chickened out. That would be awful. No, he would hear that a train had crashed, which would be worse. Still, she needed to let both her parents know she was OK. She supposed by the time all of this got sorted out, it would be too late to head up to Aberdeen this weekend. Hopefully her dad would be willing to buy her another ticket. *Although, really, the train company should give me one for free at least,* she thought. Joan would be even less willing to let her go after this, though. Maybe her dad could come down to Glasgow instead.

But then something else made her pause. If there was no town nearby and it was already late afternoon, what were they going to do once it got dark?

She gazed around her, hunting for signs of civilization. Tristan was right: nothing.

"You said you'd been here before," she began. By now they had traipsed to the top of the hill and were going down a particularly sheer section of the other side, so Dylan kept her eyes on the ground, watching every step. If she had been looking at Tristan's face, she would have seen the wary, cautious look that came into his eyes. "When was that, exactly?"

Nothing but blanket silence from the boy walking beside her.

"Tristan?"

Tristan ambled on without answering.

SO MANY QUESTIONS, SO EARLY ON. IT SEEMED AN OMINOUS sign to him. He tried to lighten the mood by laughing, but Dylan drew her mouth into a grimace, and this time she really did look at him. He rearranged his features into a more convincing expression.

"DO YOU ALWAYS ASK THIS MANY QUESTIONS?" HE RAISED AN eyebrow.

Dylan was stung into silence. She turned away from him, looked up at the sky where the clouds were painted steely gray and darkening with each passing minute.

"Afraid of the dark?" he asked.

She wrinkled her nose, ignoring him.

"Look," he said, "it's going to take longer than this light will last to get where we're going. We're going to have to rough it."

Dylan made a face. She had no experience with camping but

was fairly sure that any activity that involved sleeping outdoors with no access to a kitchen, bathroom, or warm bed was not for her.

"We haven't got a tent. Or sleeping bags. Or any food," she complained. "Maybe we should head back to the tunnel and see if anybody's there looking for us."

He rolled his eyes, arrogant and patronizing again. "It's way too late to do that! We'd end up wandering around in the pitch-black. I know a sheltered spot. We'll survive. You've been through worse today."

Oddly, Dylan hadn't thought much about the train crash. Once she'd gotten out of the tunnel, Tristan had assumed control so thoroughly that she had simply followed his lead. Added to that, it had all been over so fast that she wasn't sure what had actually happened.

"See that?" he asked, pulling Dylan from her thoughts and pointing to a ruined cottage, about half a mile away, nestled in a narrow valley at the bottom of the hill. It looked long abandoned, with a tumbledown stone wall outlining the boundary. The roof had several large holes in it, the door and windows were long gone, and it seemed as if another ten years might finish off the crumbling walls.

"You want us to stay *there* tonight? Look at it! It's falling apart. I mean, it's only got half a roof! We'll freeze!"

"No, we won't." Tristan's voice dripped with scorn. "It's barely raining at all. It'll probably stop soon, and it's much more sheltered down there."

"I am not staying there." Dylan was resolute. She could not imagine anything less comfortable than spending the night in a damp, cold, ramshackle hovel.

"Yes, you are. Unless you want to keep going by yourself. It'll be dark soon. Good luck." The words were spoken coldly, and Dylan was in no doubt that he meant them. What could she do?

~~~~~

Close up, the cottage did not look any more attractive. The wilderness was reasserting itself in the garden; they had to fight their way through thistles, brambles, and tufts of thick grass just to get through the front door. Once they were inside, things improved slightly. Even without the windows or door, the wind was cut considerably, and the roof at one end was almost completely intact. Even if it rained during the night, they had a reasonable chance of staying dry. The place looked like it had been ransacked, though. The previous owner had left various possessions and a few rickety bits of furniture, but almost everything was broken and strewn carelessly across the floor.

Tristan led the way in, righting a table and chair, and upturning a bucket to sit on. He gestured to Dylan to take the chair. She sat gingerly, thinking it might collapse under her weight. It held firm, but she couldn't relax. Without the howling wind, there was a very awkward silence. Added to that, she no longer had the perilous terrain to keep her occupied. There was nothing to do but sit and try not to stare at Tristan. She felt incredibly ill at ease, trapped inside a small cottage with a virtual stranger. On the other hand, the day's trauma was beginning to sink in, and she was desperate to talk about what had happened. She eyed Tristan, wondering how to break the silence.

"What do you think happened? With the train, I mean."

"I don't know. Just crashed, I suppose. Maybe the tunnel caved in or something." He shrugged and stared at a spot over her head. Everything about his body language told her that he didn't want to talk about it, but Dylan wasn't going to give up that easily.

"But what happened to everyone else? We can't have been the only survivors. What happened in your carriage?" Her eyes burned with curiosity.

He shrugged again, standoffish and disinterested. "Same as yours I suppose." His eyes flitted away, and Dylan could see he was uncomfortable. How could he not want to talk about this? She couldn't understand it.

"Why were you there?" He looked up sharply at that, startled, and Dylan quickly elaborated. "What I mean is, where were you going on the train? To visit someone?" Suddenly she wished she hadn't asked. Something had flashed in his eyes that she didn't like—a defensiveness.

"My aunt lives in the northeast." His tone was final, shutting down the conversation.

Dylan drummed her fingers on the tabletop as she considered him. Visiting an aunt seemed innocent enough, but she wondered if it was something more sinister. Why else would he be so mysterious, so shifty? Was she isolated in the middle of nowhere with some sort of criminal? Or was she just paranoid after the shock of the day?

"What will we do for food?" she asked, more to change the subject than anything else, because his aloofness was unnerving.

"Are you hungry?" He sounded a bit taken aback.

Dylan thought about it and found, to her surprise, that the answer was no. She had last eaten on the way to the train station.

A hurried hamburger choked down with a warm Diet Coke. That had been hours ago. Although skinny, she normally ate like a horse. Her mum always joked that she'd wake up one day and her metabolism would have changed. Maybe loss of appetite was a symptom of shock.

"At the very least, we'll need some water," she said, although even as the words came out, she realized that she wasn't thirsty, either.

"Well, there's a stream out back," he answered, humor in his voice. "Can't say how clean it'll be, though."

Dylan considered drinking from a stream with mud and bugs in it; it wasn't appealing. *Besides,* she thought, *if I drink the water, I'll need to use the bathroom, and there doesn't seem to be one.* The clouds were bringing the night unusually quickly, and the idea of going out alone in the dark was not one she wanted to contemplate. There were nettles and thistles to consider, plus she would be too scared to go very far, so she would have to worry about staying within earshot. It would all just be too embarrassing.

He seemed to read the thoughts in her eyes. Although he turned his face away to stare through the window into the evening, Dylan could see the telltale lifting of his cheek. He was laughing at her. She narrowed her eyes and glowered in the other direction, out of the hole where the back window had once been. She could see next to nothing, just the outline of hills in the distance. The onset of night was making her nervous.

"Do you think we're safe here?" she asked.

He turned back to look at her, his expression unreadable. "Don't worry," he said quietly, "there's nothing out here."

The sense of isolation in his words was as chilling as the thought of unknown things scurrying about in the dark, and Dylan shivered involuntarily.

"Cold?" He didn't wait for an answer. "There's a fireplace over there. I've got matches—I can probably get it going."

He stood up and loped over to the stone fireplace, which sat under the remaining piece of roof. The chimney breast must have strengthened the wall, because this part of the cottage was in the best repair. There were still a few logs strewn about beside it, which he gathered and carefully arranged into a precarious cone shape. Dylan watched him work, captivated by his quiet concentration. As he reached into his pocket, he glanced in her direction, and she hastily went back to staring out the window. Red colored her cheeks, and she hoped he hadn't caught her staring. A low chuckle from the direction of the fireplace confirmed that he had, and she squirmed in the chair, mortified. The sound of a match striking was accompanied by a light wafting of smoke. She imagined him holding it into the firewood and trying to coax out the flames, but resolutely kept her eyes away from him.

"Barring a sudden gust of gale-force wind, we should be a bit warmer in a few minutes." He stood up and ambled back across the room to his makeshift seat.

"Thanks," Dylan mumbled, and meant it. She was grateful for the fire; it chased away the dark that was creeping over the land. She turned slightly and gazed into the flames, watching each one jump and leap over the logs. Soon the heat began to radiate out of the hearth, bathing them both in warmth.

Tristan went back to staring out the window, even though there was nothing to see. Having used up all of her nerve trying to broach conversations that had been shut down before they could really begin, Dylan did not dare interrupt his brooding. Instead she folded her arms on the table and leaned her chin on them, staring away from him and into the fire. The dance of the flames hypnotized her, and before long she felt her eyelids droop.

As the curtain of sleep closed over her, she heard the wind rushing around the crumbling walls of the cottage. Though she couldn't feel the chill of its touch, she heard the wailing as it whistled through cracks and crevices, searching for a way in. The sound was eerie, frightening. She trembled uncomfortably but tried to stifle the movement before Tristan noticed it.

It was the wind, nothing more.

SIX

WHEN DYLAN OPENED HER EYES, SHE WAS ON THE TRAIN again. She blinked, confused for a moment, but then accepted this bizarre turn of events with an almost imperceptible shrug. The train jostled and juddered as it jumped over the points, then settled down into a gently vibrating rumble. She closed her eyes again and rested her head against the seat.

It felt like only a second later, but when she opened her eyes, something felt different. Perplexed, she furrowed her brow. She must have dozed off again. The harsh lights of the carriage hurt her eyes, making her squint. Shaking her head a little to clear the cobwebs, Dylan shifted uncomfortably in her seat. The woman's bags were taking up a ridiculous amount of space, and something sharp from a bright orange carrier was digging painfully into her ribs.

She remembered promising to text her dad to tell him she was on the train and, with some difficulty, squeezed her phone out of her pocket. One of the oversize carrier bags shifted with her and rolled dangerously close to the end of the seat before the woman opposite her reached forward and shoved it back. Dylan heard her tut angrily but ignored her. Flicking the screen to life, she began to text.

Dad, on train. Got an earlier . . .

A sudden jolt of the train jarred her elbow and ripped the phone from her fingers. She made a grab for it with her other hand but only touched the bottom edge, sending it spinning farther out of her reach. With a horrible snapping sound, it clattered to the ground.

"Crap," she muttered quietly. Her fingers scrabbled around on the floor for a few seconds before they found the phone. It was sticky; some idiot must have spilled their juice on the floor. Dylan pulled the phone up to inspect the damage.

Instead of juice, her phone was covered in a thick dark red substance that trickled down her screen and dripped slowly off, falling to create small explosions on the knee of her jeans. Looking up, she met the eyes of the woman across from her for the first time. They stared back, lifeless. Blood trickled from her scalp and her mouth hung open, gray lips pulled back in a scream. Dylan looked around wildly and spotted the two Rangers fans she had tried to avoid. They were lying with their arms around each other, heads together at an angle that just looked wrong. Another jolt of the train made them flop forward like puppets, their heads held on to their necks by thin threads of sinew. Dylan opened her mouth to scream as the world was torn apart.

It began with a hideous screeching noise, a sound that set Dylan's teeth on edge and sawed at every nerve in her body as metal collided with metal and ripped apart. The lights flickered and the train seemed to buck and jerk beneath her feet. She was flung forward in her seat with incredible force, sprawling across the carriage directly into the monstrous woman in front of her. The woman's dead arms seemed prepared to embrace her, and the gaping mouth stretched wider into a hideous grin.

~~~~~

"Dylan!" The voice, unfamiliar at first, pulled her back into consciousness. "Dylan, wake up!" Someone was shaking her shoulder, hard.

Gasping, Dylan yanked her head up from the table and gazed into a pair of concerned blue eyes.

"You were screaming," Tristan said, his voice anxious for once.

The terror of the dream was still raw. The woman's death-grin hovered in front of Dylan's eyes, and adrenaline pumped through her veins. But it wasn't real. It wasn't. Gradually her breathing slowed as reality reasserted itself.

"Nightmare," Dylan muttered, embarrassed now. She pulled herself upright, away from his stare, and glanced around. The fire had long since died, but the first light of dawn had begun to brighten the sky and she was able to see her surroundings clearly.

The cottage looked colder in the morning light. The walls had been painted cream at some point, but that had long since faded and begun to peel away. The holes in the roof and the missing windows had allowed damp to seep into the walls, and now patches of green moss were spreading across the surface. The careless abandon of furniture and possessions was sad somehow. Dylan imagined someone, at some point, lovingly arranging the room with items that held meaning and emotion.

For some bizarre reason, the idea made her choke up. Her throat tightened and tears threatened to spill down her cheeks. What was wrong with her?

"We should get going." Tristan broke through her thoughts, bringing her back to the present.

"Yeah." Her throat was husky with emotion, and Tristan glanced over at her.

"You OK?"

"Fine." Dylan took a deep breath and attempted to smile at him. It felt unconvincing, but she hoped that he didn't know her well enough to see through it. He narrowed his eyes slightly but nodded.

"So, what's the plan?" she asked brightly, trying to gloss over the awkward moment. It worked, to an extent.

He lifted half of his mouth in a smile and moved over to the door. "We walk. That way." He pointed and then stood with his hands on his hips, waiting for her to join him.

"Now?" Dylan asked, incredulous.

"Yup," he replied shortly, and disappeared out the door.

She stared at the door frame he had just vacated, aghast. They couldn't just go. Not without having a drink from the stream and trying to find some food, or maybe even having a quick wash. She wondered what he would do if she just sat there and refused to follow him. Keep walking, probably.

"Dammit," Dylan muttered, getting hastily to her feet and chasing clumsily after him.

"Tristan, this is ridiculous."

"What now?" He turned to look at Dylan, exasperation clear in his eyes.

"We've been walking for hours and hours and hours."

"And?"

"Well, the train only crashed an hour north of Glasgow. There is nowhere in this part of Scotland that you could start from, walk as far as we have, and find *nothing*."

He looked at Dylan, evaluating her shrewdly. "What's your point?"

"My point is that we must be walking round in circles. If you really knew where you were going, we'd have gotten there by now." Dylan hitched her hands on her hips, ready to argue, but to her surprise Tristan's face looked almost relieved. That confused her. "We can't just keep going," she continued.

"Do you have a better idea?"

"Yes, my better idea was to stay at the train tunnel, where someone would have found us."

Again he smiled. The concern from this morning had long since disappeared, and the arrogant, mocking Tristan was back.

"Too late now," he snickered, and turned and walked onward.

Dylan looked at his back with disbelief. He was so rude and presumptuous, it was unbelievable. "No, Tristan, I'm serious. Stop!" She tried to add a ring of authority to her voice, but it sounded almost desperate even to her own ears.

Even from ten yards away, she could hear his sigh of impatience.

"I want to go back."

He turned to face her again, and she could tell that it was only with great difficulty that he was keeping his calm expression under control. "No."

She gaped at him, astonished. Who the hell did he think he was? He was a teenage boy, not her mother. She couldn't believe he thought he could boss her around like this. She folded her arms across her chest and set her feet, bracing herself for a fight.

"What do you mean, no? You don't get to just decide where I go. Nobody put you in charge. You're just as lost as me. I want to go back." She enunciated each syllable in the final sentence, as if the force of her words could make it so.

"You can't go back, Dylan. It's gone."

Mystified by his words, Dylan frowned and pushed her lips together into a thin line. "What are you talking about? What's gone?" His cryptic sentences were beginning to get on her nerves.

"Nothing, OK? It's nothing." He shook his head and seemed to be struggling to find the right words. "Look, trust me." His eyes burned into hers. "We've come this far. It would take just as long to go and find the tunnel again. I do know where I'm going. I promise."

Dylan shifted from foot to foot, undecided. She desperately wanted to go back to the site of the crash, certain that someone in charge, someone who could *fix* this, would be there. On the other hand, she would never be able to find it alone, and she was terrified of being deserted in the wilderness. He seemed to sense her uncertainty. He walked back toward her, coming uncomfortably close, bending his knees so that he could look into her eyes. She wanted to step backward, but she was frozen like a rabbit in headlights. Echoes stirred in Dylan's memory, but he was far too near, and she lost her train of thought.

"We need to go this way," he whispered. "You have to come with me." He looked intently at her, and Dylan's mind fogged. She watched him smile a satisfied smile. "Come on," he ordered.

Without her thinking about it, Dylan's feet obeyed.

Trudge, trudge, trudge. They continued over boggy marsh-land that seemed, somehow, to be always uphill. Dylan's legs were screaming, and every step she took was accompanied by a cold squelch in her sneakers. The bottoms of her jeans had soaked up water almost to her knees, and they were dragging with every pace.

Tristan, however, was unfazed by her dark looks and grum-bling. He kept up the pace ruthlessly, always staying a few feet ahead of her, silent and determined. Occasionally, if she stumbled, he would whip his head round, but as soon as he ascertained that she was fine, he would continue to march resolutely onward.

Dylan began to feel more and more uncomfortable. The silence between them was like a brick wall, totally impenetrable. It felt like he resented being stuck with her, like she was an incon-venient little sister he'd reluctantly promised to babysit. There was nothing to do but take on the role and traipse along after him, the sulky little girl who wasn't getting her way. Dylan was far too intimidated to try to confront him about his hostile behavior. She tucked her chin into her hoodie and sighed. Looking down at the long grass, trying in vain to pick out the holes and oddly shaped clumps that longed to trip her, she muttered miserably under her breath and plodded in Tristan's wake.

At the peak of yet another hill, he finally paused. "Do you need to rest for a bit?"

Dylan looked up, a little disoriented from lumbering with her head down for so long.

"Yeah, that'd be good." She felt like she should whisper after the prolonged silence, but the wind whipping around them snatched her words as soon as they left her mouth. He seemed to understand though, because he ambled over to a large rock that protruded from the grass and heather, and arranged himself nonchalantly against it. He stared out across the landscape, as if on sentry duty.

Dylan didn't have the energy to look for a suitable dry spot. She sank to the ground where she stood. Almost instantly the wet seeped through her jeans, but she was already so cold and soggy that she barely registered the change. She was too tired to think, too tired to argue. Robbed of spirit, she was ready to blindly follow wherever Tristan chose to lead her. *Perhaps that had been his plan all along,* she thought angrily.

It was odd; somewhere at the back of her mind, she knew that there were several things wrong. There was the fact that they had walked for the better part of two days and not met anybody, the fact that she hadn't eaten or drunk anything since the crash yet she didn't feel hungry or thirsty, and finally—most frightening of all— the fact that she hadn't spoken to her mum or dad for thirty-six hours and they had no idea that she was all right. Somehow these thoughts stayed at the back of her head, nagging her, but only vaguely, gentle tugs on the tail of a charging stallion. She couldn't focus on them.

Suddenly Tristan looked in her direction, and she was too absorbed in her thoughts to look away in time.

"What?" he asked.

Dylan bit her lip, wondering which of a million questions to put to him first. He was very hard to talk to, and he hadn't asked one single question about her. Wasn't he at all curious? He probably wished he'd started walking as soon as he'd left the tunnel, instead of waiting to see if anyone else would appear. Dylan wasn't sure if that wouldn't have been better for her, too. She could have stayed by the tunnel mouth, and if nobody had come, then eventually she'd have persuaded herself to go back through the tunnel and out the other side. By now she'd be home again and fighting with her mother about making another trip to Aberdeen.

A distant howl erupted somewhere to her left. It was high-pitched, mournful, like an animal in pain. The noise seemed to echo off the surrounding hills, giving it an eerie quality. It made her shiver.

"What was that?" she asked Tristan.

He shrugged, apparently unconcerned. "Just an animal. They introduced some wolves here a while back. Don't worry," he added with a small smile, looking at her nervous expression. "There are plenty of deer around here for them to eat. They aren't going to bother with you."

He looked up at the darkening sky. It had melted into late afternoon without Dylan really noticing. Surely they hadn't walked for that long? She folded her arms across her chest, hugging herself for warmth. The wind seemed suddenly stronger. Swirling around her, it tugged stray strands of hair across her face, making them dance in front of her eyes like rippling shadows. She tried to brush them aside, but her fingers found nothing but air.

Tristan pushed off from the rock he was leaning against, his eyes searching the oncoming night. "All the same, we should get a move on," he said. "We don't want to be stuck on the top of a hill when it gets dark."

It really had gotten very dark in a short space of time. Dylan found it hard to see as they made their way down the hill. This side of the peak was covered in gravel that skidded out from under her feet, and rocks that were slick with recent rain. She tried to pick her way, shuffling forward a small step at a time, keeping one foot firmly on the ground while she felt her way hesitantly with the other. It was slow going, and she could feel Tristan's impatience. Still, he dropped back to walk by her side, one arm half-extended, ready to grab her if she fell, and that was comforting. Above the wind and the sound of her breathing, she occasionally caught the faint baying of animals prowling in the night.

"Stop." Tristan flung his arm out in front of Dylan. Shocked by his abrupt halt, she turned to gaze at him, wide-eyed. Taking in his stance, she felt a nudge of apprehension thrill through her. He was standing stock-still, absolutely alert. Every muscle in his body was tense, ready for action. His eyes were focused intently on something ahead, darting in small, quick movements as he scanned the scene in front of them. His eyebrows were furrowed, his mouth set in a grim line. Whatever it was, it wasn't good.

SEVEN

"WHAT IS IT?" DYLAN SQUINTED IN THE DIRECTION TRISTAN was looking, but could see nothing out of the ordinary through the gloom. She could just make out the shape of hills in the distance and the path that they were descending. Though she stared for a long time, everything was still. She was about to open her mouth to ask what he had seen when he held up his hand, motioning for quiet.

Dylan closed her mouth and watched him. He was still frozen, his eyes searching the darkness. Dylan glanced once more in the direction of Tristan's gaze but still couldn't see anything. His tension was infectious, though, and she felt her stomach tightening. Her heart started to beat faster, and she had to concentrate on inhaling through her nose to keep her breathing under control.

Tristan continued to stare keenly forward for another moment, then turned to look at her. For an instant, his eyes glowed vividly, like blue flames. Dylan gasped. But the next second, they were black as coals in the night, and she wondered whether she had imagined it.

The wind seemed to pick up, whipping around them as they stood there. The noise rushed in Dylan's ears, but above it she thought she detected a faint howling. The same animal noises they'd heard earlier. Tristan may have said they were nothing to worry about, but his rigid posture told her otherwise.

"*Wolves?*" she mouthed, too frightened to speak.

He nodded.

Dylan looked at the landscape in front of them, searching the black grasses for silhouettes. It was still empty. Anxiety had pushed her unconsciously closer to him, seeking protection, and she was able to murmur into his ear. "What are we going to do?"

"There's a derelict wooden cabin at the bottom of this hill." His words were whispered, too, but fervent. "We need to reach it. We're going to have to go a little faster, Dylan."

"But where are they?" she whispered back.

"It doesn't matter right now; we just have to move."

His words frightened Dylan. She scanned the dark, half hoping that the danger would reveal itself, half hoping that it wouldn't. The darkness was thickening somehow. Even the ground at her feet was now just a shadow. If she tried to go faster, she would fall, possibly taking Tristan down with her.

"Tristan, I can't see." Fear made her voice catch.

"I've got you," he said, and the certainty in his voice gave her courage, warmed the chill in her chest. He reached for her hand, fingers curled around hers, and gripped tightly. Dylan realized with a start that this was the first time they had touched. Despite the horror of the moment, she felt almost jittery from the contact. His hand was very warm, and the hold he took on her fingers was strong. Immediately she felt safer. His confidence, obvious in every word, every movement, gave her confidence, too.

"Let's go," he said.

He led the way forward at a much faster pace. Dylan tried to keep up, but she couldn't see, and she tripped and stumbled often, unbalanced on the steep incline. At one point she put her foot down heavily on a patch of gravel, and it slid right out from under her. Her other foot tried to find purchase on the ground, but it hit the hill at an awkward angle. She was forced to put her full weight on it, and the muscles in her ankle wobbled and strained. She felt a sharp pain as the joint twisted under her. With a whimper, she felt herself falling, her leg buckling. But Tristan's hand kept a firm grip on hers, and he tensed his arm, yanking her to a halt and stopping the back of her head from smacking against the cold ground. At that moment he seemed to be impossibly strong. With just one arm, he pulled her back upright, almost lifting her off the ground before settling her back on her feet. In the next second, he was urging her forward again.

"Almost there," he said, slightly breathless.

Looking forward, Dylan thought she could make out the faint outline of a building not far ahead. It was, like Tristan had said, a wooden cabin. As they moved closer, the details began to appear. This place had a door still intact, with a window on either side. The roof was a steep apex with a little lopsided chimney at one end. They would reach it in just a couple of minutes at Tristan's pace.

The ground leveled out, and Dylan felt more comfortable trying to stride forward. Her ankle throbbed with every step, but she was sure that it was only twisted, not sprained. Tristan pressed on faster, encouraging her into an uneven jog.

"You're doing great, Dylan, keep going."

The animal wailing was getting louder, closer. It was now a constant, interweaving orchestra of noise. Dylan couldn't guess how many creatures were circling them. She still hadn't caught even a glimpse of a wolf, though her eyes darted left and right. Still, they were almost there now. They would make it. The cabin looked a lot sturdier than the tumbledown cottage they'd been forced to sleep in the night before. There would have been no way to keep wolves out of that one. They were so close now that Dylan could almost make out the reflection of her own frightened face in the windowpane.

That was when she felt it. It began as a chill around her heart, and then her breath seemed to freeze in her lungs. In the dark she couldn't see them; she could merely make out the movement in the air, shadows upon shadows. They whirled before her, and she felt the air stir against her skin as they snaked around her. Testing, tasting the air.

These were not wolves.

"They're here." Tristan's voice was full of dread, and so quiet that the words seemed not to be for her ears. Nonetheless, Dylan heard them, and they scared her more than anything else. There was something odd about the way he spoke. It was as if he had known these creatures were coming, as if he knew what they were. What secrets was he keeping from her?

Something rushed past her. Although she yanked her head back quickly enough to snap her jaw shut, the thing slashed across her face, causing a burning across the bridge of her nose and her cheek. She wiped her hand roughly across her skin and felt wetness there. She was bleeding.

"Tristan, what's happening?" she shrieked, casting her voice above the wind and the howling, which was rising in a frightening crescendo, interspersed with hisses and screams. The ice in her chest made it painful to breathe.

Out of the gloom, a shadow appeared, heading straight for her. She didn't have time to react, to step sideways out of its path, or even to brace herself. But the impact she was waiting for never came. Amazingly, the shadow seemed to pass right through her. She wasn't sure if she imagined it, but it felt like a frozen arrow piercing her body. Dropping Tristan's hand, she grabbed her middle, expecting to find a wound or hole, but her hoodie was completely intact.

"Dylan, no! Don't let go of me!"

She felt fingers reaching for her, and searched the air for his hand, but came up empty. Then suddenly she was grabbed by what felt like hundreds of hands that seemed to have no more substance than smoke. They were strong, though, and through the sheer force of their numbers, she felt them pulling her downward. Instinctively she flailed with her arms, trying to knock them away, but her hands found nothing in the air. What was going on? These were not animals or birds. She stopped moving and felt the substance-less things return immediately. How could she fight something she couldn't touch? Under the combined strength of the creatures, her legs collapsed and she sank to the ground.

"Dylan!"

Although he was standing right next to her, Tristan's voice seemed very far away. It barely registered over the sound of jubilant snarling and shrieking. The things were swarming all over her now. She could feel them on her arms, her legs, across her stomach, even on her face. Everywhere they touched her burned like frozen metal on bare skin. More and more of them were passing through her body, chilling her bones. There was no adrenaline in her fear. Instead, terror weakened her. She had no power to struggle against the unbeatable.

"Tristan," she whispered. "Help."

Her voice had less strength than a murmur. She felt weak all over, as if something had drained her of energy. It was hard to refuse the weight of the coaxing hands. Down, down, down toward the ground, then, astonishingly, past it. The dirt and rock did not seem as solid as it should. Dylan felt she could slip through it as if it were liquid.

"Dylan!" Tristan's voice could have been coming from underwater. It was distorted and fuzzy. "Dylan, listen to me!"

She could hear a note of panic, and she wanted to comfort him. She felt almost calm, weightless, and tranquil; he should be calm, too.

A hand grabbed the front of her hoodie roughly. It hurt. The air around her was filled with angry hisses, and Dylan agreed— the hand should stop. The fist shook harder and then yanked her upward. She felt like she was trapped in a tug-of-war.

The hissing intensified and the pulling hands transformed into ferocious talons, digging in like needles all over her body. They tore at her clothes and tangled into her hair, wrenching her head back and pulling a cry of pain from her lips. The unknown assailants seemed to enjoy that, and the hissing transformed into cackling, a menacing screech that drove straight into Dylan's heart and chilled it.

Suddenly Dylan was hauled upward. The hand holding the

front of her hoodie pulled her upright, and an arm snaked under her knees and lifted her into the air. Her feet dangled and her head lolled backward until she could summon the strength to lift it. She knew she was in Tristan's arms. She didn't have time to be embarrassed, although he had her pinned tightly to his chest, shielding her, because the creatures had not given up the fight. They snapped at her feet and circled around Tristan. They grabbed at his clothes, his hair, slashed angrily in front of his face. Ignoring them, he began to run. The claws lost their grip, but they tried to grasp her again and again. Dylan could feel the things whooshing around her; they were close enough to slash shallow gashes across her skin, but could not grip her as Tristan stormed toward the cabin.

The screaming reached fever pitch as Tristan and Dylan neared the shelter. The things realized they were about to lose their prey and doubled their efforts. Tristan seemed impervious to their attacks. They scratched and tore at Dylan, focusing on her head and her hair. She tried to hide her face in Tristan's shoulder.

Almost there. Tristan's feet thumped against a paved path as he flew across the final few yards. Not letting go of her, he somehow opened the door and dashed inside. Dylan heard a thunderous chorus of screams. There were no words, but the emotion was clear in their screeching clamor: they were furious.

EIGHT

DYLAN KNEW THE MOMENT THEY CROSSED THE THRESHOLD into the safety of the cabin because the noise stopped instantly. Tristan slammed the door behind him and immediately dropped her to her feet, almost as if having her in his arms had scalded him. Leaving her standing there, her mouth gaping wide in shock, he walked quickly to the window and stared out of it.

The cabin, like the cottage the night before, was sparsely furnished. There was a bench along the back wall, and Dylan stumbled over to it. She dropped heavily onto the rough wood and hid her head in her hands, small sobs escaping from between her fingers as she tried to control the rush of fear that coursed through her veins. Tristan glanced over, an unfathomable expression on his face, but he stayed at his lookout post by the window.

Pulling her hands away from her face, Dylan examined her arms. Even in the almost-dark, she could see crisscrossed scratches all over her skin. Some had barely grazed her, but others had gouged deeper, causing small droplets of blood to ooze through. Her skin stung all over, burning. Still, the pain hardly registered as the adrenaline that flooded her system made her hands tremble.

This cabin had a fireplace, and after a few minutes Tristan crossed over and bent down to it. There were no logs, and Dylan didn't hear the sound of a match scratching, but soon there was a fire blazing in the grate. The flickering gave the cabin an eerie atmosphere as shadows played against the walls. Dylan didn't question the sudden arrival of the fire. There were too many more important—impossible—thoughts in her mind, jostling for space. Those ideas niggling at the back of her consciousness were fighting to break through, demanding to be heard.

They continued like that for a long time—Tristan statue-like and composed back at the window; Dylan curled up in a ball on the bench, occasionally crying and gasping quietly—the after-effects of the adrenaline rush. There was no sound from outside. Whatever the things had been, they seemed to have retreated for now.

Eventually Dylan lifted her head. "Tristan."

He didn't look over. He seemed to be bracing himself for something.

"Tristan, look at me." Dylan waited, and finally he turned his head, slowly and unwillingly. "What was that?" She tried to keep her voice calm, but it was still husky from crying and it cracked a little as she spoke. Her green eyes shimmered as tears still lingered, but she held his stare, willing him to be truthful. Whatever those things had been, Tristan had recognized them. He had been speaking to himself when he'd muttered, "They're here," and he had known what would happen when she let go of his hand. How had he known? What else was he hiding from her?

TRISTAN SIGHED. HE HAD KNOWN THAT THIS POINT HAD BEEN coming; he'd postponed it as long as possible. But there were no parlor tricks or games that could gloss over what had happened. Dylan had seen and felt those things. They could not be explained away as wild animals. He had no choice but to be honest with her. He wasn't sure where to start, how to explain in a way she would understand, how to break it to her and yet cause the least amount of pain.

Reluctantly he crossed the room and sat down on the bench beside her. He didn't look at her but stared at his interlaced fingers, as if hoping to find the answers there.

Normally, when revealing the truth became an unavoidable necessity, he just blurted it out. He told himself that a short, sharp shock was better than drawing it out painfully. But in reality, it was because he didn't care. Whether they cried, sobbed, begged, or tried to bargain, there was no changing things. He just turned away and waited it out until they accepted the inevitable, and then the two of them could go forward together in mutual understanding. But this time . . . this time he didn't want to.

Sitting close enough to feel her breath on his face, he turned his head and gazed into her green eyes, a luscious, deep green that made him think of forests, and felt a twist in his stomach. He didn't want to hurt her. He wasn't quite sure why, but he felt a yearning to protect this one, more than he'd ever felt for any of the others.

"Dylan, I haven't really been honest with you," he began.

He saw her pupils dilate slightly, but there was no other reaction. She already knew this, he realized. She just didn't know what the deception was.

"I wasn't on the train."

He paused, gauging her response. He expected to be interrupted by a stream of questions, of demands and accusations, but she just waited, still as stone. Her eyes were pools of fear and uncertainty; she was afraid of what he might say but determined to hear it, nonetheless.

"I was . . ." Tristan's voice trembled and died. How to say it? "I was waiting for you."

Her eyebrows puckered together in confusion, but she didn't speak and he was glad of that. It seemed easier to get the words out without hearing her voice. He refused to do her the disservice of not looking in her eyes, though.

"You didn't walk away from the crash, Dylan." His voice had dropped to a whisper, as if he could lessen the blow by turning down the volume. "You were one of the ones not to."

The words were spoken clearly, but they seemed to float in Dylan's brain, refusing to settle into meaning. She tore her eyes away from his, staring at a broken tile on the floor.

Tristan shifted uncomfortably beside her, waiting for a reaction. A full minute passed, then another. She didn't move. Only the occasional tremor of her lips stopped her from being a statue.

"I'm sorry, Dylan," he added, not as an afterthought but sincerely. Although he didn't understand the reason, he hated inflicting pain on her, wished he could take it back. But there was no undoing what had been done. He didn't have the power to change things, and it would be wrong to do so even if he could. It was not his place to play God. He watched her blink twice, saw the realization settle into her being. Any second now the flood of emotion would begin. He hardly dared to breathe. He was afraid of her tears.

She surprised him.

"I'm dead?" she asked finally.

He nodded, not trusting himself to speak. Expecting an outpouring of anguish, he lifted his arms out toward her. However, she remained oddly calm. She sighed, then made a tiny smile to herself. "I think maybe I already knew, somewhere."

NO, THAT WASN'T QUITE RIGHT, DYLAN THOUGHT. SHE HADN'T *known* . . . but somewhere deep down, her subconscious had been keeping tabs on all the things that were wrong, all the things that just didn't add up. And though she couldn't explain why, she felt no terror at finally acknowledging the truth. Only relief.

She thought about never seeing her mother again, or Katie, of never getting to know her father and enjoying the relationship they might have had, of never having a career, a marriage, children. She felt sadness tug at her heartstrings, but overshadowing these mournful thoughts was a sense of inner peace. If it was true, and she knew in her bones that it was, then it was done and unchangeable. She was still here, she was still her, and that was something to be thankful for.

"Where am I?" she asked quietly.

"The wasteland," Tristan replied. She looked up at him,

waiting for more. "It's the land between worlds. You have to cross it. Everyone does. Their own personal wilderness. It's a place to discover the truth that you have died and come to terms with it."

"And those things?" Dylan gestured toward the window. "What are they?"

Although the noise had gone, Dylan was sure that the creatures had not left. They were simply waiting, biding their time and hoping for another opportunity to attack.

"Demons, I guess you'd call them. Scavengers, wraiths. They try to snatch souls during the crossing. The closer we get to the other side, the worse the attacks will become as their desperation grows."

"What do they do?" Her voice was barely more than a whisper.

Tristan shrugged, seemingly unwilling to answer.

"Tell me," she pressed. It was important to know, to be prepared. She didn't want to be in the dark anymore.

He sighed. "*If* they catch you, which they won't, then they pull you under. The ones they've caught, we never saw again."

"And once you're under?" Dylan raised a questioning eyebrow.

"I don't know exactly," Tristan replied quietly.

She grimaced, dissatisfied, but sensed he was being honest.

"But when they're finished with you," he continued, "you become one of them. Dark, hungry, without a conscience. Monsters of smoke."

Dylan stared into nothingness. She was horrified at the thought of becoming one of those things. Screaming, desperate, violent—they were hateful creatures.

"Are we safe here?"

"Yes." Tristan answered quickly, as if wanting to reassure her as much as he could. "These buildings are safe houses. They can't come inside."

DYLAN ACCEPTED THIS QUIETLY, BUT TRISTAN KNEW THERE would be further questions, more truths that she needed to know. And he would give them to her, where he could. She deserved that much at least.

"And you?"

That was all she said, but it implied a thousand questions. Who was he? What was the life that he led? What was his place in this world? Tristan was forbidden to reveal most of these answers, and in truth he didn't know all of them, but there were some things that he could tell her, some things that she had a right to know.

"I'm a ferryman," he began. He had been staring at his hands, but he snuck a quick look at her face. It was simply curious. He took a deep breath and continued. "I guide souls across the wasteland and protect them from the demons. I break the truth to them, then deliver them to wherever they're going."

"And where is that?"

A key question. "I don't know." He smiled ruefully. "I've never been."

Dylan looked incredulous at this. "But how can you know that it's the right place? You just drop people off and walk away? For all you know, it's the gates of hell!"

He nodded indulgently, but there was a finality about his answer. "I just know."

She pursed her lips and looked unconvinced, but didn't argue the point further. Tristan exhaled a relieved breath. He didn't want to lie to her, but there were some things he just wasn't allowed to share.

"How many people have you . . ." Dylan paused, unsure how to phrase her question. "Guided over?"

He looked up, and this time there was a definite sadness in his eyes. "I honestly couldn't tell you. Thousands, hundreds of thousands, probably. I've been doing this a long time."

"How old are you?"

This was a question that he could answer, but he didn't want to. He sensed if she knew the truth, if she knew how long he had lingered here—not learning, growing, and experiencing the way a human did, but simply being—then the delicate connection between them would break. She would see him as old, someone strange and other, and he found that he didn't want that. He attempted to make a joke out of it.

"How old do I look?" He held out his arms and offered himself up for inspection.

"Sixteen," she said, "but you can't be. Is that when you died? Can you not age?"

"In technical terms, I've never really lived," he replied, a wistfulness in his eyes. Quickly that gave way to a more guarded expression. He had already let slip more than he should. Mercifully, she seemed to read that in his expression and asked no more questions.

LOOKING AROUND, DYLAN TOOK NOTICE OF HER SURROUND-ings properly for the first time. The cabin was one long room, with mismatched furniture suffering the wear and tear of abandon.

Still, it was in better repair than last night's cottage. The doors and windows were intact, and the fire burning strongly in the grate had warmed the room. Beside the bench, there was an old bed, devoid of blankets but with a mattress. Although it looked like it had seen better days and was coated with numerous stains, it was inviting at that moment. There was also a kitchen table and sink at the other end.

Stiffly Dylan stood up—she must have been sitting on the hard bench for longer than she'd realized—and crossed the room to the little kitchen area. She felt grimy, uncomfortable. She wanted to clean up, but the sink looked like it hadn't been used in years. Both taps were covered in rust. Still, she grasped one and twisted. Nothing happened so she tried the other. When it stuck as well, she increased the pressure, feeling the edges of the tap digging into her palms. She felt something start to give and so squeezed and twisted a little harder, hope burgeoning. With a scrape and a clunk, the handle of the tap came away entirely in her hand, the metal weakened by rust.

"Oops." She turned and grimaced at Tristan, showing him the broken handle.

He grinned at her and shrugged. "Don't worry about it."

Dylan nodded, guilt alleviated, and tossed the broken piece into the sink. Then she turned and walked over to the bed. She felt Tristan's eyes on her and, when she twisted round to sit down on the mattress, noticed his gaze evaluating her.

"What?" she asked, smiling slightly. Now that the truth was out in the open, she felt, oddly, much more comfortable around him. It was as if the secret had been a wedge keeping her in the cold.

He smiled back at her. "I'm just astonished at your response, that's all. Not one tear." His voice trailed off as her smile fell, and sadness took its place.

"What good will crying do?" She sighed, with the wisdom of a much older soul. "I'm going to try to sleep."

"You're safe here. I'll keep watch."

And she did feel safe, knowing he was there, alert. Her protector.

"I'm glad it's you," she mumbled, just as sleep overcame her.

TRISTAN WAS CONFUSED, UNSURE OF HER MEANING, BUT IT made him happy all the same. He watched her sleep for a long time, looking at the shadows of the fire flicker and play across her face, untroubled in unconsciousness. He felt a strange longing to touch her, to stroke down her smooth cheek and brush away the hair that fell over her eyes, but he didn't move from where he sat. He was her guide, her temporary protector. Nothing more.

DYLAN DREAMED AGAIN THAT NIGHT. ALTHOUGH HER ENCOUNter with the demons had given her ample fodder for a nightmare, she dreamed instead of Tristan.

They were not in the wasteland, but Dylan had the strangest feeling she'd been here before. They were in a forest. It was filled with large oak trees with gnarled trunks and wide, sprawling branches that interwove to create a canopy above them. It was night, but the moonlight filtered down through the trees, dappling gently and casting rippling shadows as the leaves swayed. The light breeze ruffled her hair, tickling her neck and shoulders. A carpet of leaves underfoot rustled as they walked. At some point recently it must have rained, because the air smelled slightly of dampness and nature. Somewhere to her left, she could hear the faint trickle of a slow-running stream. It was exquisite.

In the dream, Tristan held her hand as they walked, slowly weaving in and out of the trunks, following no set path but simply choosing a winding route to nowhere. Her skin seemed to burn where his hand touched it, but she was frightened even to twitch her fingers in case he let go.

They didn't speak, but it didn't feel uncomfortable. They were content just to be near each other, and words would have ruined the peace of this beautiful place.

IN THE CABIN, AS SHE SLEPT, TRISTAN WATCHED HER SMILE.

NINE

THE FIRST LIGHT OF THE MORNING SENT THE SUN'S RAYS
streaming through the windows of the cabin. Even filtered by the
dust and grime on the panes, it was strong enough to wake Dylan.
She stirred feebly, brushing her hair from her face and rubbing her
eyes. For a moment she wasn't sure where she was, and she lay still,
taking stock of her surroundings.

The bed was unfamiliar and narrow, the mattress lumpy. The
ceiling above her was raftered with solid pieces of timber that
looked like they had stood strong for a hundred years. She blinked
twice, trying to get her bearings.

"Good morning." The soft voice came from her left and made
her snap her head sharply toward it.

"Ow!" The quick movement pinched a nerve in her neck. As
her hand rubbed the cramping pain away, Dylan stared in the
direction of the voice, comprehension dawning.

"Morning," she replied softly, a blush warming her cheeks.
Although they had shared so much last night, she felt awkward
again, unsure of herself.

"How'd you sleep?" Tristan's normal, polite question seemed somehow out of place: decorum in the midst of such strangeness. She couldn't help but grin.

"OK, you?"

He smiled. "I don't need to. One of the oddities of the wasteland. You don't really, either. Your mind just thinks it should, so it does. Eventually it will forget. Takes a while to adjust."

She stared at him, speechless for a moment. "No sleep?"

He shook his head. "No sleeping, no eating, no drinking. Your body is just your mind's projection. You left the real thing back on the train."

Dylan's mouth opened and closed a few times. This sounded like some bizarre science-fiction movie. Had she landed in the Matrix? What Tristan was telling her seemed incredible, unbelievable, but as she stared down at her hands, she realized that, even though they were encrusted with mud, they were smooth, unblemished. The deep scratches left by the wraiths had healed.

"Huh" was all she could manage. She looked toward the window. "Is it safe to go outside?" She wasn't sure if the monsters—demons—from last night were still a threat during the day.

"Yeah, they're not too keen on the sunlight. Of course, if it was a cloudy, dark day, they might surface, if they were desperate enough." Tristan looked at her frightened expression. "We should be OK today, though. Sunshine." He gestured toward the window.

"So, what now?"

"We move. We still have a long way to go. The next safe house is ten miles away, and the darkness comes quickly here." He frowned at the window, as if chastising the weather for placing them in danger.

"Did I die in the wasteland winter?" Dylan's eyes were slightly amused but also intrigued. She wanted to know more about this strange place.

TRISTAN STARED AT HER, DELIBERATING OVER HOW MUCH TO tell. Guides were supposed to deliver souls across the wasteland and do nothing more. Most souls, when they discovered where they were and what had happened to them, were too absorbed in their own sorrow and self-pity to show much interest in this road between the real world and the end. Dylan was not like any other soul he'd encountered. She had accepted the truth calmly, with no outbursts. Now the eyes that examined him were simply question-ing, curious. A little more information might make it easier for her to accept and understand, he argued with himself. But in truth, he wanted to share it with her. He wanted a way to be closer to her. He took a deep breath and chose.

"No." He smiled. "It's your fault."

He had to bite his lip to stop himself from laughing. Her reaction was exactly as he had expected: perplexed and a little bit outraged. Her eyebrows furrowed and her lips pursed, her eyes narrowing to green slits.

"*My* fault? How is it my fault? I haven't done anything!"

He chuckled. "What I mean is, the wasteland is what you make it." Her expression turned to one of startled confusion as her eyes widened to sparkling pools in the sunlight. "Come on." He lifted himself from the chair, walked over to the door, and opened it. "I'll explain on the way."

THE AIR WAS WARM AS DYLAN STEPPED OUTSIDE, BUT A breeze crept around the walls of the cabin and tickled her hair.

The sun shone down, brightening the colors of the wasteland. Drops of dew caught the light and glinted in the wet grass, which was a luscious shade of green. The hills cut into the blue sky, their ridges razor-sharp against the heavens. Everything appeared to be washed clean, and Dylan drew in a deep breath, reveling in the freshness of the morning. But dark clouds dotted the sky toward the horizon. She hoped the sun would banish them before they could steal the beautiful day.

She picked her way down the path behind Tristan, trying to avoid the thistles and nettles that snuck up between the cracked stones. Tristan waited just a few yards away, shifting from foot to foot in a way that told her he was eager to be off.

Dylan made a face. More marching. Understanding where they were going, and why it was so important to get there quickly, did not make the journey any more appealing.

"Why can't the wasteland be a bit flatter?" she grumbled as she approached Tristan.

He smirked but didn't reply. Instead he turned on his heel and began to lead the way. Dylan sighed and hitched up her jeans a little higher, hoping that it might stop them from getting wet quite so quickly, but knowing it was a futile gesture.

Their journey began on the other side of the cabin, following a narrow dirt trail that snaked across a beautiful meadow of long grass nestled between the hills. There were wildflowers: hidden drops of purple, yellow, and red in an ocean of green. Dylan wanted to wander slowly, to drink in the scenery and trail her fingers, letting the grass and flowers tickle her hands.

For Tristan, however, the meadow was simply another obstacle to overcome, and he strode through the surrounding splendor without glancing left or right. It took about ten minutes to cross, and Dylan soon found herself at the foot of the first hill of the day. Tristan had already started the ascent, and Dylan hurried to draw level.

"So," Dylan began as soon as she had caught up with his long, purposeful strides. "Why is all this"—she gestured to the land-scape—"my fault?"

"It's also your fault that it's all uphill." Tristan chuckled darkly.

"Well, that's just typical," Dylan muttered, already out of breath and cross at Tristan's enigmatic answers.

Instead of being abashed, he laughed. The scowl on her face deepened.

"I said before that your body was your mind's projection. The wasteland is sort of the same thing." He paused to grab her elbow as she stumbled. She was too focused on what he was saying to watch her feet. "When you came out of the tunnel, you expected to be halfway to Aberdeen—somewhere in the Highlands, some-where remote, hilly, and wild—so that is what the wasteland became. You don't like exercise, so all the walking is putting you in a bad mood. This place, it reacts to how you feel. When you got angry, that brought the clouds, the wind . . . and the dark. The darker your mind, the longer and darker the nights." He looked across at her, trying to read her reaction. She stared back at him, drinking in his every word. A sly smile spread across his lips. "In fact, even I look like I do because of you."

She frowned at that and turned her head to concentrate on the ground, processing what he was saying, but also unable to keep from looking at his face.

"Why?" she asked finally, failing to make sense of his last comment.

"Well, a soul's guide should seem safe. You have to trust us, to follow us. We automatically form ourselves to look appealing to you."

Dylan kept her head down, but her eyes popped wider and her face blushed scarlet, giving her away.

"So," Tristan continued, enjoying himself immensely, "if I've done it right, you should have a thing for me."

Dylan stopped dead in her tracks, hands on her hips, the blush deepening. "What? That's . . . well, that's just . . . I do not!" she finished hotly.

He walked forward a few more steps, then whirled to face her with a huge grin on his face.

"I don't," she repeated.

His grin widened. "OK."

"You are such a . . ." Appropriate insults seemed to fail Dylan, and she stormed onward, stamping angrily up the hill. She didn't even turn round to check if he was following. The dark clouds that had ringed the horizon just ten minutes earlier rumbled forward, coating the sky and darkening the atmosphere.

Tristan glanced up and frowned at the change. He started after Dylan, making light work of the steep incline.

"I'm sorry," he said as soon as he'd caught up. "I was only teasing."

Dylan didn't turn or acknowledge that she'd heard him.

"Dylan, stop, please." He reached out and grabbed her arm.

She attempted to shrug his hand off, but he held firm. "Let go of me," she hissed through her teeth, embarrassment sharpening her anger.

"Let me explain," he said, his voice gentle and almost pleading.

They stood facing each other, Dylan breathing heavily, Tristan exuding calm, only his eyes wary. He took another quick glance at the sky; the clouds were almost black. Drops of rain began to fall, thick heavy globules of cold water that left dark circular stains on their clothes.

"Look," he began, "that was mean. I'm sorry. But you see, we have to make you follow us. If you refuse to come with us, if you wander off on your own . . . well, you've seen those things. You wouldn't last one day, and you'd never find your way across even if they didn't get you. You'd wander here forever."

He searched her eyes, watching for a reaction, but her expression remained unchanging.

"I appear in a form I think will be helpful. Sometimes, like with you, I choose a form that should be attractive, sometimes I'm a form that is intimidating. It depends on what I think will best convince that specific person."

"How do you know?" Dylan asked curiously.

Tristan shrugged. "I just know. I know *them*. Inside. Their past, their likes. Dislikes. Their feelings, hopes, and dreams." Dylan's eyes widened as he spoke. What, then, did he know about her? She swallowed as a list of secrets, of private moments, flashed in her head, but Tristan wasn't finished. "Sometimes I take the form of someone they've lost, like a spouse." Catching sight of her face, he immediately realized that he'd said too much.

"You pretend to be someone's love, their soul mate, to trick them into believing you?" Dylan spat the words at him, nauseated. How could he use a person's most treasured memories, toy with their emotions like that? It made her sick to her stomach.

His face hardened. "It's not a game, Dylan." He spoke in a low, passionate voice. "If those things get you, you're gone. We do what we have to."

The rain was falling harder now, bouncing off the ground. It had soaked through Dylan's hair and ran down her face like phantom tears. The wind had picked up, too, sweeping off the mountain and exploiting every hole in their clothing. Dylan shivered, folding her arms across her chest in a vain attempt to hold in some warmth.

"What do you really look like?" Dylan demanded, wanting to see beyond the lies, to see his real face.

A change of emotion flickered in his eyes, but Dylan was too caught up in her outrage to notice it. He didn't respond, and Dylan raised her eyebrows with impatience. Finally he dropped his gaze to the ground.

"I don't know," he whispered.

Shock dissolved Dylan's anger. "What do you mean?"

He raised his head to look at her, and pain seemed to darken the blue of his eyes. He shrugged, and his words came out stiltedly. "I appear to each soul in the most suitable way. I keep that shape till I meet the next soul. I don't know what I was before I met my first soul, if I was anything. I exist because you need me."

As Dylan gazed at him, the rain began to lighten. Pity swelled in her chest, and she reached out a hand to comfort him. Watery rays of sunshine broke through the clouds. Tristan pulled back from her touch, and the sadness was replaced by a mask of indifference. She watched him shutting down.

"I'm sorry," she whispered.

"We should go." Tristan looked toward the horizon and thought of the distance that they still had to travel. Dylan nodded mutely and followed him up the hill.

~~~~~

They spent the rest of the morning walking in silence, each caught up in their own thoughts. Tristan was angry. Angry at himself for making fun of her and causing the whole conversation that had made her face twist into an expression of disgust and abhorrence. She had made him feel deceitful, like a common trickster. He didn't expect her to understand, but she had seen the demons, she knew the stakes. Sometimes it was necessary to be cruel; sometimes the end did justify the means.

DYLAN WAS FULL OF GUILT AND PITY. SHE KNEW SHE'D HURT him when she accused him of being uncaring. She hadn't meant the words to come out so viciously, but the idea of someone pretending to be your mother, your father, or, worse still, the love of your life . . . It was an appalling thought. But maybe he was right; here, the consequences were frightening. It was life or death. *More* than life or death. A far cry from the petty squabbles that had seemed so significant in her old life.

She was also trying to imagine how it would feel not to have your own identity. To be defined entirely by those around you, never to have a moment alone. Not even knowing your own face. She couldn't envisage it and, for once, was glad to be herself.

At midday they took a break, halfway down a hill on a little ledge that offered shelter from the wind and breathtaking views of the rolling countryside. There was a dense covering of clouds, but they didn't look like they held any rain. Dylan sat down on the rocky outcrop, not caring that it chilled her through the thick denim of her jeans. She stretched out her legs and leaned back against the rugged hill. Tristan didn't sit but stood at the front of the ledge, staring out across the hills with his back to her. It might have looked like a protective gesture, but Dylan was sure that he was simply avoiding conversation. She chewed on a jagged nail, wanting to smooth things over but not sure how. She didn't want to bring the subject back up again for fear of making things worse, but she couldn't think of anything to say that wouldn't sound false. How could she bring back the mood from earlier? Reawaken the jokey, teasing Tristan? She didn't know.

He turned abruptly and stared down at her. "Time to move."

TEN

THAT NIGHT THEY STAYED IN ANOTHER COTTAGE, ANOTHER
safe house on the route across the wasteland. The afternoon had
passed quickly, and they marched at a pace that made Dylan think
Tristan must be trying to make up for time lost during their argument. They reached the cottage just before the sun disappeared
over the horizon. During the last half mile, Dylan thought she
could hear distant howling, although it was difficult to tell over
the wind. Tristan had increased the pace once again, grabbing
her hand to speed her up, confirming her suspicions that danger
lurked nearby.

As soon as they entered the confines of the cottage, he instantly
relaxed. The muscles in his jaw, clenched tight in concern, loos-
ened into a slow smile, and his eyebrows unfurrowed, smoothing
out the creases in his forehead.

This cottage was much like the others: broken furniture strewn
about a single large room. There were two windows on either side
of the front door, and two more at the rear of the cottage. They

were made up of small panes of glass, and several in each window were broken, allowing the wind to whistle noisily through the room. Tristan snatched some scraps of material from beside the bed and began to stuff the small holes, while Dylan crossed to a chair and flopped down, exhausted from the day's exertion.

If she didn't need sleep, should she really be tired? *Whatever,* she thought. Her muscles hurt—or *felt* like they did. Trying to shift her muddled thoughts, she watched Tristan work.

Once he had finished with the windows, Tristan built a fire. He took much longer than the previous night, fiddling with the lay of the logs and snapping twigs into a perfect pyramid. Even when it was crackling away merrily, he still didn't move from the fireplace but crouched over it, staring into the flames as though mesmerized. He was avoiding her, Dylan felt sure—a feat that was next to impossible in the small room. She decided to try a stab at humor to bring him out of his reverie.

"If this place is my making, why are all these cottages so crappy? Couldn't my imagination come up with a slightly better resting spot? Maybe something with a Jacuzzi or a TV?"

Tristan turned and gave her a very small, forced smile. Dylan grimaced back, lost as to how to pull him out of his terrible mood. She watched as he crossed the room, plonking himself on the opposite side of the small table. He mirrored her position so that they were face-to-face, just a couple feet apart, with their elbows on the table. They stared at each other for a short moment. Tristan's mouth twisted to the side as he read the slight awkwardness in her eyes, and with some effort he offered her a genuine smile. Dylan took courage from the gesture.

"Look," she started, "about before—"

"Don't worry about it," he said abruptly.

"But . . ." Dylan opened her mouth to continue and then lapsed into silence.

TRISTAN SAW THE REGRET, GUILT, AND—WORST OF ALL—PITY in her eyes. On the one hand, he felt a kind of perverse pleasure that she cared enough about his pain to feel sorry for him, but on the other, he also felt a niggling frustration that she was making him think about things that he'd long since accepted. For the first time in a long while, he felt aggrieved at his lot. At the never-ending circular prison his existence amounted to. All of those self-ish souls who had lied, cheated, wasted the lives they had been given—a gift he longed for and could never have.

"What's it like?" Dylan suddenly asked him.

"What's what like?"

He watched her purse her lips, searching for words to phrase her question.

"Ferrying all these people, taking them all the way across, and then watching them disappear, or go over, or whatever. It must be hard. I bet some of them don't even deserve it."

Tristan stared at her, astonished by the question. Nobody, not one soul of all the thousands he'd guided over, had ever asked him that. And what answer to give? The truth was hard, but he didn't want to lie to her.

"At first, I didn't really think about it. I had a job, and I did it. It seemed like the most important thing in the world to protect each soul, to keep it safe. It took a long time before I started to see some of the souls for what they really were. Who they really were as people. I stopped pitying them, stopped being kind. They didn't deserve it." Tristan's voice twisted as bitterness coated his tongue. He breathed in deeply, pushing the resentment back down, glossing over it with the facade of indifference that he'd perfected over time. "They cross over, and I have to watch them walk away. That's how it is."

It had been like that for a long time now. Then this one had come along, and she was so different that it was knocking him out of the role he usually played. He'd been fairly horrible to her—sneering, patronizing, making fun of her—but he couldn't help it. She had him off-balance, off-kilter somehow. She wasn't perfect, he knew that—saw it in the million different memories of hers that played in his head—but there was something unusual—no, special—about her. He felt guilt stir in the pit of his stomach as she squirmed uncomfortably in the chair, compassion and borrowed sorrow etched across her face.

"Let's talk about something else," he offered, to spare her feelings.

DYLAN AGREED QUICKLY, GLAD OF THE CHANCE TO TURN THE conversation. "OK. Tell me some more about you."

"What do you want to know?"

"Hmm," she said, going through a list of the questions that had been swimming around her head all afternoon. "Tell me about the weirdest form you've ever taken."

He grinned at once, and she knew this had been the right question to lighten the mood.

"Santa Claus," he answered.

"Santa!" she exclaimed. "Why?"

He shrugged. "It was a little kid. He died on Christmas Eve in a car crash. He was only about five, and Santa was the person he trusted more than anyone. He'd sat on his knee in a store a couple of days before, and it was one of his favorite memories." A humorous light sparkled in his eyes. "I had to keep jiggling my belly and shouting, 'Ho! Ho! Ho!' to keep him happy. He was very disappointed when he found out Santa couldn't sing 'Jingle Bells' in tune."

Dylan laughed at the idea of the boy sitting in front of her dressed up as Santa. Then she realized that he wouldn't have been just dressed up as Santa—he would have *been* Santa.

"Tell me . . . tell me about your first-ever soul," she said.

Tristan twitched his lips to the side in a wry smile.

"Well, it was a long time ago," he began. "A young man. His name was Gregor. Do you want to hear the story?"

Dylan nodded eagerly.

IT WAS A VERY LONG TIME AGO, BUT IN HIS MIND'S EYE, TRISTAN could still see every detail. His first memory of existing was walking, walking in a landscape of brilliant white. There had been no floors, no walls, no sky. The fact that he was walking was the only evidence that any surface existed at all. Then out of nowhere details had begun to appear. The ground beneath his feet was suddenly a dirt road. Hedges sprang up on either side of him, high and unruly and rustling with the sounds of living creatures. It was night, the sky above him inky black interspersed with twinkling stars. He recognized and could name all of these things. He also knew where he was going, and why he was there.

"There was a fire," he said. "A thick plume of smoke was

winding its way up into the sky, and that was where I was headed. I was walking up a lane, then from out of nowhere two men came flying past me. They ran so close to me that I could feel the air stirring, but they couldn't see me. When I got to the source of the flames, I saw that the two men were trying to draw water from a well, but their efforts were in vain. They couldn't defeat a fire like that. It was a vicious inferno. No one could hope to survive such a thing. That was why I was there, of course."

He smiled thinly at Dylan, who was staring at him with rapt attention.

"I remember feeling . . . not nervous, but uncertain. Was I supposed to go in and get him, or stand there and wait? Would he know who I was, or would I have to convince him to accompany me? What would I do if he got upset or angry?

"But in the end it was easy. He walked straight through the wall of the burning building and came to a stop in front of me, totally unscathed by the fire.

"We were supposed to set off. But Gregor didn't seem to want to leave. He was waiting for something. No . . . some*one*."

Dylan blinked, confused. "He could see them?"

Tristan nodded.

"I couldn't," she mumbled, looking down thoughtfully. "I didn't see anyone. I was . . . I was alone." Her voice died on the final word.

"Souls can still see the life they've left for a little while. It depends on their moment of death," he explained. "You were unconscious when you died, and by the time your soul woke up, it was too late. Everyone else was gone."

Dylan gazed at him, eyes wide pools of sadness. Then she

swallowed audibly. "What happened to Gregor?"

"People started to arrive at the house, and though Gregor gazed at them mournfully, he didn't move from my side. Then a woman came sprinting up the drive, her skirts hitched up to leave her legs free to run, a horror-struck expression on her face. She screamed his name. It was a heart-wrenching, tortured sound. She dashed past the watching crowd and made as if to run into the house, but a man grabbed her. After struggling for a few seconds, she slumped in his arms, sobbing hysterically."

"Who was she?" Dylan whispered, captivated by the story.

Tristan shrugged. "Gregor's wife, I guess, or a lover."

"What happened next?"

"The hardest part. I waited as Gregor watched her outburst with an agonized look burned across his face. One arm stretched out toward her, but he seemed to realize that he couldn't offer comfort, and he remained next to me. After a few seconds, he turned and said, 'I'm dead, aren't I?' I just nodded, not trusting myself to speak. He asked if he had to go with me, looking back at the crying woman, and I said yes. Then he asked where we were going, and I panicked," Tristan confessed. "I didn't know what to say."

"What did you tell him?"

"I said, 'I am just the ferryman. I do not determine that.'

"Thankfully the man accepted this answer, and I turned and began walking away into the dark night. With one last look at the woman, Gregor followed."

"Poor woman," Dylan muttered. "That man, Gregor, he knew he was dead. Right away he knew." She looked incredulous.

"Well," replied Tristan, "he had just walked through the wall of a burning building. Besides, back then, people were much more religious. They didn't question their church, and they believed what it taught them. They saw me as a messenger from above—an angel, I guess you'd call it. They didn't dare question me. People nowadays are much more troublesome. They all seem to think they have rights." He rolled his eyes.

"Huh." Dylan looked up, seemingly unsure whether to ask her next question.

"What?" Tristan saw her hesitation.

"Who were you for him?" she blurted out.

"Just a man. I remember being tall and muscular, with a beard." He paused at the look on her face. Her lips were twisted together to stop herself from giggling. "Lots of men had beards then, big bushy ones. I had a mustache, too. I quite liked it; it was nice and warm."

This time she couldn't contain the laughter, but it died away quickly.

"Who's been the worst soul?" she asked quietly.

"You." He smiled, but the gesture didn't reach his eyes.

ELEVEN

THAT NIGHT DYLAN SLEPT LITTLE. SHE LAY AWAKE THINKING about souls, about Tristan and all the other ferrymen that must exist, about where she was going. She supposed her body was getting accustomed to not needing sleep, but in truth there were so many thoughts running wild in her head that sleep would have evaded her anyway.

She sighed, shifting on a worn and lumpy armchair.

"You're awake." Tristan's voice was low in the semi-dark, coming just from her left.

"Yeah," Dylan murmured. "Too much stuff in my head."

There was a long moment of silence.

"Do you want to talk about it?"

Dylan swiveled round so that she could look at Tristan. He was sitting in a chair, staring out into the night, but when he felt her eyes on him, he twisted round to face her.

"It might help," he offered.

Dylan bit her lip, considering. She didn't want to lament her bad luck, not when he had it so much worse. But there were a million uncertainties buzzing round her head, and Tristan might be able to answer at least some of them. He smiled at her encouragingly.

"I was thinking about what's beyond the wasteland," she began.

"Ah." Understanding broke across Tristan's face. He grimaced at her. "I can't really help you with that."

"I know," she said softly.

She tried not to show her frustration, but it was something she was getting increasingly anxious about. Where was she going? Having seen the demons that loitered in the darkness ready to pull her under, she doubted it was anywhere bad. It must be a good place; why else would demons try to stop her from getting there? And it must be *somewhere*, too. If oblivion lingered at her destination, what would be the point of crossing the wasteland?

"Is that all that's worrying you?"

Hardly. Dylan huffed a breathy laugh. It didn't last long, though. She looked down at where flickers from the fire were playing across the old, cracked stone floor. They danced in a way that was eerily familiar.

"Those demons," she began.

"You don't have to worry about them," Tristan told her firmly. "I won't let them hurt you."

He sounded completely confident, and when Dylan looked up, she saw that his eyes were wide and glowering, his jaw clenched. She believed him.

"OK," she said.

Silence stretched between them again, but more thoughts were bubbling in Dylan's mind.

"You know what I can't get my head around?"

"What?"

"That you don't actually look like you. I mean," she went on, realizing that didn't make any sense, "I can see you. I can touch you." She held up a hand, fingers searching in his direction, but she didn't have the courage to reach out and make contact. "But what I see, what I feel, it's not really you."

"I'm sorry." It was impossible to miss the wistfulness in Tristan's voice.

Dylan chewed on her tongue, realizing she'd been thoughtless. Wanting to make up for it, she added, "But what you look like doesn't matter. Not really. Who you are, it's in your head and your heart, you know? Your soul."

Tristan stared at her, his expression fathomless. "Do you think I have a soul?" he asked quietly.

"Of course you do." Dylan answered quickly but honestly. Tristan saw that in her face and smiled. She smiled back, but it turned into an ear-splitting yawn. She threw her hand over her mouth, embarrassed.

"I guess my body still thinks it needs sleep," she said sheepishly.

Tristan nodded. "You'll probably feel horrible tomorrow, really exhausted. It's all psychological, though . . ." He trailed off.

The silence deepened and felt almost tangible.

Dylan hugged her knees, curled up in the armchair, and stared beyond Tristan toward the fire. She wondered whether she ought to say something, but she couldn't think of anything that wouldn't sound pointless. *Besides,* she thought, *he might want to think. This might be as close to being alone as he ever gets.*

"I guess it's easier at the start," she mused.

"What do you mean?" Tristan turned back to look at her.

She didn't meet his gaze but kept her eyes fixed on the fire, letting it lull her into a semi-trance. "At the beginning," she said, "when the souls sleep. I bet it's nice to get a bit of peace and quiet. You must get tired of always having to talk to them."

She faltered right at the very end, because it occurred to her suddenly that that's what she was: one of *them*.

Tristan didn't respond for a moment and she cringed, reading the worst possible meaning into his silence. Of course she was just another soul to him. Chagrin washed through her, and she squirmed in the chair.

"I'll stop talking," she promised.

Tristan's lips twitched. "You don't have to do that."

SHE WAS RIGHT, THOUGH. HE DID PREFER THE START OF THE journey when the souls drifted out of consciousness and he could be almost alone. Sleep was like a curtain, shielding him, even if only for a few hours, from their selfishness, their ignorance. He was staggered that this . . . this *girl* would have the compassion, the selflessness to think about *his* feelings, *his* needs. He glanced over at her, huddled in the chair, looking for all the world like she wanted to disappear into the ancient cushions. He felt moved to take the awkward blush from her cheeks.

"Do you want to hear another story?" he asked.

"If you like," Dylan responded shyly.

An idea occurred to him.

"You asked me before who was the worst soul I've ever ferried across," he began, "but I lied. It wasn't you." He paused for just long enough to shoot her a quick look.

"No?" Dylan rested her head on her knees, her eyes amused as she watched him.

"No," he promised. Then the jokiness dropped out of his tone. "It was a little boy."

"A boy?" Dylan asked.

Tristan nodded.

"How did he die?"

"Cancer," Tristan murmured, unwilling to recount the tale any louder than a whisper. "You should have seen him, lying there. It was heartbreaking. He was tiny and frail, white-faced with a bald head from radiation."

"Who were you for him?" Dylan asked gently.

"A doctor. I told him . . ." Tristan choked off, not sure whether he dared to admit to this. "I told him I could make the pain go away, that I could make him feel good again. His little face just lit up. He leaped out of the bed and told me that he felt better already."

Tristan hated guiding children. Although they came the most willingly and were the most trusting, they were also the hardest. They did not complain, though he felt that they deserved to the most. What an injustice, to die before you had had the chance to grow, to live, to experience.

"Tristan." Dylan's voice jerked his head upright from where he'd dropped it to his chest. "You don't have to tell me if you don't want to."

But he did want to. He didn't know why; it wasn't a pleasant tale, and there was no happy ending. He wanted to share something of himself with her. Something meaningful.

"We walked out of the hospital together, and it had been so

long since he'd felt the sun, he couldn't take his eyes off it. The first day was fine. We made the safe house easily, and I kept him amused with magic tricks: conjuring a fire from nowhere, making things move without touching them. Anything to capture his attention. The next day he was tired. His mind still felt like it was ill, but he wanted to walk. He hadn't been allowed to walk for months because he'd been so sick. I couldn't refuse him. I should have."

Tristan hung his head in shame.

"We were too slow. I was carrying him by the time the sun went down, but it wasn't enough. I ran. I ran as fast as I could, and the poor kid was getting jostled about. He was crying. He could feel my anxiety, and he heard the howling of the demons. He trusted me. And I let him down."

DYLAN WAS ALMOST AFRAID TO ASK. BUT SHE COULDN'T LEAVE the story here like this. "What happened?"

"I tripped," Tristan croaked, eyes glistening in the muted light from the flames. "I tripped and I dropped him. I let him go to break my fall. Just for a second. A split second. But it was enough. They got him and they dragged him under."

His voice died, but the silence was still punctuated by his ragged breathing, hitching and breaking as if he were crying, though his cheeks were dry. Dylan gazed at him. Of its own accord, her hand reached out and wrapped itself around his. The room was warm, but his skin was cold to the touch. Dylan trailed her fingertips across the back of his hand. He looked at her for a heartbeat, his expression somber, then he flipped his hand over and wound his fingers around hers. He held her there, one thumb tracing slow circles around the heart of her palm. It tickled, but Dylan would have rather lost her hand than pull away.

Tristan looked up at her, shadows dancing across his face from the fire.

"Tomorrow is a dangerous day," he murmured. "The demons are gathering outside."

"I thought you said they couldn't come in?" Dylan's voice was half-strangled with sudden panic. The fact that he was warning her surely must mean he was worried. And if Tristan was worried, then the danger must be very real. Her stomach tightened.

"They can't," he promised, a serious expression on his face, "but they know we have to come out eventually."

"Will we be safe?" Dylan's voice rose up into an embarrassing squeak.

"We should be OK in the morning when the sun is up," he said, "but in the afternoon we'll have to go through a valley, and it's always dark down there. That's where they'll make their attack."

"How do you know? I thought you said that the landscape came from me?"

"It does, but there's an under-terrain that always stays the same, and you project your landscape onto it. That's why the safe houses are always in the same place. And the valley will be there. It's always there."

Dylan bit her lip, curious yet cautious, and decided to ask her question anyway. "Have . . . have you ever lost anyone in the valley?"

He looked up at her. "I won't lose you."

Dylan heard the unspoken reply to her question and pressed her lips together, trying not to show her anxiety.

"Don't be frightened," he added, feeling the change in atmosphere. His fingers squeezed her hand with gentle pressure, and Dylan flushed.

"I'm fine," she replied, too quickly.

Tristan clearly saw through her denial. He got up from the chair and crouched in front of her, still gripping her hand. He looked her straight in the eye as he spoke. Dylan was desperate to look away, but she was hypnotized.

"I will not lose you," he repeated. "Trust me."

"I do," Dylan responded, and this time there was truth in her words.

He nodded, satisfied, and stood up, relinquishing both her eyes and her fingers. Dylan stuffed her hand between her jean-clad knees, trying not to show that she was trembling, the skin on her palm tingling. She tried to quiet her breathing as she watched Tristan approach one of the windows and stare off into the night. She wanted to call to him, to pull him away from the glass and the demons that lurked just beyond, but he knew much more about them than she did. Still, nothing could draw her that close to those things. She hunched a little deeper in the chair, shuddering slightly.

"It's always the same," Tristan suddenly said. He didn't turn, though, and Dylan wondered if he was speaking to himself. He lifted one hand and pressed it to the glass. Immediately the noise from the circling wraiths doubled.

"What's always the same?" Dylan asked, hoping to draw his attention—and his hand—away from the window. The wailing and screeching was scaring her.

To her relief, he did turn, dropping his hand.

"The demons," he told her. "They are always hungrier, more voracious, when it's a soul . . ." He paused. "A soul like you."

Dylan frowned. The way he said it, it was like there was something wrong with her.

"What do you mean, a soul *like me?*"

He considered her for a short moment. "The wraiths, they'll take any soul, and gladly. But pure souls are like a feast to them."

Pure souls? Dylan rolled that around her head for a moment, waiting for it to make sense. *Pure* wasn't exactly a word she'd use to describe herself.

"I'm not pure," she said.

"Yes, you are," he assured her. "I don't mean that you're perfect. A pure soul . . . you're a good person."

Dylan shook her head, ready to deny his words again. He looked as though he really meant it. Her mouth opened and closed a few times, but no sound came out. Tristan was watching her carefully, but she seemed to have no control over the muscles of her face or the flush on her cheeks.

"Any time a pure soul comes into the wasteland, the wraiths are more aggressive, more dangerous." He looked at her, making sure he had her full attention. "They want you—you specifically. To them, your soul would be a feast. More desirable, more delectable, than the bitter taste of a soul who'd lived too long."

Dylan just gaped at him. How the hell did he know anything about her? Was her life written across her forehead? But then she remembered, how he'd told her he knew each soul. Inside and out. She cringed. And the way his lips kept twitching as he watched her squirm; he was laughing at her embarrassment.

Mortified, she writhed in the chair, but that wasn't enough. She was still trapped by his gaze like an ant under a magnifying glass. She bounced out of her seat, and her momentum carried her forward a few steps until she was facing the window Tristan had been looking through just a few moments before. She approached it, purposely avoiding his reflection, and pressed her forehead to the frigid glass, trying to cool her red-hot embarrassment.

TWELVE

WHEN THEY EMERGED FROM THE COTTAGE, THE WRAITHS
were nowhere to be seen. Dylan looked around her, eyes wide and
frightened, and then sighed with relief. Though she knew there
was still the valley to travel through.

It was a gloomy morning. The sun's rays were unable to break
through the thick, swirling mist. Tristan took a long, measured look
around and then glanced back at Dylan, smiling sympathetically.

"You're nervous." It wasn't a question.

Dylan gazed at the mist and comprehension dawned. "I made
this?"

He nodded. He walked over to her and grasped both of her
hands in his. "Look at me," he commanded. "You don't have to be
afraid. I will protect you. I promise." He bent his legs a little so
that he could look into her eyes. She tried to hold his gaze and felt
a glow tingle into her cheeks.

"You're cute when you blush." He laughed, his words causing
the blush to go into overdrive. "Come on." He let go of one hand as
he turned, but kept hold of the other, gently tugging her forward.

Dylan stumbled after him, dimly aware of the mist thinning and the sun's rays fighting their way through. She thought she understood why, and so her blush was slow to fade. Two minutes later she had convinced herself that his words were nothing more than a strategy—to lighten her mood and evaporate the mist, lessening the risk from the demons. Still, his hand remained tightly folded around hers as he led her on.

At the top of the first hill, Tristan paused and surveyed the landscape. He fixed his gaze on something to the left and pointed toward it.

"See those two hills over there?" Dylan nodded. "The valley we have to pass through lies between them."

"That's a long way," Dylan said dubiously. It was already mid-morning, and the hills looked fairly distant. Surely it would be dusk before they reached them? She certainly didn't want to be caught in there in the dark.

"Optical illusion, it's much closer than it looks. We'll be there in about a couple hours. We'll be fine as long as your good mood holds out." He smiled down at her and squeezed her hand.

Dylan felt as if the sun shone a little brighter. *How humiliating, to have your emotions made so obvious,* she thought.

A narrow path wound its way down the side of the hill, wide enough for only one of them to negotiate at a time. Tristan led, finally letting go of her hand as he picked his way over small stones and clumps of weeds. Dylan walked slowly and cautiously behind, leaning back slightly to compensate for the slope and taking tiny shuffling steps as she sought out safe footholds. She held her hands out, both to help keep her balance and to save herself if she fell.

It took them about half an hour to make their way to the bottom of the hill, and Dylan sighed with relief when the ground evened out and she was able to stretch her legs and take longer, bounding steps. From here, the two hills guarding the valley appeared to tower above them. Tristan had been right, they seemed much closer now. All that stood before the hills was a flat expanse of marshland. Large puddles shimmered at intervals, and reedbeds grew in sporadic clusters. Dylan internally cursed, imagining the cold mucky water that would soon be seeping into her socks. She glanced at Tristan.

"I don't suppose a piggyback is part of your guide duties?" she asked hopefully.

He gave her a withering look and she sighed. Plunging her hands into her pockets, she rocked back on her heels, reluctant to take the first step.

"Maybe we should just take a little rest here?" she suggested.

"That's a great idea." He frowned at her, unimpressed. "We can just wait till midafternoon and then hit the valley at nightfall. Live dangerously, why not?"

"OK, it was just a suggestion," Dylan grumbled as she took the first step into the marsh. Her sneaker squelched ominously. She winced, but her foot stayed warm and dry. *Not for long,* she thought as she continued to trudge along.

The marsh was not more than a couple of miles across, but they made slow progress. Carving a path through the large puddles and reeds, and slogging through the mud that at times sucked her down ankle-deep, was hard work. Tristan seemed to have much less trouble. His feet found the firm ground more easily, and even when Dylan trod in the same spot as him, she was sure she sank deeper. The mud stank, too, unlike anything she'd ever smelled before. It was putrid and wafted up with each step.

About halfway across, they hit a patch that was boggier than the rest. Dylan sank down almost to her knees, and when she tried to jerk herself free, nothing happened. She rocked backward and then threw her weight forward several times. Still nothing.

"Tristan!" she yelled, even though he was just a few yards from her.

He turned and looked at her. "What?"

She raised both arms in a gesture of hopelessness. "Stuck."

A wicked look came across his face. "And what do you want me to do about it?"

"Don't be funny, get me out!" She put her hands on her hips, giving him an angry look. He grinned and shook his head. Dylan decided to try a different tack. She dropped her arms, hung her head, and looked up at him from underneath her lashes, pouting.

"Please?" she whimpered.

He laughed louder but began to slosh his way over to her. "You're pathetic," he joked. He grabbed hold of both her arms, locked his knees, and braced his body, then leaned back and heaved. Dylan heard a sucking, squelching sound, but her feet remained firmly stuck.

"Bloody hell," he panted. "How did you do this?"

"I stepped," she snapped, slightly peeved at his mocking attitude.

Tristan dropped his grip on her arms and took a step forward. He wound his arms around her waist, hugging her tightly, their full bodies touching. Dylan froze a little at the close contact, her pulse racing. She hoped he couldn't feel it. Squeezing her hard, he pulled backward. Dylan felt the mud start to loosen its grip on her legs. With a disgusting, plopping sound, the bog finally released her. Without the marsh to hold her, Tristan's pulling launched her forward. She let out a sound that was a cross between a yelp and a cackle as he staggered backward, trying to keep his balance. Splotches of muddy water splashed up and spattered their faces and hair.

Tristan's arms tightened around her as he tried to stop the two of them from falling into the marsh. Taking a few awkward steps backward, he finally managed to steady them both.

LOOKING DOWN, HE SAW DYLAN'S MUD-FRECKLED FACE STARing up at him and was caught for a second in the dazzling green of her eyes as she laughed.

HELD TIGHT IN TRISTAN'S EMBRACE, DYLAN SWAYED, NOT YET sure of her feet and still a little giddy. She grinned up at him, momentarily losing her shyness. He was staring right back at her. The moment deepened and the laughter died in Dylan's throat. Suddenly it was hard to breathe. She drew in shallow gasps and her lips parted slightly.

The next instant, he had released her. He stepped away and gazed off toward the hills.

Dylan stared at him, confused. What had that been? She had thought he'd wanted to kiss her, but now he didn't even seem to want to look at her. It was very puzzling, and not a little embarrassing. Had she just made a fool of herself? She wasn't sure. She shifted her stare to the only safe place: the ground.

"We should get going," he said, his voice oddly rough.

"Right," Dylan mumbled, still slightly dazed. He turned and splashed on, and she traipsed after him.

TRISTAN WADED AHEAD THROUGH THE BOG, TRYING TO PUT A little distance between them to give himself time to think. He was perplexed. For decades, maybe even centuries—it was hard to accurately measure passing time in the wasteland—he had protected and guided souls as they made their journey. At first, he had cared for each one, listened to their stories, and tried to comfort them as they grieved for their lives and futures and, of course, as they felt the pain of leaving behind those they loved. Each soul that waved goodbye at the end of the journey had taken a small piece of him with them, torn off a tiny piece of his heart. After a while, he had hardened. He no longer reached out to them, and so they could not get inside him. In the past few years, guiding souls had been little more than a chore. He had spoken as little as possible and attempted to hide the truth for as long as possible. He had been a cold machine. A GPS for the dead.

This girl had somehow managed to reach his old self; he felt it resurfacing. She had uncovered the truth at an astonishingly early stage and had accepted it with more maturity than many who had spent a full life on earth. She treated him like a person. Here in the wasteland, that was a rare thing. Souls were usually too wrapped up in their own demise to even entertain the thought that their guide was some*one*. She was a soul worth protecting. A soul worth caring about. A soul that he wanted to give a piece of himself to.

But there was something more than that. He couldn't define the feeling. Holding her in his arms had caused odd feelings to stir, feelings that had him thinking about her instead of the sun lowering dangerously in the sky. He felt almost . . . human. That couldn't be right, but Tristan had no other word for it. Human.

But he wasn't. He shook himself awake with a jolt. Feelings like this were dangerous; they could cause him to lose his focus. They put Dylan at risk—they needed to be smothered.

"Tristan." Dylan's voice broke through his reverie. "Tristan, it's going to get dark soon. Maybe we should wait and go through the valley tomorrow?"

He shook his head and kept on walking. "Can't," he replied. "There's no safe house this side of the valley. We'll just have to go as fast as we can."

DYLAN HEARD THE REPRESSED PANIC IN HIS VOICE AND FELT A tight knot in the pit of her stomach. She knew her fear would not help—in fact, it might make the situation far worse, but she couldn't smother the emotion.

Ten minutes more of trudging and the ground started to firm up beneath their feet. The grass held Dylan's weight when she stepped on it. She tried to scrape off some of the mud that now coated her sneakers. She didn't dare stop to do the job properly; she could feel Tristan's impatience. At last the puddles became less frequent, and Dylan was astounded to see, when she looked up, that they were in the shadow of the two hills. Before her was the valley Tristan had warned her about.

It looked unremarkable. A fairly wide path wound through it, and the sides sloped gently upward. Dylan had expected a narrow crevice, claustrophobic and tight. She felt relieved, but a glance at Tristan's tense posture had her stomach somersaulting again. She reminded herself that he was a much better judge of where the danger lay. Grimacing, she tried to shuffle faster, closing the distance between them.

Dylan was anxious to begin with, wanting to dash through as quickly as possible, but Tristan paused. He seemed to be bracing himself. Dylan eyed him surreptitiously. Was he thinking about the other souls he'd taken through this place, some that he'd lost? How many? Feeling nervous, Dylan stretched out her fingers and curled them around his left hand. She smiled timidly up at him and squeezed. He returned the smile tightly and then gazed back down the valley, looking almost defiant.

"Almost there," he muttered, so low that Dylan wondered if she'd even been meant to hear it.

THIRTEEN

IT SHOULD HAVE BEEN A FAIRLY PLEASANT WALK THROUGH THE valley. The path was flat and wide, made of little pebbles that made Dylan think of country walks on long abandoned railway lines. It wound its way gracefully down the trough between the two hills that gently undulated upward, covered with short grass and wild-flowers. It was picture-perfect. Or would have been if it wasn't for the sheer cliff walls that erupted from the grassy slopes and curved inward as they rose up, pinching the sky until it was little more than a narrow slit of light. Darkness enveloped this place. Dylan shivered as the cold shade embraced her.

Beside her, Tristan remained silent and tense, moving quickly and glancing constantly around. His stress triggered her own. She didn't dare look at her surroundings, but stared straight ahead and willed the two of them to pass through without incident. In her peripheral vision, she could just make out the swooping blur of bats. No, not bats, she realized. Wraiths. They scythed down the rocky face, then circled low overhead. Dylan gripped Tristan's fingers tightly, trying not to look at them.

But she couldn't ignore them. She found herself listening for the familiar but haunting howling that she now associated with the demons, but there was no high-pitched wailing echoing in the air. There were, however, other noises.

"Can you hear that?" she asked tersely.

Tristan nodded, his expression grim.

It sounded like the gentle rumbling of a thousand whispers. Although there were no distinct words, the sound was nonetheless menacing.

"What is it?" she warbled. Her head jerked about as she scanned the sky, the cliffs, hunting for the source of the noise.

"Not from above," Tristan told her. "It's beneath us."

At first the only sound Dylan could hear was the crunching of their feet disturbing the gravel and small pebbles that littered the trail. But now that she was listening for it, she realized the eerie hissing was, in fact, coming from the ground.

"Tristan, what's happening?" Her voice was almost inaudible even to herself.

"The demons. They're gathering beneath us. As soon as they spot an opportunity to attack, they'll rise up in a mass. It's what they do here. Always."

"Why?" Dylan whispered.

"We're in the heart of the wasteland," Tristan explained. "This is where they lurk, thousands of them. The shadows almost never die here. They know they'll get their chance."

"What sort of opportunity do they need?" she choked out.

"As soon as we're deep enough in shadow, they'll strike." His voice was matter-of-fact, but there was a note of panic there that frightened Dylan more than the words.

"What can we do?"

He barked a humorless laugh. "Nothing."

"Shouldn't we run?" Dylan was not a strong runner. She was thin, but she wasn't fit. She had always insisted that she would only run if she were being chased. *This situation seems to qualify*, she thought ruefully.

"Not till we have to. Save your energy for when you really need it," he said, smiling slightly. The smile didn't last long. "Hold on to me, Dylan. Don't let go. And when I tell you to run—run. You follow the path, and when you're through the valley, there's another cottage. You run toward it and you don't look back. Once you're in the door, you're safe."

"Where will you be?" she whispered.

"Right beside you," he said grimly.

Dylan's eyes were wide with panic. She tried to focus them on the path in front of her. Her hand was wrapped so tightly around Tristan's that her fingers were throbbing. The rumbling seemed to grow louder, and it appeared as if the ground was bubbling, melting to let the demons through. It took a moment for her eyes to make sense of the pattern on the ground, then she realized that it was shadows. Dark shadows. Her breathing began to come in shallow, ragged gasps as she saw that the valley was darkening around them, the cliffs pressing in more tightly. They were deep within the heart of it. How long before the demons broke free?

The air seemed to chill instantly. A gust of wind drove up the valley and lifted Dylan's hair around her face. The breeze whispered in her ears, echoing the noise from the ground, and she picked out the distinct howling of other demons, keening somewhere above them. They were gathering on all sides.

For a heartbeat she felt as if time had stopped, suspended on the brink of chaos. Every nerve in her body was stretched tight, adrenaline pumped through her veins. Her muscles seemed to tingle, ready to respond to her commands. She took a long, deep breath, and the air rushing into her lungs thundered in her ears.

Before she could exhale, before she could blink, time sprang back into being and everything seemed to happen at once. The ground smoked as countless demons erupted through the surface like black, wispy snakes, twisting and hissing and writhing in the air. The howling from above descended from the sky, diving and weaving around her. Hundreds of them. Thousands. The air was black with wraiths, blinding her. Dylan simply gaped; this was nothing like she'd seen before. Her heart turned to ice as one demon glided straight through her chest, snatching inside her before breaking out of her back. Faceless things caught in her hair and tugged and pulled at her, causing needle-like pains in her scalp. Claws grasped at her shoulders and arms, wrenching and hauling at her.

"Dylan, run!" Tristan's voice broke through the confusion of sound and movement, straight to the center of her brain.

Run, she repeated to herself. *Run!* But she couldn't move. Her legs were frozen, as if they had forgotten how to function. She had always laughed at the victims in horror movies who were helpless with fright and ran afoul of the ax-murdering villain, but here she was, indisputably immobilized by fear.

A yank on her hand made her stumble into motion, jerking her legs into action. They caught up with her before she fell and began to pump her forward. *Run, run, run,* she thought, tearing as fast as she could down the path, one hand glued to Tristan's. The screaming demons still swirled around her, but they were unable to get a firm grasp.

The path stretched in front of her, and although she couldn't see the cottage, she knew it couldn't be too far. It had to be close now. She was running at full tilt and knew she wouldn't be able to keep up the pace for long. Her legs were already burning, protesting now at every step. Each time she lifted a foot, it felt heavier and heavier. Her breathing came raggedly and unevenly, each intake causing cold, stabbing pains to rip across her chest. Her arms punched forward rhythmically, trying to keep her going, but she was slowing with every stride. The clawing demons were beginning to find purchase, pulling backward and slowing her further. She knew she would not be able to hold out unless the cottage was very close.

Something pulled on her hand hard enough to almost topple her backward. Dylan yelped as her shoulder was wrenched in its socket, then, a heartbeat later, she realized what had happened. Both her hands were clenched into fists. Empty fists.

"Tristan! Tristan, help!" She coughed feebly between breaths.

"Dylan, run!" She heard him holler. He was no longer beside her. Where had he gone? She didn't dare turn round to search for him in case she fell. Instead she concentrated on doing what he'd told her: running. Running as hard and as fast as she could.

What was that? Directly in front of her, about four hundred feet away, was a murky square shape. It had to be the cottage. She sobbed in relief and tried to galvanize her exhausted muscles into one last effort.

"Come on, come on, come on, come ON!" she muttered under her breath, ordering her body to keep going. Ignoring the pain, she moved her legs even faster, forcing them to sprint the remaining feet. The door was already open, inviting her in.

"Tristan, I can see it! Tristan!" But that final thought choked in her throat as several demons dived at her at once and ripped their way into her body. They seemed to have no substance, yet she could feel them grabbing at her heart. She stuttered and stumbled, finding it hard to control her limbs.

"No," she gasped. "No, no, please. I'm there! I'm there!"

It was impossible to move. Cold hands gripped her insides and twisted, chilling her to the bone and taking her breath away. Every inch of her longed to stop. To lie down on the ground and have the demons pull her gently downward to where it would be dark and she could sleep. A place where she could cease struggling and be at peace.

Suddenly Tristan's words burst into her head. *You run toward it and you don't look back. Once you're through the door, you're safe.* With them came an image of his face.

Sheer will drove her forward, step by step, toward the open door. Every movement was agony, every breath stabbing pain. Her body screamed at her to stop, to give in, but she doggedly pushed on. As she inched closer, the screaming, howling, and hissing intensified. The demons doubled their attack, pulling and ripping and scratching at her. They swirled around her face and attempted to blind her. Just a few feet away, she fell to her knees, exhausted. Screwing her eyes shut tight, she forced her aching lungs to pull in air and began to crawl. The ground was cold under her hands, small stones scraping at her palms and digging into her knees. *Move,* she thought desperately. *Just move.*

She knew instantly when she had crossed over the threshold.

The noise died away immediately, and the cold chill inside her dissolved into a numb ache. Spent, she collapsed onto the floor, gasping hard.

"Tristan, we made it," she croaked, unable to lift her head from the floor.

He did not answer. And there was no sound of breathing behind her, no movement in the cottage. The ice in her heart returned, multiplied tenfold. She was afraid to turn around.

"Tristan?" she whispered.

Dylan rolled over onto her back. She lay there for a moment, too scared to open her eyes, afraid of what she might see. Her need to know won out. She forced her eyelids open and surveyed the scene before her.

No.

Unable to speak, she let out a pitiful whimper. The doorway was empty, the night outside black.

Tristan hadn't made it.

FOURTEEN

DYLAN DIDN'T KNOW HOW LONG SHE LAY ON THE FLOOR. SHE couldn't take her eyes from the doorway. Any moment Tristan was going to walk through it, windswept, breathless, but fine. He was going to smile and take control. He had to. Her heart was crashing in her chest; her muscles felt locked in stone. Completely drained from her exertions, her body started to shake.

After what may have been mere minutes, but felt like an eternity, the cold seeped through the floor and penetrated to the very core of her bones. Her trembling limbs began to seize up, and she knew she had to shift them.

She groaned as she pulled herself up into a sitting position, not daring to take her eyes from the doorway. Tristan was going to arrive any second, as long as she kept looking. Somewhere at the back of her mind, a small voice told her that this was ridiculous, but she held on to the belief, because it was the only thing keeping the panic from rising up in her throat and erupting in screams.

Dylan managed to get her quivering legs underneath her and,

with the support of the door frame, hauled herself to her feet. She kept a firm hold on the rotting timber and stood, swaying, on the threshold. She could hear whispering and screaming outside, although the safe house dulled the noise. Keeping her feet firmly inside, she leaned her head out, searching the night for a glimpse of blue eyes or tousled blond hair. Her eyes found nothing, but her ears were assaulted by a barrage of outraged shrieking as the demons attempted to assail her but were frustrated by the safe-house boundary. Gasping with shock, she yanked her head back and the noise instantly diminished.

Dylan backed away from the door slowly. Her feet caught on something on the floor and she almost tripped. She tore her eyes away from the doorway for a fraction of a second, but it was almost pitch-black, and she couldn't make out what she'd stepped on. Another wave of terror. She could not bear a night alone in the dark here. She would go insane.

Fire. There was always a fireplace in these cottages. But she was going to have to turn away from the door, and that meant facing the fact that Tristan might be gone. *No,* she told herself. He would come. She should just get the fire going for when he arrived. She felt her way across the cottage, and sure enough at the other end of the room was a stone fireplace. Kneeling, she searched with her fingertips. Her fingers brushed against ash and lumps of wood in the grate. To the left of it she found some dry logs but no matches, and no electronic switch like the one back home.

"Please," she whispered, aware that she was begging an inanimate object to work but unable to stop herself. "Please, I need this." On the last word, her composure broke. Her chest convulsed with strangled sobs, and her eyelids squeezed together as the first teardrop slipped down her cheeks.

A crackling noise made her open them, momentarily afraid, but what she saw made her gasp with shock. There were flames in the fireplace. They were small and flickered in the draft from the open door, but they refused to be put out. Dylan's hands reached out and grabbed a couple of logs. She placed them delicately on the fire, holding her breath in case her clumsy actions smothered the fledgling flames.

They held but continued to sputter because of the draft. Dylan turned and looked at the door. Closing it felt like closing the door on her hope—on Tristan. But she couldn't lose the fire. Feeling as if she were moving in slow motion, she rose and walked over to the door. She paused there, fighting a desire to run out into the night to find him. That would mean surrendering herself to the demons, though, and Tristan wouldn't want that. Unable to watch, she shut her eyes, and then the door.

As the latch clicked closed, something broke within Dylan. Tears filling her vision, she blundered across the room until she met what felt like a bed. She threw herself onto it and gave way. Panic engulfed her. She battled desperate cravings to run and scream and break things.

"Oh God, oh God, oh God," she repeated again and again in between gasping sobs. What was she going to do? Without Tristan she had no idea where she was going. She would get lost, wander till it was dark, and then be a sitting duck for the demons. Or would she have to stay here and wait? But who would come for her? If she didn't need to eat or drink, would she wait here for an eternity, like a cursed princess in some ridiculous fairy tale, hoping for a prince to rescue her?

The loneliness and fear dragged up feelings that hadn't had a chance to surface since the crash. Visions of her mum swam before her eyes. Had there been a funeral yet? She pictured Joan receiving the call at the hospital, saw the devastated look on her face, her perfectly arched eyebrows crumpling, her hand reaching up to cover her mouth as if she could hold the truth out. Dylan thought of all the arguments they'd ever had, of all the mean things she'd said and never meant, and all the things she wanted to say and never had. Their last real conversation had been a fight about seeing her dad. She could still remember telling her mother she was going to visit him, could remember the look on her face. Joan had stared at Dylan as if she'd betrayed her.

This thought wove into another. Her dad. How had he reacted? Who had told him? Had he mourned for the daughter he'd never really known?

All of a sudden her situation, her death, hit home. It wasn't fair. Her future, her family, her friends . . . all were gone. Now her ferryman, too? No, not just her ferryman. Tristan. Stolen away, just like everything else. Dylan didn't think she had any tears left, but as his face surfaced in her mind, more bubbled over, hot and salty on her cheeks.

It was the longest night Dylan had ever endured. Every time she closed her eyes, haunting images flashed through her head: Joan, Tristan, a father figure who was terrifying without a face, flickers of the nightmare from the train. Slowly, sluggishly, it passed. The fire dimmed to an orange glow, and the dark outside dissolved into a soft light that filtered through the windows, but Dylan didn't notice. She continued to stare at the logs till the warm colors of heat had dimmed to gray ash and the spent pieces of wood could do nothing but smoke softly in their grate. Her body seemed to have turned to stone. Her mind was shell-shocked and took refuge in stupor.

It took until midmorning for her to realize that the light meant she was free to escape her haven that was somehow also a prison. She could search for Tristan. What if he was lying somewhere in the valley, hurt and bleeding? What if he was waiting for her to come and find him?

She eyed the door, still closed against the terrors of the wasteland. Tristan was out there, but so were the wraiths. Were the valley's shadows deep enough and dark enough for them to attack? Would the morning light be strong enough to keep her safe?

When she thought about going out into the wasteland, on her own . . . her entire being shied away from the idea.

But Tristan was out there.

Get up, Dylan, she told herself. *Don't be so pathetic.*

She hauled her tired body, grumbling from yesterday's enforced exercise, off the bed and over to the door. She paused with her hand on the knob, took a deep breath, then another, and tried to make herself grip the doorknob, twist, and pull it open. Her fingers refused to obey.

"Cut it out," she muttered.

Tristan *needed* her.

Holding that thought in her head, she swung open the door.

The air caught in her lungs as she froze. Her heart stopped beating, then began thumping double time as her eyes struggled to take in the scene before her.

The wasteland that had become almost like home over the past few days had vanished.

There were no rolling hills, no long grasses tickled with dew drops to soak into her jeans and make tramping up and up and up as miserable as possible. The leaden sky had disappeared, and the graveled pathway that had led her to safety last night was gone.

Instead, the world had turned into many dazzling shades of red. The two hills remained, but now they were coated with burgundy dirt. There was no vegetation, but the steep sides were pierced with sharp, jagged rocks that burst from the ground in unique formations. The graveled path had been replaced by a slick black walkway that looked like boiling tar. It appeared to be constantly bubbling as if it were alive. The sky was bloodred, with black clouds that didn't drift so much as race to the western horizon. The sun glowed red-hot like a burning oven ring.

But these were not the most frightening things. Gliding across the surface, climbing the hills, and wandering up the pathway were hundreds upon hundreds of what looked like . . . well, Dylan couldn't even find the words. They were human and yet looked formless, only the briefest outline identifying their age and gender. Dylan looked closely at the ones nearest to her. They seemed not to see her, not even to be aware that *they* were really there. They were intent on only one thing—on following the brightly glowing orb that radiated in front of each of them.

Every figure was shadowed by a host of black specters that hovered around their heads and circled in front of them. Dylan drew in a panicked breath as she watched them, fearful for each of the figures, but though the wraiths swirled in the air around them, they kept their distance. It was the orbs, she realized suddenly. The wraiths didn't want to get close to the pulsing balls of light, though where the shadows were heaviest, she noticed they glowed less brightly and the demons dared to swoop more closely. Little cogs clicked into place at the back of her head as she stared.

She was one of those things. This was the real wasteland. And Tristan was her orb. Without her orb, could she even step outside safely? If she left the safe house now, could the demons attack her even though it was daytime? The only way to be sure was to step outside. Could she do that? She swayed gently in the doorway as she thought about it. No. Tilting out, she caught the hiss and wail of wraiths. That was enough. Horrified, she stepped back and slammed the door. She leaned her spine against it, as if she could hold the wraiths at bay. Her strength lasted only a few more seconds before she sank to the ground, wrapped her hands around her legs, and dropped her head to her knees.

"Tristan, I need you," she whispered. "I need you!" Her voice cracked and broke as tears tumbled forth. "Where are you?"

She was trapped. Not only did she not know where she had to go, if she stepped outside, the demons would get her. The only safe place was here, but how long could she wait for Tristan?

Minutes sauntered by. After a while Dylan pulled herself together a little. She stood up and dragged a chair over to the window. She settled into it and leaned her head on her folded arms, which she rested against the windowsill. The view was the same as from the front door. A crimson desert dotted with drifting souls blindly following and being followed. It was mesmerizing to watch. Seeing the demons still made her stomach churn as she remembered the scratch of their claws.

The thought of facing them again caused a trickle of sweat to slither down her back. She knew that she would not be able to walk outside today. It was still possible that Tristan was out there, trying to make his way back to her. She had to hold on to that hope. She could wait at least another day.

After a brilliant sunset of oranges, reds, and burgundies, the sky grew black. With the darkness came the whistling and screaming around the cottage. Dylan lit the fire—this time with matches she had found on top of the mantelpiece. It had been a much longer process than the previous night, but finally she had coaxed the flame to grow and devour the twigs. Now the large logs had caught, and the fire was crackling and spitting, providing warmth and comforting light. She had abandoned her post at the window. The darkness frightened her, and she could not tell who was outside, watching her. Instead she lay on the bed and gazed at the flames till her eyes drooped and she slipped into semiconsciousness.

~~~~~

When Dylan woke hours later, it was still pitch-black outside. She looked up at the ceiling, and just for a few moments she could have been anywhere. In her cramped room at home, surrounded by posters and teddy bears, or in a strange room in Aberdeen getting ready for another day of chatting with her dad. But she wasn't in either of these places. She was in a safe house. And she was dead. A steel band wrapped itself around her ribs. She couldn't breathe.

The cottage was warm. The fire that she had so carefully constructed still blazed in the grate and sent shadows rippling across the walls, but that wasn't what had pulled her from sleep. Turning over onto her side to watch the flames, she saw the true reason for her waking. A figure was silhouetted against the light of the fire, unmoving. Fear flooded her and she froze, but as her eyes adjusted, the outline began to take shape, a familiar shape sitting on the floor. A shape that Dylan had feared she would never see again.

FIFTEEN

"TRISTAN!" DYLAN GASPED. SHE JUMPED OFF THE BED, ALMOST falling in her haste to cross the room. He stood as she approached and, forgetting herself, she threw her arms around him in relief. Quiet sobs escaped her, making her chest shake. She nestled her head into his shoulder and let herself drown in the ocean of safety and pleasure that engulfed her.

Tristan stood immobilized for a moment, but then wrapped his arms around her and squeezed her tightly to him. He rubbed her back with one hand as she continued to cry into his chest.

Eventually Dylan felt the rush of emotions subside into calm, and, as the awkwardness returned, she drew herself away from him. She had little experience of being held by boys, and her head was a whirlwind of confusion. A blush warmed her cheeks, but she forced herself to look up into his eyes.

"Hi," she whispered.

His back was to the flames, his face hidden in shadow.

"Hi," he replied, the smile evident in his voice.

"I thought . . . I thought you were gone." Dylan's voice caught with emotion, but she plowed on, desperate to know. "What happened? You were just behind me."

There was a pause. Dylan's eyes searched in the darkness, but she couldn't see enough to read his expression.

"I'm sorry," he whispered. He took her hand and led her back over to the bed, sitting beside her. The light from the fire now flickered across his face, illuminating it for the first time and causing Dylan to draw a sharp intake of breath.

"Oh my God, Tristan, what happened to you?"

Tristan was barely recognizable. One eye was puffy and almost closed, the other bloodshot. His jaw was bruised and swollen, and one cheek had a deep gash running the length of it. He struggled to smile, but the attempt clearly hurt. Even in the dark, his eyes conveyed the suffering he had endured. Dylan reached a hand up to stroke his face but hesitated, afraid to cause him any more pain.

"It doesn't matter," he replied. "It's nothing."

Dylan shook her head slowly. It wasn't nothing. Tristan's face had been ravaged, mutilated. Was that because of her?

"Tristan . . ."

"Shh," he soothed. "I told you, it's nothing. You're still sleeping," he commented, an obvious attempt to change the subject.

She nodded. "It was just to pass the time."

"Do you think you could sleep more?" She shook her head before his sentence was finished. "Well, at the very least you should lie down and rest. Tomorrow we have far to go."

Dylan stared at him with pleading eyes. She knew he was trying to avoid discussion of where he'd been, but it came across as though he didn't want to talk to her about anything. She felt rejected. She'd thrown herself at him and made obvious her joy at his return. Now that seemed foolish. Her eyes smarting, she folded her arms across her chest. As if sensing her emotions, he reached and caught one of her hands, pulling it gently away from her side.

"Come on, lie down. I'll stay with you."

"I . . ." She was hesitant, uncertain.

His voice was a low murmur in the dark. "Lie down with me," he repeated. "Please."

He shuffled backward till he was lying down, leaning against the wall. He pulled her over beside his chest. She nestled into his side, feeling self-conscious but safe. He didn't seem to want to speak, but was content to lie there beside her. Dylan smiled and allowed herself to relax for the first time in two days.

~~~~~

In the morning light, Tristan's injuries looked even worse. His left eye was a blur of blue and black shadows, and his jaw was covered in shades of purple, brown, and yellow. The gash down his cheek was beginning to close, but the dried blood stood out starkly against his pale skin. He also had several long scratches down his arms. As the morning chased the gloom from the cottage, Dylan traced her fingers down one particularly vicious-looking wound that ran the length of Tristan's forearm. She still lay in his arms, and though she felt incredibly comfortable and secure there, she was afraid to speak and break the silence.

"We should get going," Tristan whispered in her ear. His voice was soft and low, and his breath tickled her neck and sent a shiver down her spine. Embarrassed, she jumped off the bed and away from him, coming to a standstill in the middle of the room, across from a window. She glanced out of it and saw that the wasteland, *her* wasteland, was back.

"It's changed," she gasped.

"What do you mean?" Tristan looked up sharply.

"Yesterday, before you came, I looked out of the door and . . . and . . ." Dylan didn't know quite how to describe the world she had seen. "Everything was red—the sun, the sky, the ground. And I could see souls, thousands of them, traveling with their guides. I saw the demons, they were everywhere . . ." Caught in the memory, Dylan's voice trailed off into a whisper.

"You only see the true wasteland when you lose your guide," he said to her. "I am the vessel that creates your projection."

"So it's fake? Everything I see is fake? It's just in my head?" Tristan had told her that already, but Dylan had never really appreciated just what it meant. Until now. She didn't like it. Although the wasteland of yesterday had been horrifying, she couldn't stand the thought of being tricked by Tristan.

"Dylan," he said tenderly. "You're dead. What you see in your mind is all you have. This place, here, this is the only way you can make the journey. This is what's real."

Dylan looked at him, and her eyes were pools of helplessness. He held out his hand to her.

"Come on," he said. "Let's go." He gave her a warm, reassuring smile that she returned with slightly trembling lips.

She stepped forward to take his hand, thrilling a little at the contact, and faced the door. This cottage had been both jail and shelter to her, and she had mixed feelings about leaving, but

Tristan strode out confidently and pulled her once more into the wasteland.

There was no sun today, but the layer of clouds that covered the sky was light and fluffy. Dylan wondered what it revealed about her mood. If she had to identify it herself, she would say pensive and curious. She was confused by what Tristan had said about the wasteland and her mind, but although she did not want to be deceived by this artificial place, she felt a lot safer in the familiar landscape of hills. Of course, the presence of Tristan played a vital role in that. She looked at him again, at the back of his head and his strong shoulders as he led her forward. What had happened to him? Dylan felt responsible for every bruise, every scratch. After all, he was here protecting her.

"Tristan," she began.

He looked back at her and slowed so that they were walking side by side. "What is it?"

Under his gaze, she chickened out and asked something else instead, something else she was curious about. "All those souls . . . I could see them walking, but they weren't coming to me. To the safe house, I mean."

"No."

"So, where do they stay? How does that work?"

Tristan shrugged nonchalantly. "Each ferryman has their own points of safety, of protection here. The way we look, that's you. But the place you and I stop, that will always be *my* safe house."

"Oh." Dylan was quiet for a minute, but she continued to sneak looks at Tristan, wondering if it was all right to pose the question that she really wanted to ask.

He caught one of her sidelong glances. "You want to know what happened to me," he guessed.

She nodded.

TRISTAN SIGHED, THE DESIRE TO BE HONEST AND SHARE WITH her fighting the knowledge that she should not know more about this world than was necessary for her to travel through it. He could not remember a time when a soul had seen and guessed so much about this world. No soul had ever been separated from their ferry-man and survived a demon attack before. Dylan should be lost to him, and yet here she was. He was astounded, and palpably grateful. How could this seemingly ordinary soul be so extraordinary?

"Why does it matter?" It wasn't so much a question as a stalling tactic whilst he tried to decide what to do: what was right, or what he wanted.

It worked. Dylan was silent as she thought about it.

"Because, well . . . because it's really my fault. You're here because of me, and if I had been faster, or kept the sun out longer, shining more brightly, then . . . well, then it would never have happened."

Tristan looked surprised, and he was. This was not the answer he had expected. He'd thought it was simply curiosity about this world—the human need to know *everything*. But it was because she cared. A glow began in his chest, and he knew his decision was made.

"You didn't tell me they could hurt you," she said softly, her green eyes wide with empathetic pain.

"Yes," he replied. "They can't actually kill me, but they can touch me."

"Tell me what happened to you." It was a demand wrapped in velvet, and he couldn't resist her a third time.

"They were everywhere, and you were frozen. I could see that you couldn't move, and you needed to run."

DYLAN NODDED. SHE REMEMBERED THIS PART. HER CHEEKS burned with disgrace at the memory. If she had just run when he'd told her, if she'd been braver and hadn't been immobilized by fear, they would have both made it.

"I pushed you, and you seemed to come out of a trance. Then, when we ran, I thought we would be OK." He grimaced. "I didn't mean to let go of you," he whispered.

Dylan chewed on her lip, guilt rising like nausea inside of her. *He* felt bad, was blaming himself, when it had been all her fault.

"Tristan—" She tried to interrupt, but he shushed her with his hand.

"I'm sorry, Dylan. I'm sorry about that. As soon as they saw that I'd let you go, they surrounded me, got between us. I couldn't get through them to catch up. Then you were running, but the cottage was too far. You weren't going to make it." His eyes had a faraway look at this point, as if he was reliving it. The set of his mouth told Dylan that it was painful. Her guilt increased as she realized dredging this up was hurting him again. She began to question her motives. Was it simply nosiness? She hoped not.

"The demons were everywhere," he continued. "You can't touch them, but I can. Did you know that?"

She shook her head, not trusting herself to speak, not wanting to break his rhythm.

"I ran after you and pulled as many of them back as I could. I couldn't get them all; I've never seen them swarm in such a number. It wasn't working. Although I can touch them, I can't damage them. Every time I yanked them away, they would simply circle off and attack from another angle."

He broke off at this point and seemed to be struggling internally. Dylan wasn't sure if he was debating whether to say something or simply trying to work out how to say it. She waited patiently. Tristan looked up at the sky. It seemed to hold his answer: he nodded curtly and sighed.

"There are some things that I can do in the wasteland . . . things that aren't normal, things you might call magical."

Dylan held her breath. This was the sort of confession she had been waiting for, something that would make sense of it all.

"I conjured up a wind." He paused as Dylan's eyebrows furrowed together, confused. She hadn't noticed that. "You wouldn't have felt it; it was only for the demons."

"You conjured a wind?" she asked, astonished. "You can do that?"

Tristan grimaced. "It's difficult, but I can."

"What do you mean it's difficult?"

"It takes a lot of energy, drains me, but it worked. They were being buffeted all over the place. They couldn't get a grip on you." He sighed. "But it didn't take them long to figure out what was causing it. The majority of the swarm turned and began to attack me."

"You should have stopped," Dylan blurted out. "You should have stopped the wind and . . . and fought them, or—"

Tristan shook his head, stopping her words. "I had to make sure you were safe. You are my number-one priority in the wasteland." He smiled at the horrified expression on her face. "I can't die, and I am duty-bound to protect the soul first, myself second."

Dylan nodded numbly at this. Of course he wasn't just putting himself in danger specially for *her*. It was his job.

"They tried attacking me, slashing at me with their claws and flying straight at me, kind of like a full-body punch. They can't go through me like they can you. There were still some around you, but you were so close to the cottage. I managed to keep it going until I saw you cross the threshold, but then the entire swarm focused on me and there were too many to fight. They dragged me under."

Dylan pictured it in her head as he spoke. The demons plummeting downward, curling viciously around him, pulling and scratching at his face. She imagined him trying to fight them off, thrashing his arms and trying to run. The demons swarming all over him, grabbing tighter and pulling him down, down into the ground. Although, even in her imagination, he should have been too far away for her to see, every feature of his expression was crystal clear: his face a mask of terror and panic, eyes wide and mouth gaping open in horror. Blood trickled down his face, running into his left eye, where one of the demons had mauled him. In her mind's eye, Tristan slowly disappeared. How much had they hurt him? How much pain had there been in each blow, each clawing talon? And he went through all of it for her.

"The last thing I heard was you calling for me. I tried to fight them off to get to you, but there were too many of them. At least I knew you were safe." He looked at her, blue eyes piercing straight to her core.

Dylan could do nothing but gaze back, lost in awe, lost in the depth of his stare. So of course she fell. Her foot caught on a clump of grass.

"Oh!" she gasped, as she felt herself falling forward toward the ground. She closed her eyes and waited for the thump—but it never came. Tristan's hand had darted out and grabbed the back of her hoodie, bringing her to an abrupt stop just above the ground. She opened her eyes and peeked at the path. As she'd thought—wet and mucky. She hadn't even sighed with relief before she was yanked backward. Tristan appeared to be trying very hard to keep a straight face, but a laugh escaped his clenched jaw.

Dylan huffed and marched away with the little dignity she had left. She heard the laughing intensify behind her.

"You are *so* clumsy," he joked, catching up with her easily.

She put her nose up in the air and continued to walk, praying she wouldn't trip again. "Well, no wonder. Look at this place. Couldn't the wasteland be paved?" she hissed, trying to hold on to her anger.

Tristan shrugged. "It's your fault—you made it like this."

Dylan made a face. "I hate hiking," she muttered. "And I hate hills."

"Aren't Scottish people meant to be proud of their hills?" He looked at her quizzically.

Now it was her turn to shrug. "Our PE teacher would put us into a minibus every year, drive us out to the countryside, and force us up mountains in the freezing cold. It was torture. I'm not a big fan of uphill."

"Ah, I see." He grinned. "Well, you'll be relieved to know we're past halfway. You'll be out of here soon." He meant it to cheer her up, but Dylan's face fell a little at this news.

Then what? What was beyond this wasteland? And did that mean she would never see Tristan again? The thought of this was more upsetting than her fear of the unknown. Tristan had become the only person in her world, and she couldn't bear to lose this final thing.

Her musings took her to the top of the hill, over a few lumps and bumps, and into a natural hollow. The perfect spot for a little rest. She looked hopefully at Tristan, and he smiled, understanding. With the smile came a shake of his head, however.

"Not today," he told her.

Dylan pouted, staring up at Tristan petulantly.

"I'm sorry," he said. "We don't have time, Dylan. I don't want us to get caught again."

He held out a hand, an invitation. Dylan gazed at it morosely, but he was right. They had to try to stay ahead of the night, and the wraiths that came with it. She didn't want Tristan to suffer any more because of her. Reaching out, she took the hand he offered. It was covered with scratches and bruises, mirroring the faded marks on Dylan's own arms. He pulled her up out of the hollow, and at once she was assaulted by the strength of the wind stinging her ears. It made conversation difficult as they descended. Dylan had hoped to get Tristan back to what had gone on beneath the earth, but it seemed she would have to wait for a more peaceful moment. It wasn't the sort of tale that could be shouted over the wind.

Besides, though she was desperate to hear what happened next, she was afraid of discovering what else he had endured. For her.

SIXTEEN

THANKFULLY THEY MADE IT TO THE NEXT SAFE HOUSE WELL before the sun went down. It was another stone cottage, and Dylan began to wonder if the look of the safe houses was part of her projection. Were they supposed to be her idea of sanctuary, of home? She tried to think about where she might have made that connection. The flat she lived in—*had* lived in—with her mother was a red sandstone tenement surrounded by countless other identical buildings. Her gran had lived in the countryside before she died, but that had been a modern bungalow with over-fussy landscaped gardens dotted with ridiculous stone lions and gnomes. She couldn't think of anywhere else that had been like home.

Except, well, her dad had mentioned his place when they'd talked on the phone. A small stone house, he'd called it. Old-fashioned, with just enough room for him and Anna, the dog. Was this the image her mind had conjured up of that place? Perhaps her subconscious was trying to give her a little of the thing she'd hoped for but had never managed to attain. For a moment she imagined the door opening and a man walking out. He was handsome, strong, and kind-looking. She smiled at the thought, then realized that was all it was. She'd never even seen a picture of her dad, couldn't remember what he'd looked like before he left. A random Google search had brought up over a dozen James Millers, and she hadn't wanted to ask her mother which one was him. Shaking her head to chase these hard thoughts away, she followed Tristan to the front door.

Although slightly tumbledown, there was something comforting about this cottage—it felt almost like coming home after a long, hard journey. The front door was solid oak, weather-beaten but strong. The windows were encrusted with the sort of grime that accumulates through long-term exposure to the fierce Scottish weather, but they were wooden sash and looked in good repair. There was no garden, but a little paved path led up to the front door. Weeds and grass peeked up through the cracks, but had not yet reclaimed the ground.

Inside, the cottage did not have the same abandoned, disordered look the others had had, and Dylan wondered idly if it was because she was becoming more at home in the wasteland. There was a bed at one end with a table beside it, which held a large but half-burned candle and an old chest of drawers. A table and chairs sat in the middle of the room in front of the fireplace, and at the other end was a small kitchen with a chipped and grubby Belfast sink. Dylan approached it, eyeing the old-fashioned taps and wondering whether they worked. Her jeans were still encrusted with mud and the gray zip-up hoodie that she had chosen back in the flat before any of this death nonsense had started was now a patchwork of stains, mud splashes, and little rips. She didn't even want to think about what her face looked like.

Although the taps were rusted and the sink was caked in mud, Dylan felt optimistic as she turned the cold tap. At first nothing happened, but then there was a groaning and gurgling. She stepped back warily, just as the tap spurted out a torrent of brown water. After a few seconds of spewing, the flow settled down into a trickle that looked fairly clean.

"Oh, yes," said Dylan, looking forward to being able to have a wash for the first time in days. She tried the hot tap, too, which also poured forth mucky water before turning clear, but it never heated up. She splashed the water on her face, shivering at the icy temperature. Playfully she scooped up a handful of the water and turned to throw it at Tristan. She stopped short, the water falling through her slackened fingers to bounce off the flagstoned floor. The room was empty.

"Tristan!" she screamed, panic-filled. The door was standing open and, though it was still light, night was fast approaching. Did she dare go outside? She could not be alone again. That thought was her deciding factor—she started purposefully forward, just as Tristan appeared in the doorway.

"What?" he asked innocently.

"Where the hell did you go?" Dylan demanded, relief quickly turning to anger.

"I was just outside." He looked at her stricken face. "Sorry, I didn't mean to scare you."

"I just . . . I was worried," she muttered, feeling overdramatic now. She turned and waved at the sink behind her. "The tap works in here."

Tristan gave her a half smile, then glanced back at the door.

"There's still twenty minutes of light left. I'll stay outside and give you some privacy. I'll be just by the front door," he promised. "You'll be able to talk to me if you want to." He smiled reassuringly and walked back outside.

Dylan wandered over to the doorway and peeked outside. He was seated on a rock. He glanced up and caught her looking at him.

"You can shut the door if you want. I promise not to look if you want to leave it open, though." He winked, embarrassing her.

Fidgeting where she stood, she considered the idea of washing—she was desperate to clean up—with the door open and him just outside. Uncomfortable. But then she thought about shutting the door and being alone inside. The terror of being abandoned was still too raw. Even the thought made her heart flutter with alarm. She closed the door halfway, shutting out his smirking face but leaving a small gap. Just in case.

Eyeing the door uncomfortably, she stripped off her clothes and, using a sliver of soap that she found by the sink, began to wash as quickly as possible. It was freezing and she considered getting Tristan to start the fire, but she knew that by the time it was lit, they'd both have to be inside for safety. Gritting her teeth to stop them from chattering, she tried to be thorough and speedy. Then there was no option but to put her dirty clothes back on. Dylan wrinkled her nose as she yanked on her mud-caked jeans. She was just pulling her T-shirt over her head when Tristan knocked on the door. Although the T-shirt was fairly baggy and not at all see-through, she snatched up her gray hoodie and yanked it on, zipping it right up to her chin.

"You done?" He snuck a quick look through the door. "It's just that it's getting dark."

"I'm done," she mumbled.

Tristan walked in, shutting the door firmly. "I'll get the fire going."

Dylan nodded gratefully. She was still cold from washing in the freezing water. Again it took him a ridiculously short time, and flames were soon roaring in the grate. He stood up and observed her.

"How was the bath? Better?"

She nodded. "Wish I had a change of clothes, though." She sighed.

Tristan smiled wryly and walked over to the chest of drawers. "There's some stuff in here. Not sure how good the fit will be, but we could try and wash your clothes if you want. Here." He tossed a T-shirt and some joggers at her. They were a little big, but the thought of being able to wash her own clothes was very appealing.

"No underwear, though," Tristan added.

Dylan mulled it over and decided that going commando for one night was a fair price to pay for some clean clothes. She was going to have to change, though, and it was too dark to ask Tristan to go back outside. She squirmed from foot to foot, holding the clothes against her chest. Tristan spotted her discomfort.

"I'll go and stand over here," he said, crossing the room to the sink. "You can change by the bed." He stared out of the small kitchen window. Dylan scurried over to the bed and, after a quick glance at Tristan, she whipped off her clothes as fast as possible.

Tristan stared resolutely at the glass, into the nothingness of the night. Dylan wondered what he was thinking about . . . He blew out a steadying breath.

When Dylan was done, he turned to face her and smiled.

"Nice," he commented.

She flushed and tugged at the T-shirt. She felt awkward being braless and folded her arms across her chest.

"Want help with the laundry?" he offered.

Dylan widened her eyes, mortified at the thought of him getting a peek at her ratty underwear. Why, oh why, hadn't she died in some glorious Victoria's Secret ensemble?

"No, it's OK." She grabbed the dirty clothes from the bed and held them tightly against her body as she crossed the room, trying to keep her bra and underwear hidden in the center of the ball. She plonked them down on the counter and spent five minutes scrubbing the sink with an old scouring pad to try to clean off the muck before uncoiling the rusty chain and stuffing in the plug. She turned both taps on full—the stream from the hot tap still icy cold—but couldn't get more than a dribble. The sink was going to take an age to fill.

While she waited, the heat of the fire lured her to the middle of the room. Tristan was already seated in one of the chairs, leaning back comfortably with his feet propped on a stool. Dylan sat on the second chair and drew her knees up to her chest. She wrapped her arms around her legs and looked over at Tristan. Now was the time to get the rest of the story.

"So," she said softly.

He looked over at her. "So?"

"Tell me the rest, Tristan. What happened when they dragged you under?"

He stared into the flames, but Dylan felt that he wasn't seeing the fire; he was back outside with the demons.

"It was dark." His voice was low, hypnotic, and Dylan could immediately see everything he described in her mind's eye. "They pulled me down through the ground, and I couldn't breathe. The dirt filled my mouth and nose. If I hadn't known better, I'd have thought I was dying. It seemed to last forever, just going down and down, deeper into the earth. Finally, the force of the demons pulled me through something, and then I was falling. They were slashing at me again, cackling in delight and diving close to me so that I twisted and somersaulted through the air. Then I hit something, something hard. It felt like I'd broken every bone in my body. Of course I hadn't, but the agony . . . I've never felt anything like it. The demons were swarming all over me, and I couldn't even defend myself—" Tristan broke off suddenly, looking over toward the kitchen. "The sink's about to overflow."

HE NEEDED TO TAKE A BREAK, TO PAUSE AND GATHER HIS thoughts. It disconcerted him. Tristan had never been caught before, had never been overpowered by the demons. He'd told Dylan that protecting the soul came first, and that was true, but only to a point. Self-preservation always took over, and so sometimes souls were lost. Not this one, though. He would sacrifice himself to keep her safe; these pains were a small price to pay.

"Oh!" Dylan had been mesmerized by his words and the look in his eyes, and had forgotten about the sink. She scurried out of the chair and, with some difficulty, twisted the rusty taps to stop the water. She dipped the soap in and rubbed it vigorously between her palms, trying to coax some suds out of it. She managed to make a decent lather. Next she dunked her clothes in and left them to soak while she skipped back and plonked herself down across from Tristan, looking at him expectantly.

He smiled slightly.

"How did you get away?" she asked.

He smiled. "You."

"What?" Dylan looked at him, aghast.

"You needed me. That brought me back. I . . . I didn't know that could happen—it never has before—but you called to me. I heard you. I heard you, and the next thing I knew, I was back at the entrance to the valley. You saved me, Dylan." He stared at her, eyes warm and full of wonder.

Dylan opened her mouth, but shock robbed her of speech. A sudden vivid memory of cowering on the floor, her back against the door and crying for Tristan. Is that what had done it?

"Why did it take so long?" she whispered. "I waited for you all day."

"I'm sorry," he murmured softly. "I came back at the other side of the valley. I . . ." He shifted uncomfortably. "I was moving a little slower. It took all day to walk to you."

"I was so glad to see you. It was terrifying being alone. But more than that . . ." Dylan blushed and looked away from him into the flames. "I was frightened that they were hurting you, wherever you were. And they did." She reached out to touch his battered face, but he pulled away.

"We need to get your clothes out of the water or they won't dry in time," he said.

Dylan pulled her arm back quickly and dropped it in her lap. She stared down at her knees as her cheeks burned and her stomach twisted.

TRISTAN SAW THE EMBARRASSMENT AND DEJECTION ON HER face and felt a stab of regret. He opened his mouth to say something, but Dylan had already spun away to the sink, hiding her humiliation by pounding the dirt viciously out of her clothes.

THANKFUL TO HAVE A TASK THAT WOULD KEEP HER EYES AWAY from him, Dylan took her time wringing every drop of water out.

"I'll help you hang them." Tristan wandered up behind her, and his voice in her ear made her jump and drop her bra on the stone floor. He bent to pick it up for her, but she snatched it out of his reaching hand.

"Thanks, but I can manage," she mumbled, pushing past him.

There was no drying rack, so Dylan turned the chairs round and hung her clothes over the backs and arms to dry beside the fire. She tried to find a discreet place to hang her underwear, but in the end gave up and settled for a spot that at least ensured they would be dry. With the chairs taken up, there was nowhere to sit except the bed. Tristan was already there, lounging lazily and watching her with a strange expression on his face.

IN FACT, HE WAS FIGHTING WITH HIS CONSCIENCE. DYLAN WAS human and he . . . wasn't. Not really. He'd been created to do this, just this, for eternity. He wasn't a person, not like she was. She was going through something momentous and frightening, and he was there to help her, nothing more. As her protector, he would be taking advantage of her vulnerability if he acted on his feelings.

She had feelings for him—he thought he could read it in her eyes. But he could be wrong. It could be nothing more than her fear of being alone. The trust she put in him could be merely born out of necessity—what other choice did she have? Her need to be close to him, the way she wanted to touch him, could be nothing more than the comfort a child yearns for when they are afraid. But he could not be sure.

There was one final consideration, and it was a clincher. He could not follow where she was going. He would have to leave her at the border, or, more correctly, she would have to leave him. If she did feel for him, then to give now what he would soon have to take away was cruel. He would not put her through that. He must not act on what he felt. He looked at her, saw her watching him with those green eyes, dark as the forest, and felt his throat constrict. He was her guide and protector. Nothing more. Still, he could comfort her. That much he could allow himself. He smiled and held out his arms.

DYLAN CROSSED OVER TO HIM SHYLY AND CLIMBED ONTO THE bed, curling up into his side. Absentmindedly, he stroked her arm, sending a tingle jolting into her core. She dropped her head onto his shoulder and smiled to herself. How could it be that here, in the midst of all this chaos and fear, having lost absolutely *everything*, she suddenly felt . . . whole?

SEVENTEEN

"TELL ME SOMETHING." DYLAN'S VOICE WAS SLIGHTLY CROAKY from sitting so long in companionable silence.

"What do you want to know?" Tristan asked, breaking out of his reverie.

"I don't know." She paused, considering. "Tell me about the most interesting soul you've ever guided."

He laughed. "You."

Dylan poked him in the ribs. "Be serious."

He thought about it for a moment.

"OK, I've got one. I had to guide a German soldier from the Second World War once. He was shot by his commanding officer for refusing to carry out his duties."

"A Nazi?" Dylan asked, shocked. Her knowledge of history wasn't great, but she couldn't imagine how guiding a German soldier could be something you'd want to remember. She might have been tempted to let the demons have him.

"You're judging. When you're a ferryman, you cannot stereotype like that. Each soul is individual and has its own merits and faults." Dylan gave him a skeptical look, so he continued. "Jonas was conscripted into the army; he didn't have a choice about it. His very first assignment was in a concentration camp in occupied Poland. As soon as he saw what was happening, he refused to follow orders. He tried to help one of the prisoners instead, and his superior shot him. He was only eighteen. It was such a waste."

"He shouldn't have joined in the first place. He should have—"

"I told you, he didn't join up voluntarily," Tristan corrected gently. "He received the order for training and so he went."

"Well, he shouldn't have. He could have run or something."

"He didn't really understand. Do you think they were completely open about what they were doing, what was actually happening to people? His father said he'd endanger the family if he didn't present himself at the barracks, so he went, and they tried to fill his head with their ideas. Then, as soon as he set foot in the concentration camp, he saw what was really happening."

Dylan stared at him, riveted now. Her eyes were wide and her eyebrows furrowed. Her disdain had melted into pity.

"I met him outside the gates of the camp. All he could think about was the man he hadn't been able to save. He was destroyed with guilt even though he was among the few soldiers to resist. He wished he'd stood up to his father and refused to join, wished he'd been able to help the people he'd left behind. At times, he wished he'd never been born. I'd never seen a soul in so much despair for such selfless reasons. He died in a Nazi uniform, but he was not a Nazi soldier. He was one of the most admirable and noble souls I have come across."

The end of his story was met with silence. Dylan was captivated, her head a whirlwind of images, thoughts, and emotions.

"Tell me another," she begged, and so the night passed that way. Tristan regaled her with tales from the thousands of souls he'd guided, handpicked to make her laugh, or smile, or pause in wonder—keeping to himself the ones that still cut into his heart. The light snuck up on both of them, but the blazing sunshine was glorious and caught Tristan's eye, making him smile wryly.

"More marching," Dylan grumbled when he slithered off the bed and pulled her with him.

"Yes." He smiled. "But today there's no uphill."

"What do you mean?" she asked.

"We've got one small hill, barely an incline, then it's flat all the way. Wet, though." He wrinkled his nose.

"More marshes?" Dylan complained, unable to keep the whine out of her voice. She hated the mud that coated everything and dragged her feet.

"Nope, no mud—water."

"I hope we're not swimming," she muttered, wandering over to the smoking fireplace to check her clothes. Although not particularly clean, they were dry and still fairly warm. She turned to Tristan and pointed at the door. "Out!" she ordered.

He rolled his eyes but bowed obediently and stepped outside. Dylan shut the door firmly before whipping off her borrowed clothes and pulling on her old outfit. They had stiffened in the heat of the fire, but it was nice to have freshly washed clothes. It made her feel almost human again. *Or freshly dead at least,* she thought, laughing to herself.

As soon as she was dressed, she splashed her face and neck at the sink. Taking another scoop of water, she held it in her hands and stared at it. What would happen if she drank it? She glanced at the door but it was still shut. She could ask Tristan, but he'd probably laugh at her. She looked back at the water. Although she wasn't thirsty, she remembered the feeling of drinking, of the refreshing taste, the icy sensation of water dropping down her gullet into an empty stomach, making her shiver. Leaning forward, she opened her lips, ready to take a drink.

"I wouldn't."

Tristan's voice made her jump, and the water sloshed down her front, soaking her hoodie.

"Bloody hell! You almost gave me a heart attack!" She paused, catching her breath. "Why shouldn't I drink it?"

He shrugged. "It'll make you puke. It's toxic. It comes from a well that goes deep into the ground, and the ground is where the wraiths live. They poison it."

"Oh." Dylan turned off the tap. "Well, then, thank you."

"You're welcome."

His smile was warm and genuine, and stopped her heart momentarily. Just as quickly, though, it seemed to freeze on his face and he turned away. Confused, Dylan followed him silently out.

Although the sun stayed strong, a chilly breeze crept up behind her and gently ruffled her hair. She frowned at the sky to chastise it for the cool wind, but was rewarded only by fast-moving clouds that quickly covered the sun. She concentrated on keeping up with Tristan, who was setting a brisk pace across a meadow of grass.

Soon he stopped and gestured. "Well, here it is. Your last hill."

Following his pointing finger with her eyes, Dylan wrinkled her nose in disgust.

"*Barely an incline?*" she imitated. "You liar! It's huge!"

The hill looked more like a mountain. There was no gentle

ridge to climb, but a sheer face with large rock formations. It reminded her of her mother's disastrous attempt to get her to enjoy the outdoors by going on a trip to the Cobbler. She'd told Dylan it would be more fun to climb the front face, a wall of granite interspersed with slippery gravel patches, than to wander up the ambling path around the rear of the hill. Dylan had skidded on the small stones, smacked her shin on a large, pointy rock, and insisted that they return home there and then. This climb looked no more appealing.

"Couldn't we go round it?" she asked, peeking up at Tristan optimistically.

"Nope," he answered, grinning at her.

"How about a piggyback?" she suggested, but her request was ignored.

Despite his injuries, Tristan walked without a hint of a limp as he crossed the meadow, and Dylan had noticed earlier that his face was healing quickly. In fact, the swelling around his eye was now only a slight purple blush along his cheekbone. His jaw was no longer multicolored but had just the faint shadow of yellow as the bruising faded.

Dylan trotted after him, and they reached the base of the hill a short time later. The incline was so uninviting, even the grass had given up just a few yards in. From then on up it was dirt, gravel, and rock. The occasional hardy plant wound its way out from under boulders, but otherwise it was inhospitable and desolate.

Dylan's calves were soon burning as she trudged up the near-vertical gradient. Though they were well worn and comfortable, her shoes rubbed a blister onto the ball of her foot in protest at the odd angle. About halfway up, the angle became even more acute, and she was compelled to climb. Tristan insisted on letting her go first. He claimed it was to catch her in case she fell, but she had a sneaking suspicion that he was merely enjoying watching her struggle.

"Almost there," he called from a few feet below. "Trust me, when you reach the top, the view'll be worth it."

"My ass," she muttered under her breath. Her arms and legs were aching, and her fingers were raw and ingrained with dirt. She hauled herself up another few feet onto a small ledge and paused to catch her breath. Foolishly, she looked down and gasped. The ground below her fell away steeply and the meadow was a long, long way down. She swayed, dizzy with vertigo, and groaned as her stomach twisted.

"Don't look down," Tristan called sharply from underneath. "Come on, keep going! I promise you're almost there."

Dylan looked unconvinced but turned back to the rock face and continued to heave herself up. A bit more climbing and she found herself at the top. She flopped over and lay panting on a small patch of resilient heather. Tristan followed moments later and stood over her, not even breathing hard. Dylan eyed him with annoyance. He ignored her look and nodded toward the horizon.

"See, I told you it was worth the climb."

Dylan dragged herself up onto her elbows and peered into the distance. The landscape on the other side was shimmering, like a million diamonds sparkling in the sun. She squinted, trying to make sense of what she was seeing. It looked as though the glistening surface was undulating. Her scrambled brain tried to apply logic to what her eyes saw. Ah, water. It was a lake—a giant lake that stretched south of the hill as far as the eye could see.

The pooling water was wide, extending miles to the east and west. There was no way they could circle it; it would take forever.

"How are we supposed to cross that?" she spluttered, recovering the use of her voice.

"Don't worry, we're not swimming." A knowing smile played its way across his lips. Dylan frowned. He always had to be so secretive. "Come on, time to go."

"Urgh," Dylan groaned, pulling herself up to a sitting position against the will of her tired muscles. She scrambled to her feet and glared at the descent. It looked more inviting than the climb up, but not by much. On this more sheltered side, grass and small bushes grew in clumps all the way down the hill, intersected by rivers of gravel.

The short rest had obviously not been part of Tristan's plan, as he strode confidently and securely down to the lakeside, not even glancing at the ground beneath his feet. Dylan slipped and slid behind him, yelping in surprise when a sudden six-foot skid made her throw her arms out to stop from falling. Tristan didn't even look round, but shook his head at her clumsiness. Dylan stuck her tongue out at him. She was sure he could have carried her if he really wanted to.

At the base of the hill, the water spread out before them. It was majestic, with small waves rippling across its surface in the breeze. It spread as far as the horizon, and seemed to Dylan almost to be breathing. Like a living thing, the shore moved and whispered, the water lapping quietly against a narrow beach of shiny black pebbles. Beyond this, the water was silent. Eerily noiseless. There was no wind rushing in her ears, and without it Dylan was abruptly aware of the absence of wildlife. There were no gulls diving across the surface of the water, screeching as they searched for food, or ducks paddling in the shallows. It seemed empty, and although magnificent, the lake frightened Dylan a little.

Tristan turned left just at the boundary of the stones and headed toward a small wooden building. Dylan didn't even bother to ask but followed dutifully after him. It was a windowless shed with an apex roof. Tristan reached it several steps before her and opened two huge doors wide, revealing what was hidden within.

"You are kidding," Dylan blurted, looking with horror.

It was a small dinghy—if you could call it that—made of roughly hewn wood. It had once been painted white with red-and-blue trim, but that had long since faded; only a few flakes hung on to commemorate the jaunty glory of its youth. It stood on a small wheeled trolley with a coil of frayed rope attached to the front. Tristan grabbed hold of the rope with both hands and heaved. The boat scraped forward a little with a loud groan from the trailer's rusty wheels. He turned and lifted the rope over his shoulder, pulling forward. Slowly the boat rolled out of the shed. In the light of day, it looked even less water-worthy than in the gloom of the boat shed. The wood was rotten in places, and some of the planks were split down their entire length.

"You expect me to get *in* this thing?" Dylan complained.

"Yes" was the brief and, Dylan was pleased to detect, slightly breathless answer.

Tristan maneuvered the trolley down the pebbles and straight to the water's edge. He held out his arm. "Hop in."

Dylan looked dubious. "It's still attached to the trolley."

He rolled his eyes. "We won't exactly be coming back this way. I'm just going to push it till the boat floats and comes away from it. You can wait till we're waist-deep in water to get in, if you want to."

Dylan frowned and pursed her lips, but approached the edge of the water. Now that she was close to it, she noticed something odd about the lake. The water was black—not the kind you would associate with water at night or under heavy clouds, but as if the water were made of tar—only much more fluid. She wanted to run her hand through it and see what it felt like, but she didn't dare. Still, Tristan was planning to wade out into it, so it couldn't be anything too poisonous. That thought comforted her as she prepared to set herself afloat on the strange lake.

Putting one foot on the trolley wheel, she grabbed hold of the back of the tiny boat and heaved her other leg over the side. Her momentum carried her forward, and she jarred her shoulder stopping herself from smacking face-first into the little wooden bench. She righted herself with as much dignity as she could muster and tried to find a comfortable way to perch on the one seat. She had no idea where Tristan was planning to sit. Or how he would steer. Or, yet more importantly, how he planned to make this little boat move.

AS SOON AS TRISTAN SAW THAT SHE WAS SAFELY BALANCED and upright, he began to push the boat farther into the water. It was heavier with her sitting in it, and his muscles strained with the effort. The black water was freezing cold, and unseen things tangled at his ankles, dragging each foot forward so that even standing became a momentous effort. At last he felt the boat lift away from the trolley and bob on the surface. Using the frame of the trolley, he jumped lightly into the boat. The movement made the vessel rock violently, and his swinging legs sprayed Dylan with icy droplets. She screeched and grabbed hold of both sides of the little dinghy, screwing up her eyes and turning her face away from the showery assault.

"Watch it!" she shrieked.

"Sorry," he said, grinning and not sounding sorry at all. He plonked himself down on another bench.

They stared at each other for a moment—one face annoyed, the other amused. The craft swayed gently on the lightly lapping waves and the wind was calm. It would have been extremely pleasant with the sun radiating warmth overhead, were it not for the dark water beneath them.

EIGHTEEN

"WELL, THIS IS NICE," DYLAN SAID SARCASTICALLY, TO BREAK the silence and jolt Tristan into action.

"Yeah." He sighed, looking out across the lake.

Maybe direct questioning would give a better result. "Tristan, how are we supposed to get to the other side?"

"We row," he said simply. He reached under Dylan's bench, causing her to yank her legs quickly to the side, and retrieved two battered-looking oars.

Dylan was positive this time—they had not been there when she'd clambered in. He stuck an oar into each of the rowlocks on the sides of the boat—where the hell had they come from?—and lowered them to slice through the dark waves. First Tristan used one oar to turn the boat round, and then began to row power-fully with both arms. He stopped briefly to remove his sweatshirt, and Dylan stared at the way his muscles bunched and strained as he rowed, the movement pulling the thin cotton of his T-shirt tight against the muscles of his chest. He handled the dinghy confidently, hands clenched in fists around the handles, their grip firm and strong.

Dylan felt her cheeks grow hot, and a strange urge to fidget made it hard to sit still. She swallowed, then glanced up to see him watching her. Mortified to be caught ogling, she dropped her gaze to the oars as they sliced through the rippling surface of the lake. Observing their smooth, circular motion, Dylan had a horrible thought. "You're not expecting me to take a turn, are you?"

Tristan snorted. "No, I'd like to get there before the end of time, if you don't mind."

Dylan raised her eyebrows, but since she was getting what she wanted, she didn't argue further. Instead she stared out across the water. The hill they had descended appeared to be the center of a horseshoe of peaks that circled half of the lake. They curled inward, providing a measure of protection from the weather. Maybe that was why the water was so calm, the swell barely rocking the tiny boat. The landscape ahead of them, however, was empty. It was as if the world just fell away.

Although Tristan was rowing fairly slowly, his powerful strokes were moving them quickly across, and Dylan could now barely see the shore that they'd left. The opposite side was still not in sight, and she experienced a moment of fear. What if the battered little boat started taking on water? Dylan wasn't sure she would be able to make it to shore. Her mother had forced her to take swimming lessons as a small child, but as soon as she was old enough to be aware of the fact that she had a body, she had refused to keep going. The walk from the changing room to the pool, three-quarters naked, was humiliating.

There was also the thought of having to dive into *that* water. Dylan could see nothing below the surface. There was no way to tell how deep it was or what might lurk beneath. Hanging her arm over the side, she let her fingertips trail. Within seconds, they were stinging from its freezing chill. The air temperature was lovely— the water shouldn't have been so cold. It was unnatural. It also felt, oddly, slightly thicker than water. Not quite the consistency of oil, but somewhere in between. Yes, a sinking boat would definitely be a bad thing.

"I wouldn't do that if I were you." Tristan pulled her out of her thoughts.

"What?"

He nodded toward the hand that still rippled the surface of the lake. "That."

Instantly, Dylan yanked her hand away and examined it closely, expecting it to be black or missing a fingertip. It was fine.

"Why not?"

He gave her a steady look. "You never know what's hiding under there."

Dylan gulped and put both hands firmly in her lap, but she couldn't help leaning slightly over the side and peering into the waves, mesmerized by the undulation of the water. The only sound was the gentle rhythmic splash of the oars.

TRISTAN WATCHED HER GAZING AT THE WAVES. HER EYES WERE wide, catching the light sparkling on the surface, but seeing nothing. Her face looked peaceful, forehead unlined with a slight smile playing softly across her lips. Her hands were now jammed between her knees, and the pose made him grin, although it quickly faded when he remembered why. She was right to listen to him; there were things lurking here that belonged only in her nightmares. Creatures of the deep. Still, her mood was calm, and so the weather matched accordingly. At this pace they would be safely across and out of danger long before dark. To the safe house. He couldn't bring himself to think any further ahead than that.

"How long?" Dylan murmured softly.

He stared at her, confused.

"Till we get there," she clarified.

"To the next safe house?" *Please let that be the question,* he thought, panicking.

"Till we reach the end." She looked up at that point, and her eyes bored into him.

He found that he couldn't lie. "Tomorrow," he croaked.

Tomorrow. So soon. One more night, then he would have to let her go and never see her again. His throat constricted at the thought. Ordinarily, this lake crossing was the best part of the journey. Ordinarily, he longed to be free of whatever soul burdened him, desperate to get away from the whining, complaining, and self-pity. Not this time. It would be agony to watch her go where she deserved, but where he could never follow. He watched Dylan's eyes widen as she took in his words. They seemed to shimmer slightly, and he wondered for one brief, euphoric but painful moment whether they held tears. He looked away, concentrating on where he was going. He couldn't stand to see her face anymore. His fingers trembled, and he tightened his grip on the oars as he pulled the two of them closer to goodbye.

DYLAN'S OWN MIND WAS WHIRLING. SHE WAS TERRIFIED OF stepping beyond the wasteland. Tristan could give her no idea of what might lie in wait. The tiny amount of religious teaching she'd been subjected to at school told her she was going to a better place, but who knew whether that was true or not? She could be walking into anything—heaven, hell, or perhaps just an eternity of nothingness. And she would have to make that walk—was it a walk?—alone.

The little waves of the lake began to grow, jostling the boat gently. Tristan frowned and increased the tempo of his rowing.

Dylan was deep in thought. It was not merely that she would have to go on alone that scared her—it was having to leave Tristan. The idea caused a deep pain in her chest and tears to pool in her eyes. He had become her protector, her comfort, her friend. There were also other feelings, longings to be close to him. She felt constantly hyperaware of him. A simple word had the ability to send her stomach erupting in butterflies, or drown her in a mire of self-doubt and sadness. At the back of her mind, she wondered if this was his doing, if he was playing with her emotions to keep her under control and make his life easier—but something told her it was real, and that was what she trusted.

She couldn't imagine not being with him now. It felt as if they had been each other's constant companion for much longer than a week. She stared at him, drinking in the image of his face, trying to memorize every detail. Despair clouded her thoughts, and the sky seemed instantly to darken. A biting wind whipped up, stirring her hair and pulling at her hoodie. Dylan didn't notice; she was lost in her pain.

TRISTAN, HOWEVER, GLANCED NERVOUSLY AT THE SKY AND rowed even more briskly. He wanted to get across the lake without incident; he knew Dylan was nervous of the water. But Dylan's emotions were working against him. The boat bobbed unevenly as the wind whisked up waves of deep troughs and white-capped peaks.

"Dylan! Dylan, look at me!"

She jumped slightly and focused her eyes on him. It was as if she were coming back to him from a long way away.

"You have to calm down, Dylan. Look at the weather." By now he was almost shouting over the wind. Dylan nodded at his words, but he wasn't sure that they had actually registered.

THEY HADN'T. SHE WAS LOOKING AT HIM, BUT ALL SHE SAW was him walking away from her, leaving her standing in a world of fear and uncertainty. Inside she screamed for him, begged him to come back, but he simply bowed his head and trudged on. Tomorrow he would be gone. Nothing else mattered.

THE OARS FELT USELESS IN TRISTAN'S HANDS. THE LAKE WAS so choppy now that he couldn't row anymore. Spray reared up and coated both of them in an icy shower. Beneath the surface, the water seemed to be writhing—from the turbulent weather or the awakening of unknown things, it was impossible to tell for sure.

"Dylan, hold on to the side!" Tristan commanded.

She didn't look up, still lost in her thoughts. The tiny craft was heaving wildly, and Tristan was grasping the wooden sides with both of his hands. Still Dylan sat motionless, somehow unaffected by the weather, as if she had detached herself entirely from this world.

A strong gust pushed the boat violently to the side. Tristan tightened his grasp, but the rotten planks splintered and broke. The piece he was holding came away entirely in his hand. Losing his grip unbalanced him, and he crashed against the opposite side of the boat, disturbing its delicate equilibrium. Tristan experienced a sudden weightlessness, accompanied by a sense of horror, but he was powerless to stop the boat from capsizing, and the black waves rushed to meet them both.

Tristan threw himself clear, worried that the boat would come down on top of them, and dived into the water. It was freezing cold and dark. Even just below the surface, he couldn't see the sky above him. The current twisted and pulled at him, muddling his senses. He kicked blindly in the direction that he hoped was up, and seconds later broke the surface. He bobbed there for a moment, the boat floating upside down beside him, and whipped his head from side to side, searching. He swam round the other side, a growing feeling of panic exploding within him. He could not lose her, not here, not to the churning waters of the lake.

"Dylan!" he screamed.

There was no reply, no sign of her.

Treading water, he tried to peer beneath him, but it was impossible. He had no choice but to dive once more.

DYLAN WAS LOST. HITTING THE WATER HAD SHOCKED HER OUT of her temporary inertia, but she had been totally unprepared for the impact, and the cold of the water had made her gasp. Black water had poured into her mouth and nose immediately. Instinct had shut down her windpipe before the liquid could pour into her lungs and choke her. She blew out the water and clamped her lips shut, but her lungs were already burning, desperate for air. She tried to tell herself that her body wasn't real, didn't need to breathe. It didn't matter; her lungs continued to scream at her. She opened her eyes but could see nothing. The water stung, but still she forced them to stay open, hoping desperately to see the sky or Tristan's face in front of her.

Stormy currents pummeled her from every angle, spinning her round. She had no idea which way was up, so she swam blindly underwater, hoping for a miracle. Every pull of her arm and kick of her leg was a monumental effort. The weight of her clothing dragged, and her limbs were aching.

Something rippled past her abdomen. She pulled her stomach in, expelling more precious air in the process. The thing slid along her arm, curling around it as if testing to see what it was. Another thing swam past her face, the rough texture of it scraping against her cheek. Dylan panicked and flailed under the water, swatting sightlessly at invisible things. Suddenly the water was alive with writhing creatures. Terror filled her.

This is it, she thought. *The end.*

She had always been afraid of drowning, had had nightmares about it all through her childhood. Another reason to avoid the swimming pool. Fear kept her arms and legs fighting her unknown attackers, even as the cold and lack of air weakened her. The need to breathe was building. Her lips were jammed together as tightly as she could hold them, but every nerve demanded she inhale.

Something grabbed at her hair, pulling, and the jolt and surprise caused her to forget momentarily about keeping her mouth closed. It dropped open and her lungs gratefully inhaled. Toxic water flooded down into them. They convulsed and tried to draw in air, making Dylan cough and choke. More of the foul liquid inundated her throat, and her eyes bulged in horror. Her ears popped, protesting at the depth of the water. The quick pain was replaced by a sharp ringing. A last-gasp scream appeared on her face as she began to pass out. The final thing she was aware of was one of the creatures grabbing her leg and yanking her down, down, deeper into the lake.

NINETEEN

FOR THE SECOND TIME, TRISTAN BROKE THROUGH THE SUR-
face of the water. He heaved Dylan up and pulled her head onto
his shoulder, keeping it above the waves. Her eyes were closed
and her face lifeless. Relief tangled with anxiety inside him. He
had been so lucky to find her in the inky water, his fingertips just
brushing the hem of her jeans. Not even waiting to right her, he
had grabbed a firm hold and swum back up. But he feared he was
too late. Was she truly gone?

The opposite shore was in sight, and he kicked off strongly
toward it. The swim didn't take long, and soon his feet scraped the
bottom of the lake as it became shallower toward land.

Tristan staggered up the pebbled shore, Dylan lifeless in his
arms. He collapsed a few yards from the water's edge, dropping
to his knees and laying her carefully on the ground. Grasping her
shoulders, he shook her gently, trying to rouse her.

"Dylan! Dylan, can you hear me? Open your eyes."

She didn't respond, lying there unmoving. Her hair was soaking wet and plastered all over her face. He lifted each lock carefully

and tucked it behind her ears. Tiny purple jewels that he had never noticed before sparkled in her earlobes. He leaned in and placed his cheek over her mouth. He couldn't hear her breathing. He felt it, though. She wasn't gone. *What do I do?* Tristan thought wildly.

Calm down, he told himself. *She's swallowed a lot of water.*

Grasping the shoulder farthest from him, he pulled her across so that she was lying facedown with her chest across his knees. Turning his hand flat, he slapped at her back, trying to get her to cough up the water.

It worked. Liquid began to spill from her mouth, then she started to choke and retch, finally vomiting a large quantity of the foul black liquid. Rasping gasps came from her throat, and he breathed a sigh of relief.

DYLAN CAME TO WITH A HORRIBLE SUDDEN AWARENESS OF her position. She was splayed awkwardly, chest crushed against Tristan's knees. She struggled to get her arms beneath her and, realizing what she wanted, Tristan helped her up. With his assistance, she struggled onto her hands and knees, gasping in air and bringing up the last of the water. The taste in her mouth was disgusting, as if the water had been polluted with foul, dead, rotten things. In fact, it had, she reminded herself, remembering the grasping hands and biting teeth that had tried to pull her under. A combination of shock and cold hit her all at once, and she began to tremble violently.

"T-T-Tristan," she stuttered through blue lips.

"I'm here," he replied, anxiety plain in his voice.

She reached out for him, and two strong arms gripped her round the middle and pulled her toward him. He nestled her into his arms and began to rub her upper arms and back, trying to warm her. She tucked her head under his chin, getting as close as possible to his body heat.

"It's OK, angel." The endearment slipped easily from his lips, surprising him.

Dylan felt a warm glow at the word, and the sudden rush of emotion, combined with the adrenaline of the trauma that she had just endured, overcame her. Tears welled in her eyes and spilled down her cheeks, stinging her cold skin. Her breath came in gasps, and suddenly she couldn't hold it back. Her whole body shook with each sob, and she gulped in air, exhaling raggedly in pitiful cries and whimpers.

Tristan held her tighter, rocking her gently. "It's OK, it's OK," he repeated over and over again.

Dylan understood but just couldn't seem to pull herself together. She would quiet down for a moment and lie peacefully in his embrace, but then the sobs would resurface from nowhere and she was powerless to stop them.

Eventually she cried herself out. Tristan still didn't move, keeping hold of her as if frightened to do anything that might set her off. Finally though, the darkening sky forced him to speak.

"We're going to have to move, Dylan," he whispered in her ear. "Don't worry, it's not far."

His arms released her, and it felt as if all of the warmth that had been generated by his closeness evaporated. Dylan's shakes returned but thankfully not the tears. She struggled to stand, but her legs wouldn't support her. Her near drowning had exhausted her; she had no will to fight her tired limbs. Tomorrow she would lose him. That thought was all consuming. It made more sense to simply lie here and let the demons come for her. Physical pain would be a welcome relief from internal agony.

Tristan had clambered to his feet, and he reached down and hooked his hands under Dylan's arms. He pulled her up as if she were weightless and placed her right arm over his shoulder. His left arm snaked around her waist, and then he half dragged, half carried her off the little beach and up a narrow dirt path to a cottage.

"I'll get a fire going to heat you up," he promised.

She could only nod numbly. The chill was inconsequential—a meaningless irritation that barely registered.

The door of the cottage was old, and its proximity to the water had caused the wood to swell and stick in the doorjamb. Tristan had to let go of her to open it, and she slumped against the wall, staring at the ground. He twisted the handle and shoved his shoulder against the door. It groaned and resisted at first, then gave way, causing him to stumble inside. Dylan didn't move. Going in meant beginning their final night together; it signified the beginning of the end. She was dimly aware of high-pitched howling coming from somewhere to her left, but she felt no fear.

TRISTAN ALSO HEARD THE NOISES FROM INSIDE THE COTTAGE where he was lighting the fire. He turned to check on Dylan and noticed for the first time that she hadn't followed him inside.

"Dylan?" he called. Her silence was enough to make all the hairs stand up on his arm. He leaped to his feet and was at the door of the safe house in three long, powerful strides. There she was, where he had left her, supported by the stone wall and staring into nothingness.

"Come on." He bent his knees slightly so that he could look

into her eyes. They didn't change their focus. It wasn't until he reached out and took her hand in his that she seemed to become aware of him. He could see the sadness etched in every feature of her face. He tried to smile in a comforting, reassuring way, but his muscles seemed to have forgotten how and it felt wrong to force it. He tugged gently at her hand, and she followed him in silence.

He led her inside and sat her down in the only chair, which he had placed in front of the flames, and when he shut the door, the temperature in the cottage quickly warmed up. Looking back toward the fire, he was shocked at Dylan's diminutive figure. Her legs were together, her hands folded lightly on her lap. Her head was bowed as if in sleep or prayer. It was like looking at an empty shell, a body waiting for the end. He hated seeing her sitting so alone like that and crossed the room to be with her. There was nowhere else to sit, so he settled for dropping cross-legged onto a scrap of tattered rug that lay in front of the fireplace. He looked at her and wanted to say something. Something to break the silence. Something to bring a smile back to her face. But what could he say?

"I can't do it," she whispered, looking up from the floor to stare at him with passionate but terrified eyes.

"What do you mean?" His reply was only just audible above the crackle of the flames. His whole being screamed at him not to have this conversation, to put her off; he could not deal with her pain as well as his own. But she needed to talk about it, so he would listen.

"I can't do it on my own. Walk the end of the journey, or whatever it is I do. I'm too scared. I . . . I need you."

THAT LAST PART WAS THE HARDEST TO SAY, BUT ALSO THE truest. Dylan had accepted her death with a calm that had surprised her, and grieved only a little for those she had left behind. Surely if she was making this journey, then eventually they would, too. She would meet them again in time.

Tristan, however, would walk away from her tomorrow and vanish from her life forever. He would go on to the next soul, and soon she would be a distant memory, if she was remembered at all. Dylan had asked him for stories of some of the other souls that he had guided and had seen his expression twist as he tried to dredge up long-forgotten memories. So many passed through his fingers that few had stood out. She could not bear to be faceless to him. Not when he had become everything to her.

No, she had no desire to make that final journey. She would not—could not—leave him behind.

"Can't I stay here, with you?" she asked timidly, little hope in her voice.

He shook his head and she lowered her eyes, trying desperately to prevent more tears from surfacing. Was it not possible, or did he not want her? She had to know, but what if she didn't get the answer she wanted?

TRISTAN MADE A MONUMENTAL EFFORT TO KEEP HIS VOICE level. "No. If you stay here, eventually the wraiths will get you and make you their own." He gestured outside. "It's too dangerous."

"Is that the only reason?" If he had not seen her lips move, he would not have been sure that she had spoken, her voice was so quiet. But whispered as they were, the words flooded into him and turned his heart to ice. This was the moment to tell her that he didn't care for her, and make sure that she knew he meant it. It would be so much easier for her to take that final step if she thought he was walking away without regret.

His pause made her look up, green eyes braced for pain, teeth biting into her lower lip to stop it from trembling. She looked so fragile, as if one harsh word would crush her. His resolve crumbled; he could not hurt her like this.

"Yes," he answered. He reached up and grabbed her by the wrist, pulling her down to share the tattered rug with him. Then he cupped his hand to her cheek, running his thumb across the smooth skin of her cheekbone. It warmed under his touch, flushing a gentle pink. "You can't stay here, even though I want you to."

"You do?" Hope burgeoned, lighting up her face.

What was he doing? He should not give her hope now, knowing that he would have to take it away again. He shouldn't, but he was powerless. He thought back on all the faces she had shown him—frightened yet relieved when she had walked out of the tunnel, disgusted and disgruntled when he'd forced her to walk all day and sleep in dilapidated cottages each night, anger and pique when he had made fun of her, embarrassment when she'd been stuck in the mud, the joy when she'd woken to find he'd returned. Each memory made him smile, and he locked them in his mind, ready for when she would leave him and there would be no more.

"Let's just say you've grown on me." He laughed, still grinning from his remembered thoughts. She didn't smile with him, seemingly too on edge. "But, Dylan, tomorrow you have to go on. It's where you belong. It's what you deserve."

"Tristan, I can't. I can't do it," she pleaded.

He sighed. "Then . . . I'll come with you," he said. "All the way."

"You promise?" she asked quickly, tugging at his heart with her words.

He looked straight into her eyes and nodded.

For a moment she looked confused. "I thought you said you couldn't."

"I'm not supposed to, but I will. For you."

Dylan gazed at him. One hand reached up and pressed against his, holding it to her face.

"You swear? You swear you won't leave me?"

"I swear."

Dylan smiled tentatively at him. Her hand was still on his, and the heat from her touch seemed to burn down into his bones. She released him and he immediately missed the warmth, but then she reached out, fingers hovering in the air just inches from his face. The skin on his jaw prickled with anticipation, but uncertainty was painted all over her face and she seemed too scared to close the distance. He twitched the right side of his mouth up in an encouraging smile.

DYLAN'S HEART WAS JUMPING HAPHAZARDLY IN HER CHEST, racing in spurts, then stopping altogether for the briefest moment. Her tired arm ached where she held it aloft, but overriding that dull throbbing was a tingling in her fingertips that almost verged on pain—a pain that would only be soothed by the feel of Tristan's cheeks, his brow, his lips. She was nervous, though. She'd never touched him before, not like this.

She saw him give a tiny smile, and then her fingers seemed

to move of their own accord, drawn in like a magnet. She molded her hand to the shape of his face and felt the muscles in his cheek move as he clenched and unclenched his jaw. His eyes were vivid blue, too bright for the muted light of the room, but they weren't frightening. Instead they seemed hypnotic to Dylan, and she was helpless to look away. Tristan released her face, reaching up to cover her hand with his own, pinning it against his cheek. Four, five, six seconds of silence ticked by, then suddenly Dylan sucked in a ragged gasp, unaware she'd been holding her breath.

It seemed to break the spell. Tristan moved back, just an inch or so, but he pulled her fingers away with his. His eyes were warm still, though, and rather than let go, he guided her hand round to his mouth and dropped a gentle kiss on the soft skin of her knuckles.

They didn't speak much after that, content just to be near each other in companionable silence. Dylan tried to slow time, to savor each moment. But try as she might, it was like holding back a hurricane with tissue paper. Time ticked on at an astonishing rate, and she could scarcely believe it when light began filtering through the windows. The fire had long since died out, but it had done its job in drying her clothes and warming her freezing body. Still they continued to stare at the grate, watching the charcoal-gray logs smoke. Tristan had shifted over during the night and thrown an arm around her shoulder, tucking her in against his side, cocooning her there. Their backs were to the windows, and although both could see the light trickling over their shoulders and illuminating the back wall, picking out the faded yellow paint and an old picture so covered in grime and dust that its subject was barely visible, they didn't turn. Eventually sunrays blasted through the window, causing the dust that swirled around in the air to shimmer gold in the light.

Dylan was surprisingly calm. She had spent much of the night thinking about what might be coming today and had reached the conclusion that there was little she could do but take the final steps and see where they led her. Tristan would be with her. That was enough. She could take everything and anything else so long as he stood by her. And he would. He had promised.

TRISTAN DID NOT WANT TO FACE TODAY. HE THOUGHT ABOUT what he had promised Dylan, and unease churned in his stomach. His mind battled with what was possible, what was right, and what he wanted. None of them could coexist.

TWENTY

"READY FOR THE FINAL BIT OF THE JOURNEY?" TRISTAN ASKED, with forced humor in his voice. They were standing outside the cottage, preparing to go.

"Yeah." Dylan smiled tightly. "Where do we go?"

"This way." Tristan began to walk around the cottage, away from the lake.

Dylan took one last look at the water. Today it seemed calm and peaceful again, the surface gently rippling, causing sparkles where the sun tickled the tiny wave crests. She remembered the horrors that lurked beneath and shuddered, racing after Tristan as if she could leave the bad memories behind. He had paused on the other side of the cottage, waiting for her. He stared into the distance with one hand up at his forehead, shading the glare from the sun.

"See that?"

Dylan looked in the direction that Tristan was gazing. The landscape was flat and bare. A small stream trickled its way toward the horizon, snaking lazily away from them. On the left side of the stream, a path wound parallel to the water. Apart from a few bushes, there was nothing else to see.

Dylan raised one eyebrow, puzzled. "Er, nope."

Her tone made him turn to face her. He grinned and rolled his eyes. "Look harder."

"Tristan, there's nothing there. What am I supposed to be looking for?"

He sighed at her, but Dylan could tell he was enjoying feeling superior. He moved behind her and leaned over her shoulder. His breath warmed her neck, setting her skin on fire.

"Look at the horizon." He pointed straight ahead. "Can you see that shimmer?"

Dylan squinted. The horizon was very far away. She could make out a bit of a glow where the land met the blue sky, but it could easily be a trick of the light, or just the fact that she was trying to see something.

"Not really," she answered honestly.

"Well, that's where we're heading. It's a join between the wasteland and . . . beyond."

"Oh," she said. "And then what happens?"

He shrugged. "I told you, I've never been. This has always been as far as I've gone."

"I know, but what have you seen? I mean, is it like a stairway to heaven or something?"

He looked at her incredulously. When he spoke he was clearly holding back laughter.

"You think an enormous escalator descends from the sky?"

"Well, I don't know," she huffed, embarrassed and covering it with anger.

"Sorry," he added, smiling sheepishly. "They just disappear. That's it. They take a step and disappear."

Dylan wrinkled her nose. She could tell that he was speaking the truth, but it wasn't very helpful.

"Come on, we've got to get started." Tristan gave her a little push to get her moving.

She looked at the horizon again, straining her eyes at the so-called shimmer. Could she see it? It was hard to tell. It was, however, giving her a headache, so she gave up and settled for gazing moodily at the path in front of them. It looked far. Not uphill, at least, but far.

"Since it's the last day . . ." she began.

"I am not giving you a piggyback ride," Tristan answered quickly. He overtook her slouching pace, striding off ahead.

Grumbling, Dylan stomped after him. "You know, I almost drowned yesterday," she continued, sure that he wouldn't relent and carry her, but miserable at the thought of marching all day. Her legs were stiff, and her chest ached. Her throat was raw from vomiting up the water and coughing to clear her lungs.

He looked back at her, a strange expression on his face, but then turned and kept on walking.

"OK, so I probably wouldn't have died, given that I'm already dead, but it was very traumatic."

This time he did stop but didn't turn. Dylan caught him in three strides but held back. Something about his posture made her wary.

"Yes, you would have." It was a whisper, but it carried far enough to reach her ears.

"What?"

Tristan looked up at the sky, took a deep breath, and turned to face her. "You would have died." Each word was spoken slowly and clearly, and each stabbed straight into Dylan's brain.

"I could have died, *again*?" Surely dead was dead?

He nodded.

"But how? Where would I have gone? I don't . . ." Dylan trailed off.

"You can die here. Your soul, I mean. When you're alive it's protected by your body. When you die, you lose that safety. You're vulnerable."

"And if your soul dies?"

"You're gone," he said simply.

Dylan stared off into space, aghast at how close she had come to oblivion. She had taken her body's death without too much complaining because, well, she'd still been here. To know that she might have disappeared altogether—to have lost the chance to meet the people she was counting on seeing again—shocked her into silence.

"Come on. I'm sorry, but we don't have time to stop; we need to move. There are no more safe houses, Dylan."

Hearing him speak her name jolted her out of her trance. "Right," she muttered. Without looking at him, she marched forward. Although her limbs ached and she felt exhausted, she did not want to be caught out here in the dark.

She held her head high and walked swiftly, but there was a limp to her gait, and she rubbed her throat absentmindedly.

"Hold on." Tristan jogged over to her.

She paused and turned, waiting for him. He didn't stop when he reached her, but took another step so that he was just in front of her. He smiled, then turned his back to her.

"Jump up."

"What?"

He turned and rolled his eyes at her. "Jump. Up."

"Oh." Dylan's face lit up with relief. She grabbed hold of his shoulders and jumped, circling his waist with her legs and wrapping her arms around his neck. He hooked his arms under her knees and began to trudge forward.

"Thank you!" she whispered into his ear.

"It's only because you're so pitiful," he joked.

He took long, powerful strides that gently jostled Dylan with every step. Very quickly, she became stiff and uncomfortable on his back. Her arms were pained holding on to his shoulders, and his grip under her knees was bruising her. Still, it was much better than walking. She tried to relax her muscles and concentrated on reveling in being so close to Tristan. His shoulders were broad and strong, and he handled her extra weight as if she were made of feathers. She tucked her face into the crook of his neck and inhaled deeply, savoring the musky smell of him. His sandy hair bobbed as he walked and tickled her cheek. She fought an urge to run her fingers through it.

"When we get there," he said, startling her, "you'll have to get down and walk yourself."

Her grip tightened compulsively. "I thought you were coming with me?"

"I am," he answered at once, "but you'll have to take the steps yourself. I'll be right behind you."

"Can't you go first?"

"No. You can't go through to the next world following someone else; you've got to take the step yourself. It's a thing," he added, as if that explained it.

"But you'll be right behind me?" she asked, nervous.

"I promise. I said I would."

"Tristan," she squeaked, her voice suddenly excited. "I can see it!"

About half a mile in front of them, the air seemed to change. The ground beyond it looked the same as it had before, but strangely distorted, as if there were a transparent screen in front of it. The point on the ground where the screen met the earth did indeed seem to shimmer slightly. Dylan felt her stomach tighten as she stared at it. They had arrived.

"Put me down," she whispered.

"What?"

"I want to walk."

Tristan let go of her legs, and she slithered down his back to the ground. Pins and needles stung her feet and lower legs, and she stretched out her arms. Then she squared her shoulders and turned to face the end of her journey. Without looking back at Tristan, she began to walk forward.

Her heart was racing, thudding wildly in her chest. She felt adrenaline course through her veins. Although her arms and legs had been aching, they now felt as if they did not belong to her, and she was not entirely in control. Taking deep, even breaths, she tried not to hyperventilate. The ground seemed to fly beneath her feet. As they got closer, it became easier to see the join between the two worlds, little more than a hundred feet away now. The landscape beyond the point was just slightly out of focus, like she was looking at it through someone else's glasses. It was beginning to make her slightly dizzy, so she tried to look straight at the ground, occasionally glancing up to the shimmering line across the path.

TRISTAN DELIBERATELY KEPT ONE STEP BEHIND HER, WATCH-ing her with careful eyes. Although she did not look at or speak to him, he had the feeling that she was very aware of his movements. When she got to within ten feet of the line, she halted.

She stared at it, breathing evenly. Her face was drawn, her mouth tight. Tristan could read her stress in every muscle in her body.

"Are you OK?" he asked.

She turned toward him, and her eyes were wild. He had thought she seemed calm, but now he could see that she was petrified.

DYLAN WASN'T TERRIFIED, BUT THERE WERE EMOTIONS RUN-ning through her body that she had never experienced before. The tension of the moment had brought several things to the forefront of her mind, sharpened her focus on things that really mattered. She didn't know what was on the other side of that line and, even though he had promised to follow her, there was something she had to say first.

Although the idea terrified her, and she knew by saying it she was making herself more emotionally vulnerable than she had ever been in her life, she was determined. The past few days had taught her a lot about herself; she was not the same girl who had dithered over packing her teddy bear. She was stronger, braver. She'd faced danger, confronted her fears—and Tristan had played a massive part in that. He had protected her, comforted her, guided her, and opened her eyes to feelings she hadn't known before. It was important to tell him how she felt, even though it made her stomach flutter and her cheeks burn. *Just do it,* she told herself.

"I love you."

Her eyes never left his face, trying to read his reaction. The words seemed to hang in the air between them. Dylan's every nerve was tingling and alert, her pulse thudding through her veins. She hadn't meant to blurt it out like that, but she needed to say it. She waited for a smile or a frown, for his eyes to shine or freeze, but his face was impassive. Her pulse began to beat in a disjointed pattern that made her fear that it might stop. As the silence lengthened, she started to shake, her body preparing for rejection.

She knew he didn't feel the same way. Of course he didn't. She was just a child. She had misread his words and his touch. Her eyes began to sting as tears fought their way to the surface. She gritted her teeth, curled her fingers into fists, and squeezed tightly, the nails digging into her palms. It wasn't enough. The pain in her chest was agony, like hot knives piercing her core. It rode over every other sensation and made it hard to breathe.

TRISTAN STARED BACK AT HER, BATTLING WITH HIMSELF. HE loved her, too; he knew it in every fiber of his being. What he did not know was whether he should tell her so. Seconds passed and still he couldn't decide. He saw her eyes widen and heard her breathing become ragged, and knew that she was taking the worst possible meaning from his silence. She believed he didn't love her. He closed his eyes, trying to get some perspective. If he let her think this, perhaps it would be easier for her to cross over. It was right to say nothing. His mind made up, he opened his eyes and stared into a sea of sparkling green.

No. Her pain, hurt, rejection . . . it could not be her final memory of him. He had to give her this one truth, whatever it cost them both. Frightened that his voice would shake, he opened his mouth.

"I love you, too, Dylan."

SHE GAZED AT HIM FOR A MOMENT, FROZEN IN TIME. HER heart beat triumphantly as she processed his words. He loved her. She exhaled in a half laugh and broke into a grin, her eyes dancing. The pain in her chest melted away, replaced by a soft glow. She took a cautious step forward until she could feel his breath on her face; it, too, was coming in gasps. His eyes burned blue, penetrating into her very core and making her tremble. She leaned up to him, close enough to see each freckle that patterned his nose and cheeks, then stopped.

"Wait," she said, drawing back. "Kiss me on the other side."

"No," Tristan said, his voice low and husky. His hand was suddenly wrapped around hers, his grip viselike. "Now."

With one hand he pulled her closer to his body, with the other he cupped the back of her neck, sliding his fingers into her hair. Chills erupted over Dylan's skin, and her half-hearted protest died in her throat. His thumb stroked up and down the nape of her neck, and she watched unblinking as he rested his forehead against hers. He closed the final distance between them, dropping his grip on her hand and her neck and folding his arms around her back, pulling her nearer still. Tilting her head back a fraction, Dylan closed her eyes and waited.

TRISTAN HESITATED. FREED FROM THE DEPTH OF HER FOREST-green eyes, doubts crept back into his mind. This was wrong. This was not allowed. Every feeling he had for her was wrong, though. He shouldn't be able to feel this way; it wasn't supposed to be possible. But he did. And this was going to be his only chance to experience the wonder that humans lived for, killed for. Letting his eyes slide closed, he pressed his lips against Dylan's.

They were soft. That was his first thought. Soft, and sweet, and trembling. He felt her fingers twist into the fabric of his sweatshirt, her hands shaking slightly against his sides. Her lips parted, moving against his. He heard her utter a tiny moan, and the sound sent a ripple into the pit of his stomach. He squeezed her tighter, his mouth pressing harder against hers. His heart was crashing against his ribs, his breathing ragged. The only thing he was aware of was the warmth of her, the softness. He felt her grow bolder, going up on her tiptoes to lean further into him, lifting her hands from his side and gripping his shoulders, his face. He copied the movement, his fingers trailing down her hairline, around her chin. Memorizing.

TIGHT IN TRISTAN'S EMBRACE, DYLAN WAS LIGHT-HEADED, dizzy. With her eyes closed, the world around her didn't seem to exist. Only Tristan's mouth, pressed against hers, and his hands, holding her close, stroking gently across her skin. Her blood was singing in her veins, and when he finally pulled away, she was gasping. He held her face in his hands and stared at her for a long moment, eyes glowing. Then he dropped his head again and placed two soft, gentle kisses on her lips. He smiled at her, a slow languid smile that had the muscles in her abdomen contracting.

"You were right," she said breathlessly. "Before is better."

She turned away from him and appraised the line. It held no threat for her now. Tristan loved her, and he would go wherever she was headed. Ten confident steps took her to the edge. She looked down, savoring the feeling. This was her last moment in the wasteland. She could say farewell to the demons, to the uphill marches and sleeping rough in dilapidated houses. She lifted her left foot and paused, just over the line. One more deep breath, and then she hopped across.

She stood, evaluating. It felt the same. The air was still warm with a slight breeze, the dirt path beneath her feet still crunched slightly as she shifted her foot. The sun still shone in the sky, and the hills still circled the landscape. She frowned slightly, curious but not overly concerned. She had expected something more dramatic.

She twirled back toward Tristan, a slightly nervous smile on her lips. It froze on her face. Cold hands grabbed her heart, and her mouth opened, mouthing a silent *No*.

The path was empty.

She stepped forward, but the shimmering line was gone. She reached out, feeling with her hands for the spot where Tristan had stood just a moment before. Her fingers came into contact with an invisible wall, solid and impenetrable.

She had crossed over, and there was no way back. Tristan was gone. She was alone again.

Dylan began to tremble all over, a sickening mixture of adrenaline, shock, and horror coursing through her veins. She swayed unsteadily, then fell to her knees, her hands over her mouth as if she could hold in the sobs. She couldn't: they spilled over, beginning as quiet, gasping moans and deepening into agonized wails. Searing pain tore at her heart. Tears streamed down her face and dropped onto the ground.

He had lied to her. His promises to accompany her had been nothing but deceit and treachery, and she had been his fool, believing it all. This must have been his plan all along. She saw again in her mind's eye the way he would smile at her, his eyes glowing, but then suddenly his face would become a cold and uncaring mask. He had known. But what about when he said he loved her? Was that a lie?

No, she did not believe that. Every fiber of her being told her the truth: he loved her. She loved him and he loved her, but they would never be together.

Already she found she couldn't get a clear picture of his face. Little details were trickling away, like grains of sand in the wind. She couldn't remember the exact shade of his hair or the shape of his mouth. A heart-wrenching sound escaped her lips, agony that set every nerve on fire. Knowing she was alone, knowing that there was no one to witness her grief, she gave herself over to the despair that engulfed her.

She slammed her fist against the wall in frustration, then pressed her palm against it, wishing with all her might that it would dissolve and let her travel back through.

TRISTAN STOOD ON THE OTHER SIDE OF THE LINE, WATCHING her fall apart. Like a policeman on the other side of a two-way mirror, he knew she could not see him. His deception had worked, and the pain he had caused was clear on her face. She knew he had lied to her, that he had planned this ending. She knew she would never see him again. Though it tore at his heart, he forced himself to watch every tear, listen to every sob and scream. He longed to rush forward and comfort her, to embrace her and smooth the tears off her cheeks. To feel the heat of her in his arms again, the softness of her. He lifted one hand and placed it in the air, palm to palm with hers, cold suffering—a wall of glass between them. Tristan willed his feet to move forward, to take him over the line, but nothing happened. He could not cross.

He had allowed himself to tell her that he loved her, allowed her to hope, and this was his punishment. He had caused this pain, and he would endure every second of it. He only hoped that she realized that under all the lies and pretense, his love for her had been honest and real.

He had always known that he would not be able to cross over with her. His promise had been a trick, a wicked sham to give her the courage to take the final step. It had taken everything he had to make her believe him, to watch her gratitude and relief, to let her trust him, and know that this moment was coming. To let himself kiss her and hold her, and know that he couldn't keep her. To know that when she crossed the line and looked back, she would discover his treachery.

Through the veil between worlds, he watched her cry. She called his name, and tears coursed down his cheeks. Shame, self-loathing, and despair welled up in him. He was desperate to look away, to hide his eyes from the consequences of his actions, but he would not.

"I'm sorry," he whispered, knowing that she could not hear it, but hoping somehow that she would understand.

Although every second he watched felt like hours of torture, eventually she started to fade. The edges of her beautiful figure began to shimmer and blur, and she started to lose substance, diminishing until she was little more than smoke. He watched her leave him. As her shape became a haze, he tried to memorize every detail of her face, trying to lock the exact shade of her eyes into his heart.

"Goodbye," he murmured, wishing with all he was that he could go with her. In the next blink of his eye, she was gone.

He stared at the ground where she had stood, then swallowed against the pain in his throat and took a deep breath. He turned back to the path and began to walk away.

TWENTY-ONE

AS TRISTAN WALKED, THE LANDSCAPE AROUND HIM SLOWLY faded to white. He barely noticed. The hills disappeared, disintegrating into sand that floated upward and evaporated in a thin mist. The path he was striding along was replaced by a featureless surface that reached out as far as the eye could see in every direction. A white light flashed, blinding him at its zenith.

The light dimmed, and particles of color began to form. They swirled around Tristan's head and settled on the ground, creating the world that his next mission, the next soul, was soon to leave. Tarmac formed under his feet, black and shiny with rain. Buildings erupted from the ground on either side of him. Lighted windows illuminated ill-kept front gardens adorned with overgrown weeds and broken fences. The cars parked at the curb were old and rusted. Heavy thudding music and raucous laughter spilled from open doorways. The whole place had an air of poverty and carelessness. It made a depressing picture.

Tristan felt no thrill at the prospect of collecting his next soul.

He did not even feel the disdain and indifference that had become habit in recent years. He felt only the torturous ache of loss.

He stopped at the second-to-last house from the end of the street. Amidst the shabby, ramshackle buildings, this one was surprisingly well kept. There was a neat lawn surrounded by flowers. Stepping-stones carved with birds laid an inviting path to the recently painted red door. There was only one window lit, in a room on the second floor. Tristan knew that was where the next soul was located, about to part from its body. He did not enter the house but waited outside.

Several passersby looked at the stranger loitering outside number twenty-four. They could tell he did not belong here. However, this was not the sort of place where you challenged an unfamiliar face, and so they continued on their way without comment. Tristan, staring into nothing, didn't notice the quizzical looks, didn't register that they could *see* him. He was ignorant of their curious eyes and their quiet mutterings.

He already knew everything he needed to know about the person who had lived here. She had stayed here alone for ten years, going out little except to work and make weekly visits to her mother who lived across town. She did not mix with any of the neighbors, who regarded her as snobby and aloof, when really she was just afraid. She had just been stabbed to death in her bed by a burglar who had expected to find more valuables than she had possessed and had murdered her in anger. Soon she would wake and get up, continuing her morning routine as usual. When she went outside, she would be greeted by Tristan and, one way or another, she would follow him.

All of this information was now assimilated in Tristan's mind. Facts and stories interweaving to make up the knowledge he needed to perform his job. He knew it, but he did not think about it. The journey of this soul would be completed because that was his role. He would feel no pity for this unfortunate creature. He would give her no sympathy or comfort. He would guide her, nothing more.

The moon was directly overhead, a stark white light that sought out and banished shadows. Tristan felt exposed in this raw state, as if every emotion and thought were laid bare, to be read by everyone. He knew that he could have hours to wait before the soul would emerge. He wondered how much longer he could go on. He yearned to escape and hide, to give himself over to the pain and grief. His brain told his feet to move, to leave his post and keep walking until he left his sorrow behind him.

He couldn't.

For the second time, tears sprang into his piercing blue eyes. Of course he would not be allowed to abscond. There was a higher order, a grander scheme of things. And his pain, his despair, his desire to relinquish this responsibility meant nothing. He could not control his destiny. He could not even control his feet.

"DYLAN."

She was aware of somebody behind her calling her name, but she didn't turn. Like the time she'd spent the night alone in the safe house, she couldn't tear her eyes away from the scene in front of her. If she looked away, Tristan was really gone.

Who was she fooling? He was already gone. He was gone and he wasn't coming back. She just wasn't quite ready to accept it. Dylan stared at the path defiantly. Her teeth bit down on her lower lip, cutting down hard enough to split the skin and make her taste blood. She didn't. Her senses were numb.

"Dylan."

She flinched as the voice called to her again. She couldn't guess if it was male or female, old or young. It didn't sound impatient or urgent. It was welcoming.

She didn't want to be welcomed.

"Dylan."

Dylan huffed, growing irritated. The voice was going to continue until she answered it. Slowly, reluctantly, she turned.

For a second she blinked, confused. There was nothing there. Her mouth opened, ready to call out, hoping the voice would speak again, but she closed it slowly. What the hell did it matter?

She was about to resume her sentry duty, gazing back down the path in the vain hope that Tristan would miraculously reappear, but as she looked away, something odd and out of place caught her eye. A light, glowing. For a second her heart leaped, thinking of the orbs she'd seen floating in the bloodred wasteland, but it wasn't the same. It grew and changed shape, elongating, forming. It smiled at her, and the expression, too, was welcoming. Two eyes, gold, pupilless, but warm, not frightening, watched and waited. They sat in a perfect face surrounded by a halo of hair. The body looked human enough in shape but not quite right. Like the glimpses of souls she'd seen, it was there but not there—half in, half out of focus.

She couldn't even tell if this being was a man or a woman or neither. Their body looked androgynous, but their voice had been deep when they called her name.

"Welcome," the being's voice chimed.

Dylan scowled, annoyed that they were beaming at her in an indulgent way, like she should be happy to be there.

"Who are you?"

"I am Caeli. I am here to greet you. Welcome home."

Home? Home! This was not home. Home was the place she'd just left. Twice.

"You must have questions. Please, come with me."

Slowly, determinedly, Dylan shook her head. Caeli looked at her in polite confusion.

"I want to go back," Dylan said calmly.

The confusion melted into understanding. "I am sorry. You cannot go back. Your body is gone. Don't fear, you will see your loved ones again soon."

"No, that's not what I mean. The wasteland. I want to go back to the wasteland." Dylan looked around at the flat expanse of heathland still surrounding her. A quick glance over her shoulder confirmed that the horseshoe of hills remained. It seemed like she was still there, if only the wall wasn't blocking her. "I want . . ." Dylan trailed off.

The being, Caeli, was giving her an incredulous look. "You have made the crossing."

Dylan's frown deepened. They weren't getting what she was trying to say at all.

"Where is my ferryman? Where is Tristan?" She tripped a little over his name.

"You do not need him anymore. He has fulfilled his role. Please, come with me." This time the being turned, pointed behind them. A doorway of sorts had appeared a little way down the path: a five-barred gate, a wide cattle grid at the base. It looked ridiculous hovering there without a purpose, without a fence stretching away from either side of it.

Dylan folded her arms across her chest, lifted her chin. "No." She forced the word out from between clenched teeth. "I want Tristan. I'm not leaving here until I see him."

"I'm sorry, but that is not possible."

"Why?" Dylan shot back.

Caeli didn't seem to understand the question. "It is not possible. Please, come with me."

They took a step to the side and gestured once again to the gate, smiling patiently, waiting. Dylan had the feeling they would stand there, calmly and serenely, until she moved.

What would Caeli do if she ignored them, tried to go back the way she had come, back to the lake? Would they stop her? She rose to her feet and took a half step back, gauging their reaction carefully. Caeli continued smiling, tilting their head a little to the side, eyebrows coming together slightly in puzzlement. Another step. Still they didn't move. Just watched. She was free to ignore them, then.

Taking her eyes off the being for a moment, she risked a second fleeting look behind her. The hills were still there. She thought she could just make out the outline of the final safe house, hazy through the line that divided the two worlds. There was no sign of the wraiths, no sign of danger. She could stay there.

But what would be the point? Tristan wasn't there. He was probably already with his next job, the next soul. He'd probably already forgotten about her.

No, a small voice in the back of her head screamed. *He said he loved you. He meant it.*

Maybe. Maybe not. There was no way to know the truth. And if Tristan wasn't coming back, what was the point of lingering here?

Sighing, Dylan unfurled her arms, letting them fall to her sides. Her hands throbbed, the blood rushing back into her fingertips. She hadn't realized how tightly she'd had them clenched around her, like she was holding herself together.

"OK," she whispered, taking first one step, then another, in Caeli's direction. "OK."

The being smiled at her warmly, waiting until she'd drawn level before turning and walking beside her along the path.

They reached the gate, but when Caeli pulled it aside, it wasn't just the rusting metal bars that shifted. It was as if Caeli was cutting a hole in the world. In the space where the gate had been was now a window onto a whole other place.

"Please." Caeli spoke quietly, indicating that Dylan should step through.

Once Dylan had crossed, she whispered, "Where are we?"

It was a gigantic room, almost without proportions. She couldn't see the walls, but it felt indoors somehow. The floor was clean, colorless.

"This is the records room. I thought it would be a good place for you to start, to find the souls who have come before you. Those who have died and found their way across the wasteland."

"How?" Dylan was intrigued, despite herself.

As soon as the word left her lips, the edges of the room contracted, forming definable walls, lined from floor to ceiling with bookshelves packed with heavy tomes. A carpet materialized beneath her feet, thick and dark, made for grandeur and muffling footsteps. She had a strange sense of déjà vu as she stared around her, the image stirring up echoes of a visit to a library with her mum: cavernous and quiet, mazelike to her ten-year-old eyes. She'd gotten lost and been found crying beneath a desk by a kindly janitor. Was this another one of those projections of her mind, like the wasteland?

Caeli spoke softly beside her. "I am sure you have family, friends that you would like to find?" They waited a beat. "Would you like me to help you locate anyone? Your Grandmother Moore? Your Aunt Yvonne?"

Dylan stared at them, shocked that they knew the names of her relatives. "You can find anyone?"

"Anyone who has completed the journey, yes. We have records of every soul. Every ferryman has a book of those whom they have guided over."

What? Dylan stared across the room as she processed Caeli's words. But she wasn't thinking about finding her grandmother or her aunt, who had died of breast cancer just three years earlier. She had another idea.

Dylan turned to the being, a light suddenly shining in her eyes. "I want to see Tristan's book."

Caeli paused for a moment before responding. "That is not the purpose of this place . . ."

"Tristan's book," Dylan repeated.

The being looked far from happy, their features a mixture of concern and disapproval, but they led her around looming shelving units and past countless books until they reached a dark corner. They reached for a shelf that was empty apart from one huge volume. It was a faded green color, with pages gilded in gold. The corners appeared worn, soft, as if a thousand fingers had lifted the cover and leafed through.

"Here is your ferryman's book." Caeli laid it down on an empty table. "May I ask what it is you are looking for?"

Dylan didn't reply, not entirely sure of the answer herself. Instead she reached out and lifted the front cover to reveal a ledger. Entry upon entry filled the page. Row after row of souls penned in with a neat hand. There was a name, an age, and a date on every line. Not their birth date, Dylan realized with a shock. It was the day they had died.

Wordlessly, Dylan flicked through the pages. Name after name after name. Hundreds. Thousands. Countless souls who owed their continued existence to Tristan. Grabbing a thick chunk, she waded through the book until she came to blank paper. Working backward, she found the final entry. Hers. It was bizarre, looking at her name written in a more elegant script than she could have ever managed. Was this Tristan's handwriting? No, it couldn't be. Next to it had been entered the date she'd taken the train. She touched her finger to the next blank line and wondered what name would grace that space.

Where was Tristan right now? Had he reached the first safe house yet?

Dylan sighed and went back to flipping through the book, opening a page at random. She didn't want to think about Tristan ferrying another soul. He was *her* ferryman. Hers. She smiled ruefully. That was a difficult thought to believe, faced with the ledger in front of her. She scanned through the list. Frowned.

"What's this?" she asked, pointing to a line near the bottom of the page. The entry had been scored out, the name all but obliterated by a thick black line of ink.

There was no answer. Dylan looked to her left, wondering if she had been abandoned, but the being stood there still. They were looking away from her, but seemed to be staring at nothing.

"Excuse me . . . Caeli?" She faltered a little calling the being by their name. "What does this mean? Why has the name been scored out?"

"That soul is not here," they responded, still looking away from her.

Not there? Were they the souls lost to the wraiths? If Dylan looked, would she find the little boy in here, the one who'd died of cancer, that Tristan had dropped running from the demons? She opened her mouth to ask, but Caeli turned and fixed her with a dazzling smile that halted her.

"Why are you interested in this book, Dylan? If you tell me, I can help you."

Disarmed by Caeli's golden stare, Dylan momentarily lost her train of thought. The mystery of the crossed-out entry slipped to the back of her mind.

"Do you know every soul in here?" She pointed to the book.

The being dipped their head in assent.

"I'm looking for someone, but I don't know more than his first name. Jonas. He was a German soldier in World War Two." Dylan blinked, a little surprised at herself. That hadn't been why she'd asked to see the book, but the idea had just popped into her head and she knew at once that, subconsciously at least, that had been her plan all along. She wanted to speak to someone else who knew

Tristan. She wanted to talk about Tristan with someone who knew him like she did. The young soldier from the Second World War had been the soul who had stuck most in her mind from all the stories Tristan had told her.

She expected the being to shake their head, to tell her they would need more than that, but to her surprise they moved to the desk and flicked confidently through the creamy sheaves until they came to the right page.

"Here." Caeli pointed to the penultimate line. "This is the soul you want."

Dylan peered at the scrawled name.

"Jonas Bauer," she murmured. "Eighteen years old. Died February 12, 1941. Is that him?"

Caeli nodded.

Dylan bit her lip, thinking. Eighteen. He was only a few years older than she was. Somehow, when she'd imagined this soul, she'd seen him as a man. But he could still have been at school. She thought briefly about the seniors at Kaithshall. The school captain, the prefects. She couldn't imagine them standing up to someone, knowing the decision would sign their own death warrant.

Eighteen. A boy and a man. Who would Tristan have become for him? How would he have made Jonas follow him?

Dylan lifted her head from the page and gazed at Caeli. "I want to talk to him."

TWENTY-TWO

CAELI HADN'T ARGUED OR ASKED DYLAN FOR A REASON behind her odd request. Instead they had held out an arm, gesturing through the library. Dylan hesitated, taking one last look at the page before following them. Something caught her eye—there, right at the bottom of the page, was another of those curious entries. Another soul blacked out.

She didn't have time to question Caeli about the crossed-out lines, however. They moved to a door fitted snugly in a wall. It was dark, maybe mahogany, and inlaid with elegantly carved paneling. The handle was small and round, made of burnished brass. Dylan couldn't recall the door having been there a moment earlier. She frowned and rubbed at her forehead, disoriented.

"Was that . . ."

Caeli smiled at her, waiting for the rest of the question, but Dylan didn't continue. It didn't really matter. The door was there now, and that was what she needed to concentrate on. It was all so confusing.

"Through there?"

Caeli nodded. Dylan waited for them to open it for her—not that she was used to formal manners, but they seemed to be in charge here.

Caeli didn't move. Was this another one of those things she had to do herself, like crossing the line in the wasteland? Looking at the being for reassurance, she tentatively stretched out a hand and grasped the doorknob. It turned easily in her hand, and Caeli stepped back so that she could swing it wide open. She did so, giving the being one more nervous glance before she stepped through and took in her surroundings.

A street. Dylan was instantly more comfortable. The buildings were like nothing she had ever seen: a world apart from the high red-sandstone tenement blocks of Glasgow. Row upon row of neat single-story homes, with well-manicured front lawns and pretty flower beds stretched out before her. Vehicles, almost all a glossy black with long, curved bonnets and shining silver platforms running along their flanks, were parked in driveways or at the curb. It looked like something out of the old movies her mum made her watch whenever they had one of their elderly neighbors over for dinner. The sun split the sky, and there was a quiet, companionable hum about the place.

Dylan stepped forward onto a neatly paved path that wound through a tidy lawn. There was a soft click behind her, and she turned to see the door close. She seemed to have exited from one of the buildings: a detached house with dormer windows and exterior walls clad in dark wood. Caeli was nowhere to be seen, but Dylan had a feeling that all she had to do was remember the door to find her way back through to the records room again.

She took a quick second to memorize the pot of yellow and

orange flowers to the right of the single step, the brass number nine nailed dead-center above a narrow letter box. Certain she'd be able to find the house again, she turned back to the street in front of her. There was a tinny sound ringing in her ears that she strained to recognize. It hissed a little, but beneath this she could hear the beats and chimes of a melody. It was like listening to a staticky radio station. She followed the sound, weaving through the cars until she came to a pair of legs sticking out from underneath a gleaming black vehicle. The noise was louder here, and she realized she had been right: an ancient-looking radio was propped on the top of the car. One foot bobbed in time with the music, an oldies tune Dylan didn't recognize.

She wondered if she'd found Jonas.

"Hello?" she called, bending down slightly to squint under the car. She couldn't see much, just more legs.

The foot stopped jiggling. After a second, there was a scrabbling sound, and out slid a body and, finally, an oil-smeared face. Dylan waited as he drew himself up to stand before her.

He was baby-faced, that was the first thing to register with Dylan. Smooth, rounded cheeks sat below twinkling blue eyes; his blond hair was neatly combed, split in a side part, but several locks had twisted out of place, sticking up at odd angles and making him look even more childlike. It was an odd face to sit atop such a tall and broad body.

Dylan was sure this was the soul she was looking for. He wasn't how she had imagined him, but this was definitely him, Jonas. She remembered suddenly that he was German and wondered if she'd be able to speak to him. She'd studied French in school, but her German was limited to counting to five.

"Can you understand me?" she asked.

He smiled at her, revealing teeth that were not quite straight.

"You haven't been here very long, have you?" His English seemed perfect, with just a hint of an accent.

"Oh." Dylan blushed, realizing she'd somehow made a faux pas. "Sorry, no. I just arrived."

He smiled a little wider in sympathy. "I can understand you."

"You're Jonas," she said. It wasn't a question, but he nodded anyway. "I'm Dylan."

"Hello, Dylan."

There was a moment's pause. Jonas watched her, his face politely surprised and not a little intrigued. Dylan grimaced and fidgeted on the spot. Why had she asked to see him? What did she want to ask? She was so muddled, off-balance, she couldn't get it quite straight in her head.

"I asked to see you," she began, sensing some explanation was required. "I . . . wanted to talk to you. To ask you a few questions. If, if that's OK?"

Jonas waited patiently, and she took that as a cue to continue.

"I wanted to ask you about your ferryman."

Whatever Jonas had been expecting, it wasn't that. He blinked, frowned, but gestured with a jerk of his chin that she should continue. Dylan played with her tongue between her teeth, biting down until it was almost painful. What did she want to know?

"He was called Tristan?" she asked. Best to start simply.

"No." Jonas shook his head slowly, looking as if he was trying to recall things from long ago. "No, his name was Henrik."

"Oh," Dylan managed to mumble, trying unsuccessfully to

swallow back her disappointment. Maybe it wasn't him, then. Maybe Caeli had been wrong.

"What did he look like?"

"I don't know, normal, I suppose." Jonas shrugged, as if the question was hard to answer. "He looked like any other soldier. Tall, brown hair, the uniform."

Brown hair? That was wrong, too.

"I remember . . ." He huffed a breath and grinned suddenly. "I remember he had bluer eyes than anyone I had ever seen. They were the strangest color."

"Cobalt blue," Dylan whispered, seeing the blaze of color in her head as clearly as if Tristan were standing in front of her. The face surrounding the eyes was a little fuzzy, but the cold heat of his stare still burned into her. That was him; that was Tristan. She smiled to herself. At least that one thing was real.

Perhaps he changed his name for each soul he encountered, picking a name he thought they would like. She remembered what he'd said, about how he had to make them follow him. She reddened as his words echoed in her mind, telling her she should be attracted to him. She'd liked the name Tristan; it had seemed olde-worldy, mysterious. Very different to the David and Darren and Jordan clones at Kaithshall. Was that just another part of his job, another piece of the deception? She felt her chest tighten as she realized with a sudden rush of sadness that she might not even have known his real name. If he had one.

"Right," Jonas agreed, smiling at her. "Cobalt blue. That is a good description of them."

"What . . . what was he like?" Unconsciously, Dylan raised

a hand to her face and started to chew on one of her fingernails. Now that she was coming to the important questions, she was suddenly edgy, not sure she wanted the answers, frightened to hear something she wouldn't like.

"What do you mean?" Jonas frowned, puzzled.

Dylan exhaled deeply through her nose, twisting her lips to the side. She wasn't sure how to phrase it.

"Was he . . . was he nice? Did he look after you?"

Rather than answer her, Jonas tilted his head to the side, blue eyes—duller than Tristan's but sharp nonetheless—studying her keenly.

"Why are you asking these questions?"

"What?" Dylan mumbled, stalling. She retreated a half step, till her back collided gently with another parked car.

"What is it you really want to know, Dylan?"

It was weird to hear her name in a strange accent. It sounded odd, off. Not like her. Unsettled as she was feeling, it matched her mood in a bizarre way.

"Dylan?" Jonas jolted her back from her distraction.

"I miss him," she admitted to the ground, bewildered into telling the truth. After a few seconds, she looked up to see Jonas eyeing her, his expression both sympathetic and a little baffled. "We went through a lot together and I . . . I miss him."

"When did you get here?" Jonas asked.

"Now. I mean, just before I came to see you. An hour, maybe?" Were there hours anymore?

The little line in between Jonas's eyes deepened, and he frowned harder.

"And you came straight here, to see me? Don't you have family you want to visit? People from your life you thought you'd never see again?"

Dylan looked away before she responded, a little ashamed of the truthful answer. "I don't want them. I want Tristan."

"What happened on your journey?"

"What?" Sidetracked by his question, Dylan turned back to Jonas.

He was leaning against the car he'd been working on, his arms folded across his chest, face drawn as he tried to understand. "When I met Henrik—sorry, your Tristan," he amended, seeing Dylan's face screw up, "I knew I was dead. I knew almost at once who he was, what had happened. I was glad to have his company over the journey, but then, when it was over, we parted. And that was it. I went on; he went on to the next soul. If I think of him, it is fondly. But I could not say that I missed him."

Dylan stared at him, disappointed. He didn't understand. Couldn't. In fact, she could probably go through every name in Tristan's book and still not find a soul who had felt what she felt, who knew what it was like to have this gnawing pain that churned in her stomach, like a vital part of her was missing.

That was both a comforting thought and a depressing one.

Dylan turned to the side, edging away from Jonas. He was still watching her with pitying eyes, and it was painful to see her sad reflection in them. She wanted nothing more than to get away from him now, to find a quiet space to hide and deal with the jumble of thoughts frazzling her brain.

"Look, thanks for listening to me. I'll . . . I'll let you get back to your car. You're fixing it up?"

"Yeah." Jonas grinned a little impishly, his chubby cheeks

making his eyes all but disappear. "I always wanted a car when I was alive." His choice of words jarred Dylan, but she kept her expression impassive. "Now I can play all I want. Though I think it would run whatever I did to it. Still, I like to pretend I'm making a difference. I was so excited when I crossed over and saw it, I almost didn't notice at first that I was back in Stuttgart!" He gave Dylan a slightly sad smile. "At least that's one thing about this place . . . going home."

Home. There it was again. Dylan's eyes clouded over, her lips pursing in annoyance.

"I'm not going home."

"What do you mean?" Jonas squinted at her.

"The records room, it can take you anywhere, right?"

"Well, yes." Jonas still looked nonplussed. "But when you crossed the line in the wasteland . . ." He paused, tilted his head to the side as he stared at her. "Did you not go home?"

It was Dylan's turn to look bewildered. "I was still in what looked like the wasteland."

"You are sure?" he pressed.

Dylan raised her eyebrows at him. She was pretty damned sure. "I'm positive. I was standing in the exact same spot. Only, only Tris—my ferryman had disappeared."

"That is not right," Jonas told her, his forehead creased with concern. "Everyone else I have ever spoken to—my family, my friends—their first moment beyond, it has been in the place they think of as home."

Dylan didn't know what to say. She should feel bad, she supposed, that she hadn't been taken to her old home or her granny's house.

But she didn't feel bad. She felt reassured. She was supposed to be with Tristan, that's what her brain was telling her. As much as she hated the wasteland—the cold, the wind, the *up!*—that was where she was supposed to be.

She didn't belong here. She didn't fit in, like always.

"I'm not supposed to be here," she murmured, more to herself than Jonas. She shifted away from him. She wanted to be alone. Alone to think; alone to cry. She forced false brightness into her voice. "Well, have fun with your car. Thanks again." Dylan was off before the final word was out of her mouth, quick steps taking her away, eyes searching out the flower pots, the brass number nine.

"Hey! Hey, wait!"

Letting an aggravated hiss escape between her clenched teeth, Dylan halted in her tracks. She paused for a second, then turned round warily.

Jonas pushed off from the car, closed half the distance between them. Worry aged his face, made him almost adult.

"You're not going to try it?" His voice was so low, Dylan almost didn't catch it.

"Try what?"

He looked right and left before he answered. Dylan raised her eyebrows, intrigued. *"To go back."* He mouthed the words.

"What?" Dylan barked, subconsciously moving so that they were face-to-face. "What do you mean, go back?" Go back where? To the wasteland? Was he saying there was a way?

Jonas shushed her, his hands gesturing a warning as he glanced around. Dylan ignored his panic, but she lowered her voice as she asked the question again.

"What did you mean, try to go back? I thought there was no going back?"

"There isn't," Jonas replied at once, but his expression was shifty.

"But . . ." Dylan prompted.

"But nothing." Jonas tried to back away, but Dylan wouldn't let him, shadowing each step.

"People have tried?" she guessed.

"You can't go back." Jonas repeated Caeli's words almost as if the answer was ingrained, but he couldn't hold the innocent expression.

"How did they do it?" she demanded, advancing again.

Blanket silence from the German.

"How did they do it, Jonas?"

He pressed his lips together, considering her. "I don't know."

Dylan eyed him shrewdly, too caught by sudden hope to be shy. "You're lying."

"I'm not, Dylan. I don't know how it's done. But I know that it's suicide."

Dylan laughed sourly. "I'm already dead."

He gave her a long look. "You know what I mean."

She took a second to think about it. Dead. *Really* dead. Gone. It was frightening; her heart pounded in her chest at the thought. But then . . . what was the point of being here? Yes, eventually her mother, her dad, Katie—they'd all make their way across. She could have her old life back, or some strange version of it. And she could be just as lonely, just as out of step as she'd been before— before the wasteland.

That was not worth waiting a lifetime for. If she knew Tristan was coming, then maybe she could bear to linger here. But that wasn't going to happen. He was never, ever coming. That thought sent a jolt of agony right into her core, and she shut her eyes against the pain of it. Tristan. She could still recall with crystal clarity the burning feeling of his lips pressing against hers, his arms tight around her. How ironic that that moment was the most alive she'd ever felt.

Was it worth risking oblivion to feel it again?

Yes.

"How can you be sure when you don't even know how to do it?" Dylan challenged Jonas. She refused to be put off by his negativity, not when he'd given her a hope to grasp at.

"No, Dylan. You don't understand." Jonas shook his head at her, hands aloft in alarm. "There are souls here who have watched centuries pass. They've known of hundreds, maybe thousands of souls who tried to crawl their way back, to return to their wife or their children. Not a single one has ever made it here again to tell the tale. You've seen the wraiths—you know what they do."

Dylan bit her lip, thinking. "How do you know about them? The ones who've tried?"

He waved a hand dismissively. "Rumors."

Rumors. She stepped forward, eyes piercing. Jonas tried to take a step back, but there was nowhere to go. Dylan glared at him, eyes determined. "Rumors from who?"

TWENTY-THREE

SHE LIVED IN A WOODEN BUILDING THAT DYLAN COULD ONLY describe as a shack, surrounded by miles and miles of flat plains. It was an isolated and wild place, with yapping dogs and rolling thunderclouds overhead. Eliza. The oldest soul that Jonas knew. If anyone was going to be able to give her answers, it was Eliza.

Jonas had taken her there simply by walking through another of the doors on his street. One moment they had been surrounded by buildings, the next, sand and tumbleweed. Dylan watched him close a rickety gate, warped pieces of wood held together with rusting nails.

"Have you been here before?" Dylan asked as he pointed the way to the old woman's house, where a light shone brightly from its one window. It was much darker here, and the warm glow was welcoming.

"No." Jonas shook his head. "But I don't know of anyone else who might be able to help you."

He gave her a funny look, and Dylan knew that he was hoping Eliza would try to talk her out of it rather than help her. She looked at the ramshackle house, feeling a little nervous.

"Who is she?" Dylan asked. "How does she know about these things?"

"She's been here a very long time," Jonas replied.

Dylan set her mouth into a dissatisfied line. That didn't really answer her question, but she sensed it was all Jonas knew.

Jonas stepped smartly onto a shaky-looking wooden porch and rapped on the door, but Dylan held back. Though she had confronted Jonas without any hesitation, she felt timid at the thought of speaking to another soul. Maybe it was because she was old, a proper adult. Maybe it was because she had never known Tristan. Whatever it was, it had Dylan backing away rather than stepping forward. If Jonas hadn't escorted her, she knew she wouldn't have made it this far.

She considered changing her mind, telling Jonas not to bother. Tristan seemed even farther away in this alien, unforgiving landscape. But then a voice from inside called "Come," and Jonas swung the door open, motioning with his hand for her to enter. There was nothing Dylan could do but comply.

Inside, the cabin was a little cozier, and that eased some of her nerves. A fire burned in the grate, and the walls were adorned with knitted fabrics. It was a one-room hut, with the bed against the wall at one end and a small kitchen area underneath the window at the other. In the middle sat an ancient woman, swaddled in blankets and rocking gently in an old-fashioned wooden rocking chair. Dylan continued to look around rather than return her curious stare, and wondered idly if this was what the wasteland's safe houses had looked like before they'd fallen into disrepair.

"Eliza," Jonas began, "this is Dylan, and—"

"You want to know how to go back," she finished for him, her voice feathery and weak, but when Dylan whipped her head round to gape at her—surprised that she had been so quick to guess the reason for her visit—her eyes were alert, piercing.

"How did you . . ." Dylan trailed off under the shrewd look Eliza gave her.

"People always come to me when they want to know that. I have seen a thousand others like you, my dear," she said, not unkindly.

"Can you tell me how to do it?" Dylan asked.

Eliza assessed her for a long moment. "Sit down," she finally said.

Dylan frowned. She didn't want to sit down. She was agitated, pent up. She wanted to pace, to move about and release some of the tension making her muscles twitch. She wanted to find out what the old woman knew and then get going, get started.

Eliza looked at her as if she knew exactly what Dylan was thinking. She gestured once again to the only other chair in the room. "Sit down."

Dylan sat, perching on the edge, hands jammed between her knees to stop them from tapping or fidgeting or shaking. She fixed her eyes on the old woman, not noticing Jonas settle himself discreetly on the edge of a table behind her.

"Tell me what you know," Dylan demanded.

"I don't *know* anything," the old woman answered. "But I've heard things."

"What's the difference?"

Eliza smiled at her, but the expression was tinged with wistful sadness. "Certainty."

That halted Dylan in her tracks, but only for a moment. "Tell me what you've heard, then. Please."

Eliza shifted in her seat, adjusting the shawls draped over her shoulders. "I have *heard*"—she emphasized the final word—"that it is possible to cross back through the wasteland."

"How?" Dylan whispered.

"You know how this place works by now. All you have to do is find the door."

"And where is that?" The question was out of Dylan's lips before Eliza had even finished speaking.

The old woman looked amused by her eagerness, the corners of her lips twitching. "Any door."

"What?" Dylan's voice was sharp, impatient. "What do you mean?"

"Any door will take you there. It's not about the door; it's about you."

"That can't be right." Dylan shook her head dismissively. "If any door could take you there, everyone would try it."

"No, they wouldn't," Eliza contradicted gently.

"Of course they would!" Dylan exploded. She was getting angry, feeling like this was a waste of time.

"No," Eliza repeated. "Because when most people try to open that door—and you're right, many do try—every time they try to open the door, it locks itself."

"It's this place," Dylan whispered. "It's like a prison; it won't let you out."

Eliza shook her head.

"I know most people don't want to leave," continued Dylan, "but it should let them, if they want to."

"You're wrong," Eliza said. "It's not this place. It's the souls; they stop themselves."

"How? Why?" Dylan shuffled even closer to the edge of her chair.

"They don't really want to leave. No, that's not quite right. They want to leave, but more than that, they don't want their soul to die. Somewhere deep down, they know crossing the wasteland again will likely be the end of them, and that thought stops them. Because they know if they're patient, they'll see their loved ones again. They just can't take the risk of trying and failing."

Dylan heard the warning in her words. But what Eliza didn't realize was that no amount of waiting was going to make Tristan come to her.

"So how do you make the door open?"

Eliza spread her hands out, as if the answer was obvious. "You have to want to go back more than you want your soul to survive."

Dylan considered that. Did she? She thought so. And from the sound of it, it would cost her nothing to try the door and find out. But even if she got back to the wasteland, then what? How would she find Tristan amongst all those orbs and souls? She doubted Eliza would be able to tell her that. Had there ever been a soul who wanted to be reunited with their ferryman? And what would she do when she found him? Dylan didn't care if she and Tristan came here, or if they went back to the real world. Even if they lived in the wasteland. She shuddered at the prospect of facing the wraiths again, but she would do it if it meant she could be with Tristan.

Eliza sighed, pulling Dylan from her thoughts. "It's always the young ones who want to go back," she murmured. "Always."

"Weren't you tempted?" Dylan asked, momentarily distracted.

Eliza shook her head, her eyes darkening with grief. "No, girl. I was old; I knew I would not have long to wait before my husband joined me."

"Where is he? Is he here?" Dylan asked the question before she realized how rude it sounded.

"No." Eliza's light, whispering voice almost disappeared. "No, he didn't make it across the wasteland."

"I'm sorry," Dylan mumbled into her lap, abashed.

Eliza's face had closed in on itself, and tears threatened her eyes, but then she seemed to steel herself, straightening her back and sniffing deeply.

"I suppose you want to know what happens when you get back across," she said.

Dylan shrugged. She was no more eager to return to her old life than she would be to come back here. It would look odd, though, if she didn't appear interested. She wasn't sure she wanted to confess her true intentions to Eliza. Telling her would be different than telling Jonas.

"I've *heard*"—once again Eliza sought to get through to Dylan the risk she was taking—"that if you can make it back to your body, you can climb back inside."

"Will it still be there?" Dylan made a horrified face, forgetting, for a moment, that this wasn't part of her plan. "Surely they'll have taken it away. My mum will have buried me. Oh my God, I wouldn't come back in the coffin, would I? Or what if she had me cremated?" Panic and revulsion turned her final few words into a squeak.

"Dylan, time has stopped. For you, anyway. Your body will be exactly where it was."

Dylan nodded, accepting this. Plans were forming in her mind. She could see herself rowing across the lake, picking a path through the valley. She thought about the bloodred ground, the scorched sky, but even these terrifying images couldn't sway her. She was going to try it, she knew. Somehow she was going to make the door open, and she was going to try it. She was going to find Tristan. She allowed herself a tiny smile. Looking up, she saw Eliza watching her closely.

"There's something more," the old woman said slowly. "Something you're not telling me." Her eyes searched Dylan's face. It was uncomfortable, like she was trying to see into her very core. Dylan grimaced, fighting the urge to turn away. "You don't want to go back," she mused. "Not all the way. What is it you are after, Dylan?"

What was the point in lying? Dylan bit her lip for a moment, then decided to confide in her. She had made her mind up anyway, regardless of what Eliza had to say. Perhaps the old woman would be able to help her.

"I want to find my ferryman," she said quietly.

The old woman kept her face impassive, only a slight puckering of her lips revealing her emotions as she thought through Dylan's intentions.

"That is harder," she said, after a painful minute.

Dylan's heart broke into a sprint. "But not impossible?"

"Perhaps not impossible."

"What do I have to do?"

"You have to find him."

Dylan blinked two, three times, confused. That wasn't hard.

He was ferrying another soul. She would just wait at a safe house and—eventually—he would come to her.

Then she remembered. Remembered watching shadowy outlines ghosting across the red-tinged wasteland. Remembered the hordes of black wraiths dogging their every step. And the orbs. The glowing orbs lighting the path, giving the souls something to follow, keeping them safe. Would that be all Tristan was to her now, an orb? If so, how would she tell him apart from the thousand others?

You'll know, a small voice said in the back of her head. But just once. Quietly. Because the rest of her conscious brain turned the full force of its scorn onto the voice. This wasn't some drippy, romantic movie. This was real life. If Tristan was one of those things, if she couldn't see him, hear him, she'd never be able to pick him out.

"How do I find him?" she asked. "I've seen them, the other ferrymen in the wasteland. They're not people, they're just—"

"Light," Eliza finished. Dylan nodded; it was as good a description as any. "But," she continued, "he is still *your* ferryman. Even if he has guided another soul since. Even if he has guided a thousand. If you see him, you should see him as you always did."

Dylan's eyes lit up. So there was a chance . . . it was possible. She heard a low cough from Jonas behind her and turned to beam at him. Only a hunch had led her to him—how long would it have taken her to find these answers on her own? How many long years had it taken Eliza to fully understand how this place worked?

"How do you know all this?" Dylan asked her, still smiling widely.

The old woman sighed. "I told you—and this is something you need to remember, Dylan—I don't *know*. I really don't. You would be taking an enormous risk." Her doubts couldn't diminish Dylan's sudden enthusiasm, though she was determined to try. "Even if you find him—your ferryman—how long do you think you can outsmart the demons?"

"We'll stay in the safe houses," Dylan said. "They can't come in."

"Are you sure? You're changing the game, Dylan. How do you know the safe houses will still be there, will still work for you? And what about your ferryman's duties to other souls?"

Dylan frowned, wrong-footed by Eliza's words. "Well, we won't stay in the wasteland then," she asserted, but some of the confidence had dropped from her voice.

Eliza laughed, but her expression was pitying. "And where will you go?"

"Can he come with me?" It was whispered, timid. Dylan's heart, racing before, now stopped, thumping erratically, as nervous for the answer as she was.

"Where?"

"Here. There. Anywhere. It doesn't matter."

"He doesn't belong here."

"Neither do I," Dylan shot back. She tried to ignore the sympathetic way Eliza smiled at her.

"And he doesn't belong with you, either. He's not human, Dylan. He doesn't feel like we do, doesn't bleed."

"He does bleed," Dylan said quietly. She wanted to tell Eliza that he could feel, too, that he loved her, but she knew the old woman wouldn't believe her. She didn't want to have to defend

Tristan's words when she wasn't sure just how much she believed them herself.

"What?" Eliza asked, looking uncertain for the first time.

"He does bleed," Dylan repeated. "When . . . when the demons got him, when they dragged him under, they hurt him. He came back to me, though. And he was covered in bruises and scratches."

"I have never heard of that," Eliza said slowly. She looked up at Jonas, hovering behind Dylan, and he also shook his head.

"I saw it," Dylan told her. She leaned forward, stared at Eliza. "Can he come with me? If not here, then back. Back across?"

The ancient soul rocked on her chair as she thought about it. Eventually she shook her head. Ice dropped into Dylan's stomach.

"I don't know," she said. "Maybe. That is the best I can give you. It is a risk." She looked at Dylan, hard. "Is it worth it?"

~~~~~

Tristan sat motionless on the rickety safe-house chair, watching the woman sleep. Though she was well into adulthood—she had celebrated her thirty-sixth birthday just a month before—she looked very young curled up on the narrow single bed. Her long brown hair snaked around her shoulders, the short tendrils of her bangs tickling her eyebrows. Beneath the pale lilac of her eyelids, he could see her eyes flickering from side to side, watching dreams. There wasn't space in his clouded brain to wonder what she saw; he was simply glad that her eyes were closed. When they were open, when they were looking at him, they were exactly the right and exactly the wrong shade of green, and he couldn't stand to look back.

He sighed and stood up from the chair, stretched, then wandered over to the window. It was dark outside, but that was no problem for him. It was easy to pick out the swirling shapes, shadows upon shadows, that coiled around the tiny building, sniffing, savoring. Waiting. They were frustrated. They hadn't caught so much as a whiff of the soul he was guiding. Not today, or the day before that, or the day before that. In fact, this was the easiest crossing he'd made in a long, long time. He smiled grimly to himself as he thought how much Dylan would have preferred the flat streets of this desolate urban decay. She wouldn't have been perturbed by the abandoned high-rises that had the woman craning her neck every three seconds.

He always thought of her that way, as "the woman." He didn't want to think her name, Marie. She was a job to him, not a person, although she was mild-mannered and cheerful. Her sunny disposition filled the air with warmth and kept the sky shining blue. She was meek, too, swallowing the lies he told her without question. Each night they had reached the safe house with plenty of time to spare. It was just as well, because Tristan's mind was not in the game.

Blank. That's all he could manage. Blank and emotionless. Thoughtless. If he'd been concentrating, he might have felt sorry for the woman. She seemed nice; she was pleasant, polite, shy. What had happened to her deserved his pity—slaughtered while she slept by a sticky-fingered thief—but he had none to spare.

A noise from behind made him whip his head round. It was just the woman, coughing quietly as she shifted on the mattress. Tristan watched her carefully for a moment, apprehensive, but she didn't wake up. Good. He didn't think he could face conversation.

Gazing into the night wasn't enough of a distraction. After drumming his fingers silently on the windowsill for a long moment, Tristan turned back and resumed his vigil in the hard wooden chair. He reasoned there was an hour, maybe two, before the sun rose. Hopefully the woman would sleep till then.

That gave Tristan a long time to kill. Six hours he'd been sitting here alone, and he'd managed not to think of her. He allowed himself a wry smile. That was a record. It was also as long as he was going to manage. Closing his eyes, he sifted through memories until he found the one he was looking for. Eyes the same shade of green as the soul sleeping soundly beside him, but a different face. Tristan's smile widened as he let himself get as close as he could to dreaming.

TWENTY-FOUR

"WHAT ARE YOU GOING TO DO?"

They had left the ancient Eliza in her cabin, and Dylan, without anywhere else to go, had followed Jonas back through to the street that she now knew to be a re-creation of a road in Stuttgart, the town he'd lived in as a child before his short career in the military. They were sitting on the bonnet of his car, the radio still whistling old tunes Dylan didn't recognize in the background.

She blew out a breath, trying to clear her head. "I'm going to go back."

Jonas regarded her, his expression somber, cautious. "Are you sure that is the right thing to do?"

"No." Dylan smiled wryly. "But I'm going to do it anyway."

"You could die," Jonas warned her.

Dylan's smile slipped from her face. "I know," she said softly. "I know. I should stay here, wait for my mum, my friends. Find my relatives. I should just accept it. I know I should . . ."

"But you're not going to," Jonas finished for her.

Dylan grimaced, dropping her gaze to her hands, which were

clasped tightly together. What else could she say? Jonas wouldn't understand. She couldn't blame him. It barely even made sense to her how the right thing could also be the wrong thing.

"My mum always told me I was stubborn," she said, and then she grinned. "Tristan said the same."

"Really?" Jonas laughed.

She nodded. "I think I annoyed him at first. I kept telling him he was going the wrong way."

It was funny now, looking back on those first couple of days. How many times had she made him stop and convince her?

"Did he tell you the story about Santa Claus?" Jonas asked, chuckling to himself.

"Yes!" Dylan laughed. How bizarre! When she'd imagined the story, it had been modern. She'd pictured the grotto in the shopping center downtown. Would it have been the same in—what?— the 1930s? Earlier? "He thought highly of you, you know. When he told me your story, he said you were admirable. And noble."

"He did?" Jonas looked pleased, smiling widely when Dylan nodded, confirming the truth of her words.

"I think he is admirable, too," he mused. "The job he does, the way he just goes round and round. It is not fair, the hand he has been dealt."

"I know," Dylan mumbled.

None of it was fair. Not what had happened to Jonas or to her. Tristan deserved to be freed from his . . . well, "job" just wasn't the right word. You got paid for a job. And it was possible to resign, to walk away. No, what Tristan had was an obligation. And he'd suffered enough.

"When are you going to try?" Jonas broke into her reverie.

Dylan made a face. She wasn't sure. Her first thought was that she would wait for morning. That would be better, giving her a whole day of light to try to make it to a safe house. But then another thought struck her. Tristan had told her she didn't need to sleep anymore—and how long had she been awake now? She still didn't feel tired. Was there such a thing as night here? The sun still hung as high as it had earlier, before they'd gone to meet Eliza.

So if time was no object, she supposed the answer was whenever she was ready. When would that be?

Never.

Now.

She thought about what she was facing: a door that wouldn't open, a wasteland, an army of wraiths, a hopeless needle-in-a-haystack search to find Tristan. It was a terrifying list that had her trembling.

And what could she do to prepare for it? Absolutely nothing.

Dylan experienced a moment of pure terror. Could she really do this? Her resolve wavered, the practical part of her brain fighting desperately against the idea of being obliterated, erased. The bloody skies and swirling demons that waited for her on the other side of the door. Why was she doing this?

Tristan. His blue, blue eyes. The warmth of his hand, strong around hers. The softness of his lips, burning down into her soul.

"No time like the present."

Any door, Eliza had said. Any door would take her where she wanted to go, so long as she was sure she wanted to go there. Dylan knew which door she should choose.

~~~~~

Not ten minutes later she was standing in front of it, breathing in the heady scent from the pots of orange and yellow flowers, squinting against the flare of light as the sun reflected off the shining brass number hanging dead square in the door. This was the door that had taken her into Jonas's world, wherever it was. It seemed fitting that this was the door she used to leave it.

Dylan contemplated the little round doorknob. All she had to think about was where she wanted to go, and when she opened the door, she would be there. She fixed in her head a vision of the wasteland: the high, rolling hills, the frigid wind, the cloud-covered sky. Her hand began to reach forward, but then she stopped herself. That wasn't right. That wasn't the real wasteland. Without Tristan, she knew what she was going to see. Wincing slightly, she dredged up a different image, one that was a landscape awash with different hues of red. That was where she was truly going.

Her teeth gritted in concentration, she stretched out her fingers again.

"Dylan." Jonas wrapped a hand around her wrist, pulled her to a stop.

Letting out a quick sigh of relief, secretly glad of the chance to delay, even for a few moments, Dylan twisted round to look at him.

"How did you die?"

"What?" Utterly unprepared for the question, Dylan could do nothing but gape at him.

"How did you die?" he repeated.

"Why?" she asked, bewildered.

"Well, it's just . . . if you make it, and I really hope you do" —he flashed her a quick smile—"you'll go back into your body, just as you were. Whatever happened to you will have still happened. So, I just wondered, how did you die?"

"Train crash," Dylan muttered through motionless lips.

Jonas nodded thoughtfully. "What were your injuries?"

"I don't know."

It had been so dark and so quiet. And she'd had no idea at all that she was dead. If there had been light in the carriage, what would she have seen? Had her body been there, sprawled across the seat? Had she been crushed? Decapitated?

If she was that badly injured, would it work for her?

Dylan shook her head slightly to clear her morbid thoughts before they stole her nerve. She'd already decided, she reminded herself. She was doing this.

"I don't know," she repeated, "but it doesn't matter." Tristan was all that mattered. "Goodbye, Jonas."

"Good luck." He attempted another smile, and she knew he thought she wasn't going to make it. She turned her back on his doubt, but he spoke again. "Hey, one more thing."

This time Dylan sighed in real frustration. "What?" she asked, not looking round, hand still held out toward the doorknob.

"Say hello to him for me." Pause. "I hope you survive, Dylan. Maybe I'll see you again."

He gave his farewell and backed away down the path. Dylan felt a slight stirring of panic as she turned and watched the distance grow between them.

"You're not staying?"

What she really wanted to ask was for him to come with her, but she couldn't do that. Wouldn't.

He shook his head at her, still shuffling backward.

"I don't want to see," he confessed. He gave her a quick wave and a final smile, then hurried away down the street. Dylan watched him cross the road, weaving between the cars until he disappeared inside a house. And then she was alone.

The street felt eerily quiet. Unwelcome. It was almost easy to turn her back on it and face the door for a third and final time. Heart thudding in her chest, a light dew of nervous sweat beading on her upper lip, she reached out for the doorknob. In her mind's eye, she conjured up the nightmare vision, bathed in bloody red, and as her fingers grasped the cool metal, her lips trembled, muttering, "Wasteland, wasteland," over and over again. She gripped the circular knob, took a final breath, and twisted.

Dylan expected nothing to happen. She expected to meet an immovable force, a lock she could never pick. She honestly believed she'd have to stand there for hour after hour, searching for her courage, her conviction, until she was sure, utterly sure, that she wanted to do this.

But the door opened easily.

Astonished, she swung it wide and peered through the opening.

The wasteland.

The burning burgundy wasteland. The sky was streaked with burnt orange and violet. Already midafternoon. That was frightening.

The path she'd followed on that final day with Tristan—when she'd still believed he was coming with her, when the sun was still shining—stretched out before her. Rather than the golden brown of sand and gravel, it was midnight black. It seemed to swell, like something bubbled under the surface. It glistened slightly, like treacle.

Holding her breath, Dylan lifted her foot and placed it gently down. The path held firm. After a moment's hesitation, she took another pace. Her fingers let go of the door. She didn't need to turn round to watch it; she knew when it closed. Knew to the very second.

Because she was no longer alone.

Souls. The instant she was back in the realm of the ferrymen, she was surrounded by souls. They were exactly as she'd remembered them: filmy, shadowy. Like ghosts, rippling slightly in the air. They had faces, bodies, but they seemed both to be there and not there. It was the same for their voices. When she'd watched them from the safe house, Dylan had been too far away, and protected by the cottage walls, to hear them. But now they were loud, babbling all around her. Nothing they said was clear. It was like listening underwater, or with a glass pressed against the wall. And then, surrounding them, intently circling, were wraiths.

Dylan gasped, but the demons made no move toward her. They frightened her, though. She threw an automatic glance over her shoulder, eyed the firmly closed door. Should she go back?

No.

Go, Dylan, she told herself. *Move.*

Her legs obeyed, and she started forward in a stiff walk that was almost a trot. As much as she could, she kept her eyes fixed forward. Her sights were firmly set on a ring of hills in the distance. Hills that she knew skirted the edge of a lake, on the shore of which was a safe house.

The path was sulfurous. Smoking fumes hovered in a mist above it and swirled around her feet, wisps that seemed ready to solidify into grabbing hands if she stayed too long. She wasn't sure if it was her imagination, but already her feet seemed too warm, as if heat was seeping up through the soles of her sneakers. The air, too, was uncomfortably hot. It was how Dylan imagined it would feel to stand in the middle of a desert, not even a breath of wind to stir the cloying heat. It tasted like sand and ash, and already her mouth was dry. She tried to breathe through her nose, and her lungs burned for more oxygen. She knew she was close to hyperventilating, but she couldn't stop herself.

Just get to the first safe house. That was all she had to do, and she would think no further than that. Just get to the first safe house.

Clenching her fingers into fists, she set her eyes forward. She was tempted—so tempted—to look at the souls, to see who passed, but some sixth sense told her that was dangerous.

Out of the corner of her eye, she could see the flickering shadows of the wraiths. Without the light of a shining orb to draw their gaze, they didn't seem to notice her. But if they did . . . she had no ferryman to protect her. She'd be easy pickings.

"Don't look, don't look," she repeated under her breath as she hurried on.

Forward, forward, forward she marched, looking at nothing more than the hills in front of her, watching as they grew larger and larger, and darker and darker with the setting of the sun.

~~~~~

Dylan made it to the safe house just as the sun, glowing like a hot coal, began to nudge the razor-sharp edge of the highest of the hills. She was panting and gasping, not with exertion, although she'd walked faster and faster as she'd chased the fading light, but with the stress of keeping her eyes fixed firmly ahead. The souls had continued to stream past her thick and fast, but she'd caught only snatches of conversation—meaningless phrases and words, the occasional heart-wrenching wail.

The later it had gotten in the day, the faster the souls around her were trying to travel. She sensed their urgency, seen glimpses of stunning white light—beautiful in the gloom—in the corner of her eye, coaxing them on. These souls were flirting with danger, pushing their luck. They had a long way to go to get to the line before nightfall, and their ferrymen knew it.

So did the wraiths. They emitted a sound the like of which Dylan had never heard before. Screaming and laughing blended together. Hate and delight; despair and excitement. It chilled her to her very bones. And it was almost impossible not to look, to turn toward the source of the sound, to see what creature could be so happy and yet so tortured at the same time. She was enormously relieved when she saw the safe house. In this bloody wilderness, she'd been worried that it wouldn't be there, wouldn't be the same. There it was, though, an oasis in the desert, and by the time Dylan threw herself in the door of the cottage, she was almost crying with the effort of it.

The night passed slowly after that.

She lit a fire, lay down on the bed. Closed her eyes. She wanted to sleep. Not because she was tired, but just to hide. Just to pass the time. But unconsciousness had deserted her. Instead, she whiled away the hours listening to the wraiths' cackles of ecstasy as they feasted on souls who had been too slow, whose ferrymen had failed.

TWENTY-FIVE

"I'M DEAD."

It wasn't a question, so Tristan didn't bother to answer it. He just stared straight ahead, letting the flickering light of the flames lull him into a semi-trance. He hated this part. Hated the crying and the moaning and the pleading. They'd almost reached the valley without the woman realizing what was happening. They might have made it all the way to the line—a feat Tristan had never achieved in all the thousands of souls he'd had to ferry—had it not been for the wraiths. This soul, this woman, was so timid, so docile and compliant, that she hadn't once questioned Tristan's word. It had become almost annoying, but at least it had been convenient.

The wraiths, though, would never let one so innocent and naive pass through the wasteland without a fight. They had dared to risk the sun, using the flimsy shadows of trees and bushes to attack. They had been easy to evade, but they'd been loud. And there had been nothing he could do to stop her from looking toward the noise.

"What happened to me?" The woman's voice was a frightened whisper.

Tristan blinked once, dragging himself back to the room, and looked at her. Her shoulders were hunched, her eyes huge, her arms wrapped around her chest as if she was trying to hug herself. He looked at her, at her pathetic expression, and he made himself feel absolutely nothing. Still, he was her ferryman; he had to answer.

"Your house was robbed. The burglar stabbed you while you slept."

"And those . . . things outside, what are they?"

"Demons, wraiths." He said no more than that. He did not want to have to make any long explanations.

"What will they do to me?"

"If they catch you, they'll devour your soul and you'll become one of them." Tristan looked away so he wouldn't see the terror on her face. Despite himself, he was beginning to feel sorry for her, and he couldn't afford that. Not again.

There was a silence that lasted for so long Tristan almost turned to read the woman's expression. He could hear the slight hitch of her breathing, though. She was crying. That was something he didn't want to see.

"I thought that you were going to rob me at first, you know," she said quietly, her voice steadier than he would have expected. She huffed a humorless laugh. "When I saw you outside my house, I thought you were one of the neighborhood thugs, come to steal from me. I was going to call the police."

Tristan nodded without looking at her. It was the way he was dressed: his age, face. It was all wrong for this woman. He should be older, someone gentlemanly. The type of man she would trust. He should not be the same boy who had been sent to collect Dylan from the train.

Why hadn't he changed? It didn't make sense. He'd never held on to a form before. And then, as they'd been leaving her street, he'd sworn he'd seen someone *looking* at him. He didn't understand it, but he didn't like it. It made it harder to try to forget about Dylan this way, to leave the pain behind.

"What would have happened," she said at last, "if I had tried to run away from you?"

He spoke into the flames. "I would have stopped you."

There was silence whilst the woman considered this. Tristan tried to lull himself into a trance, but he couldn't shut his mind off. He found himself wishing for the woman to speak, just to break the tension. She obliged a moment later.

"Where are we going?"

Of course she would ask that question. Tristan had compiled a stock answer to this one many years ago.

"I am guiding you across the wasteland. When you finish the journey, you'll be safe."

"And where will I be?" she prompted.

"On."

On. They always went on. And he went back. He had long since reconciled himself with this great injustice, and it had ceased to bother him. Not until . . .

He opened his mouth, his thoughts half forming a message. The woman had an eternity ahead of her: surely she could spare a few moments of it to seek out a soul for him? But before he'd even decided what he wanted to say, he closed his mouth again.

Dylan had gone where he could not reach her. Not his hands; not his words. And what point was there in sending a message when there was no way she could ever send one back?

He sighed..

"Tomorrow we have a dangerous journey to make," he began.

The valley would be treacherous. He needed to focus. He needed to be the ferryman.

~~~~~

The wasteland was no cooler in the early light of dawn. Dylan stood on the threshold of the cottage. She'd been there for a while, fighting with herself. There were wraiths outside already, swooping across the surface of the lake, like birds. Again, they hadn't come near her. The safe house seemed to be holding. She could stay here. Stay here, be safe, and wait for Tristan. But what if he didn't make it this far? What if the soul he was ferrying was too old, too slow? Besides, she was aching for him. The idea of waiting, for however long, was excruciating. She had to go and find him.

But the lake. She had almost drowned here. Tipped into the water, she'd floundered. Creatures in the deep had toyed with her, tugging, pulling, ripping. If it hadn't been for Tristan, she'd never have left the water. She remembered the taste of it. Foul, stagnant, polluted. It had been thick, like oil on her tongue. And that had been in her own heather-covered wasteland.

In this new burning wilderness, it was worse. The water churned, poisonous and smoking. It didn't look substantial enough to take the weight of the dilapidated dinghy, but the boat was

234

there where it had capsized, still bobbing gently on the surface. That was a relief. She'd been worried that it might have sunk or washed up dashed to pieces. But there it was.

In the middle of the lake.

She sighed as she considered it. There were only two options: wade in and get it, or walk round the lake. Walking was much more appealing than going into the oily black water, with the hidden things lurking in its murky depths. But it was a long way. She'd be racing against the sun, and she wasn't sure she would win.

So really it was a choice of what was worse: the water or the night?

Tristan had thought the better option was to use the little dinghy, despite the dangers beneath the surface. That had to mean it was just too far—and, in this version of the wasteland, just too hot—to make it round before dark. And she'd survived the lake's icy waters before. She'd never been out in the dead of night.

The lake, then. The crunch of her feet on the shore's tiny stones was the only sound as she trotted down the slight incline toward the water. There were no souls to see this early in the day. They would all be emerging from their safe houses, just as she was, ready to cross the lake. She'd thought about them in the long hours as she waited for dawn, as she'd tried unsuccessfully to block out the screaming of the wraiths. She couldn't see their safe houses, but she knew they must be close by. In a strange way, Dylan had been glad to be alone. The other souls made her uncomfortable. They were eerie. And, though she knew it was ridiculous, she was jealous that they still had their ferrymen, while she had yet to find hers.

Nor any idea how to do so. But she refused to think about that yet. One step at a time—that was the way to survive here. And the next step was to cross the lake.

She almost balked at the water's edge. The lapping waves painted the toes of her sneakers. Going any farther in meant letting the foul liquid touch her skin and giving any lurking creatures a chance to snatch at her. Dylan hesitated, chewing on her lip, but there was really no choice. It was go forward or go back. Taking a deep breath, she forced her feet to move.

Icy cold. Burning. The two sensations hit Dylan at once and she gasped. Thicker than water, the liquid fought against each step. It swirled around her knees, then her thighs. Though she couldn't see the lake bed, her feet felt their way along, shuffling over the shifting mixture of sand and stones. So far, so good. It was beyond unpleasant, but she was still on her feet, and she'd yet to feel the grabbing claws of any demons. A few steps farther in and she had to lift her hands clear of the surface. The tarlike water lapped at her middle, and she felt nauseated. She hoped she'd reach the little boat before she was out of her depth.

She fixed her eyes on it now. It wasn't in the middle of the lake really, but it was still at least the length of a swimming pool away from her. Her hopes of wading were dashed when another step took her up to her chest, and then her throat. She jerked her chin upright, trying to keep her mouth clear, but the noxious fumes seeped up into her nose, making her gag and retch. She was shuddering with the cold, shaking so hard she almost didn't feel something sliding slowly round her left leg, then her right ankle. Her middle.

Almost.

"Shit!" she shrieked. Her arms, still aloft, slapped down to chase away whatever had a hold of her hoodie. She felt the prickle of sharp scales against her palm before it slunk away. It circled back, though, snapping at her from behind, grabbing on to her hood so that her sweatshirt choked at her throat.

Dylan whirled in the water, kicking and slapping and flailing. Droplets of oily black splashed up, landing in her hair, on her cheeks. Spray found its way into her eyes and her mouth. Spitting and blind, she wrenched her hoodie out of the creature's maw and launched herself toward the dinghy, trying to swim and fight at the same time. It was ungainly and exhausting, but she managed to stop the creatures from getting a firm grip, and the boat was getting closer and closer. Nearly there. She reached out, fingers searching for the edge of the boat. She had it. But then suddenly she couldn't breathe. Three of the demons had sunk their teeth into her hoodie, and their combined strength was too much for her to shake free.

They dived, plunging down into the frozen lake, pulling her with them. Dylan opened her mouth to scream just as the water pooled over her face. It flooded into her mouth, thick and toxic. She panicked, blowing out all the air in her lungs, too desperate to think straight. As soon as her lungs contracted, they fought to inflate, squeezing and cramping. Dylan clamped her lips shut, fighting the desire to breathe once again. All the time going deeper and deeper, but there was no Tristan to save her this time.

Tristan. She saw his face in her mind with total clarity. It gave her the strength to fight. Yanking down the zipper of her hoodie, she twisted and writhed her way out, then kicked desperately up. Up and up and up. Surely this was too far? Was she going the wrong way—right to the bottom? She couldn't fight the urge to breathe much longer.

Just when she thought she was going to pass out, her head broke the surface and she hauled in great lungsful of air. She reached blindly for the boat, tears streaming down her face, making tracks through the black glue that coated her skin. Grabbing hold with both hands, she righted the boat and then hauled herself up and into the little dinghy.

Dylan lay panting, facedown for a moment, trying to feel if there was anything attached to her ankles before she had to turn and face the horrors, but there was no sensation other than the cold. Awkwardly, she clambered round and arranged herself on the hard wooden seat. Her whole body shook, from fright as much as the cold, and her head was spinning. She was soaked, too, her clothes coated in the viscous water. But she was alive.

Now she had to row. There were no oars since they had capsized, but then she remembered there hadn't been any oars last time, either—not at first. Dylan closed her eyes, reached down, and felt around with her fingers.

"Come on, come on," she muttered, scratching along the wooden planks. "You did it for Tristan. How the hell else am I supposed to get across?"

Nothing. Dylan opened her eyes, stared across the lake. It was at least half a mile to the other shore, and the air was completely calm, no phantom wind to push her gently across, not that she had a sail. And there was no way she was going to try to swim. Nothing was getting her out of this boat.

"Bugger off!" she shouted, her voice shockingly loud in the quiet. "I hate this place! Give me some bloody oars!"

She pounded the side of the dinghy, then turned and threw herself back onto the seat, utterly at a loss.

The oars were nestled neatly in the rowlocks, waiting for her.

Dylan stared at them, gobsmacked.

"Oh," she said. Then she looked up at the sky uncertainly. "Thank you?"

Not sure who, if anyone, she was talking to, and feeling foolish for her outburst despite the fact there had been no one there to see her, she grabbed the oars, dipped them into the inky smoke, and started to row.

Rowing was *hard*. Dylan vaguely recalled Tristan laughing at her when she'd asked if he wanted her to take a turn, saying something snarky about not wanting to be on the water forever. It hadn't looked very difficult when he'd done it, but Dylan was finding it almost impossible. The dinghy wouldn't go in the direction she wanted it to, and trying to pull through the water, strangely misty as it was, was like tugging at the weight of the world. Worse, her hands kept slipping on the oar handles, and she rubbed a blister into the skin on the inside of her thumb in the first ten minutes. It was very, very slow progress.

About halfway, she came across something to momentarily distract her from her aching limbs. A boat passed her, going in the opposite direction. It glided along slowly, its inhabitants rippling in the light. Then, once the first boat had passed, there was another, and another. Soon the surface of the lake was awash with tiny crafts, a hazy flotilla creating a fog on the surface of the lake.

It was much harder not to watch these souls. Facing back the way she'd come was the only way to row, so Dylan had no option but to stare in the direction of the receding boats. She tried to keep her eyes on the stern of her own dinghy, but she had to constantly fight the instinct to raise them.

Especially when a boat got into trouble. The water around her dinghy remained calm, but Dylan knew without even raising her head what was happening. First, the noise changed. Rather than the gentle lap of water against the side of the craft and the warped mumble of a hundred conversations, there was a shrill keening. Not the harsh, guttural sound of the wraiths, it was coming from a soul, she was sure of it. Then there was the light. The whispery glow of white from the orbs was barely making a difference to the glowing red light from the sun. But from the direction of the scream, the nearest orb brightened intensely. It was like suddenly having colored glasses removed, and the world, just for a moment, seemed normal-colored.

She saw the boat at once. It was directly in front of her, maybe a hundred feet away, and it was rocking from side to side like it was being attacked by a hurricane. It was hard to look at, because the orb floating in the middle of the boat was shining so brightly, it stung her eyes. Still she couldn't look away. She wasn't supposed to. It was calling to her. No, she realized. It was calling to its soul . . . but the soul was ignoring it.

The soul was looking into the water.

In front of her, the water rose up, forming a twisted shape that looked from where she was to be a claw. The claw detached itself from the lake, separated. Became a dozen, no, two dozen smaller beings. Like bats.

The creatures from the lake.

They swarmed over the soul, and the boat started to jump and lurch, tilting dangerously. As if they'd been waiting for permission, some circling wraiths, braving the sun, joined in the attack.

"No!" Dylan shrieked, realizing a second before it happened that the boat was about to capsize.

As soon as the word had left her mouth, she clapped her hand over her face, but it was too late. They'd heard her. The lake creatures continued to tug the soul down into the depths of the water, oblivious to the orb, which was now pulsing furiously. Then the wraiths came at her. With no orb, no ferryman, they didn't need to wait for dark to feast on her.

"Dammit! Dammit! You idiot!" She berated herself.

Dylan started rowing frantically, hauling the oars through the water as fast and as hard as she could. It wasn't enough. Not even close. The wraiths were flying, soaring across the vapors as if feeding on them. In the time it had taken her to jerk through three hurried strokes, they'd closed half the distance. She could already hear their delighted snarls.

This was it. She was going to die.

Dylan stopped rowing, stopped breathing. She stared at them, waiting. She knew exactly how it would feel when they punched a hole in her chest: like ice in her heart. In her last few seconds, she wondered how long it would last, how much it would hurt.

As they raced over the final few yards, she closed her eyes. She didn't want to see their faces.

But nothing happened.

They were still there, she knew that. She could hear them, hissing and growling and shrieking, but she couldn't feel anything. Nothing beyond the hammering of her pulse and the icy sweat slithering down her back, despite the intense heat of the sun. Puzzled, Dylan opened her eyes, just allowing the first shard of red light to penetrate.

They were still there; she could see them all around her. She squeezed her eyes tight shut again, scrunching up her whole face. Why weren't they attacking? It was hard to take in, hard to believe that they could be so close and not touch her . . . just because she had her eyes shut? But she had no other explanation. Hardly daring to breathe, Dylan reached out blindly and fumbled for the oars. Painstakingly, she dipped them in and started to row. One stroke at a time, she pulled through the water. The growling increased to a roar, but it was a frustrated noise and still nothing touched her.

"Don't look, don't look, don't look," Dylan chanted, mumbling the words in rhythm with her strokes, shaking with the effort. Worse than that, she couldn't see where she was going, and she knew she wasn't good enough to row in a straight line. Who knew where she would end up, but so long as she was off the water, she'd be happy. She tried to remember how far it was from the beach to the safe house over the hill. It hadn't seemed like a long way—just one hill. *Just one hill. Just one hill.* She focused on that thought. That, and keeping her eyes shut.

A jolt behind her almost undid all her hard work. For a second, she thought the wraiths were making their attack. Her eyes flew open in panic before she could force them closed again. She caught one quick glimpse of something black diving toward her before she squeezed her eyelids together, scrunching up her whole face to keep them shut. She tried to row, to dip the oars down into the water, but they bumped against something hard, jerking her hands, making pain shoot up both of her wrists. Then there was a loud scraping that sent another spike of adrenaline flooding through her system before reason caught up with her brain.

The shallows. She'd made it to the shallows. The dinghy was no longer rocking gently; it was beached on the shore.

Clambering out of the dinghy with her eyes screwed shut was awkward. Even run aground as it was, the little boat tipped and jostled as she shifted about, making her yelp and lose her balance. Then, when she swung herself over the side, the drop seemed alarmingly far. When her feet hit the ground, it shocked her, shooting agony and cold up both legs.

She was in the water.

TWENTY-SIX

THE TERROR OF THAT REALIZATION ALMOST UNDID HER AGAIN. Her eyes fluttered only to see wraiths swirling around her head like a swarm of flies. She shut them again at once, but she could still feel the icy chill of the lake rippling up to her knees. Was it her imagination, or was something sliding round her ankle, coiling like a snake about to constrict? Horrified, she yanked her left foot up and out of the water, but whatever it was just moved over to her other leg. This time there was no doubt about it: there was something there.

Squealing, Dylan erupted into action. She thrashed toward the shore, eyes shut, her gait clumsy because with each step she had to lift her sneaker clear and shake her ankle to get rid of anything that clung on. She knew she couldn't look, and like the empty train carriage where this had all started, her mind filled in the blanks. She imagined things halfway between an eel and a crab with seizing claws, or a huge mouth like a monkfish, filled with razor-sharp teeth. Sickened and panicked, she ran on, not stopping until she heard the dry crunch of pebbles beneath her feet.

Overwhelmed and exhausted, she dropped to the ground, propping herself up on all fours, and scrabbled at the stones with her fingers. *Dry land,* she told herself. *Dry land. You're safe.*

But still afraid to open her eyes, she was totally lost. There was a path up the hill, she knew, but that was in *her* wasteland. Not necessarily here. And even if it was, how the hell was she supposed to find it if she couldn't open her eyes?

Dylan's face screwed up in anguish, and a teardrop escaped from between her tightly clenched eyelids, plummeting down and exploding on her hand. Her lips trembled and her shoulders shook. She was stuck. Trapped. How far had other souls made it before finding themselves like this?

She stayed there for ten minutes, ten precious minutes of daylight, before an idea occurred to her. Perhaps she could see . . . just so long as she didn't *look.* If she could keep her head down, stare at nothing but the ground, at all costs resist the temptation to fix her eyes on the things that were screaming for her attention. If she could do that . . .

It was a better idea than staying here and waiting for the night to claim her. The dark, the cold, the screaming; that, she knew, she wouldn't survive.

Breathing in cautious gasps, she tentatively opened her eyes. Focusing on nothing but looking straight down, she waited. It took only three seconds. A wraith ducked low to the ground, skimming the pebbles, and flew straight for her face. Dylan blinked— an automatic reaction—but managed not to turn her gaze to the movement, to stay focused on the ground. At the last second the wraith veered off, snarling venomously in her ear as it passed, making the wind stir a loose tendril of her hair.

"*Yes!*" Dylan hissed.

But one wraith was easy. Realizing she'd now opened her eyes, the rest of the hovering demons tried the same approach, dive-bombing her one after another. The air was a confusing swirl of black, making it hard to see, but Dylan ignored them. Holding her hands out for balance, disoriented by the rush of movement, she got to her feet. Goose bumps erupted on both of her arms as the air vibrated around her.

Turning her head slowly left and right, she hunted out the path. It should be near the boat shed, but she couldn't see the dilapidated little hut anywhere. No shed meant no path, but did she really need it? She knew she had to go up; that should be enough. Would have to be, because the afternoon was bleeding away with frightening speed.

Eyes down, she concentrated on the slick black pebbles, then, as she moved farther from the shore, the burgundy dirt ground. Tufts of plants grew up the hillside, but not the heather and long grasses she'd become used to. These were purple and black, leaves tapering to thin spikes, stems armed with jagged thorns. They smelled, too—a pungent aroma of rot and decay. Now that she was moving away from the lake, the wasteland's heat attacked with renewed fervor. Her clothes dried and stiffened, stained black from the water, then began to stick to her as sweat leached out her skin. The top of her head was burning under the glare of the sun.

It was miserable. She couldn't breathe, and every few seconds the wraiths dived for her again, trying to catch her unawares. She didn't dare lift her head to see how far she had to go, but her legs were aching, her back sore from bending over. Scared and in pain and spent, Dylan screwed up her face and started to cry again. The wraiths cackled, as if they could sense how close she was to giving up, to succumbing. Dylan tried to pull herself together, tears blurring her vision, her steps becoming erratic.

As the gravel finally gave way to the rocky terrain near the top of the hill, Dylan's foot kicked a stone that refused to move, and she tripped. Throwing her arms out in front of her, she gasped, focusing her gaze to see the ground come rushing toward her.

Her hands took the brunt of her fall, then her chest hit the path. Snapping her head up, she found herself eye to eye with a wraith. There was just time to see its tiny puckered face curl into a leer, before it dived at her and she was cold all over, as if she'd been submerged in the icy lake.

Once she'd seen one, it seemed impossible to avoid looking at the rest, and they attacked en masse, pulling and tugging, penetrating down into her bones. With Dylan on the ground, the wraiths had already won half the battle. She felt herself sinking, sliding downward as if the hard, compacted dirt were quicksand.

"No!" she choked out. "No, no, no!"

She hadn't come this far to die now. Again, Tristan's face danced in front of her eyes, the vivid blue of his stare a perfect remedy to this bloody hell. It was like a gulp of fresh air, galvanizing Dylan. With monumental effort, she got her feet beneath her and exploded upward, throwing off the wraiths clinging to her hands, her hair. Then she ran.

Her legs burned, her lungs ached, and the claws of countless wraiths hooked deep into her sweat-saturated T-shirt and hair. Staring at the top of the hill, she fought against their hold. The wraiths howled and snarled, buzzing round her head like angry bees. But Dylan kept going. She reached the top, and going down, she knew, would be much easier.

In fact, it was too easy. Too fast—far too fast. Her feet couldn't keep up as gravity pulled her down the sheer slope. Unlike the wraiths, the slope was a battle she couldn't win—and didn't want to. Instead, she let herself free fall, careering forward, concentrating on nothing more than staying upright. If she fell over here, she was done for. Toppling, flailing, she wouldn't be able to think about where her eyes were focusing.

Suddenly, the safe house appeared. It was there, just in front of her. The incline leveled out, made it easier to control her speed. She was so close; she was going to make it. The wraiths knew it, too. They doubled their efforts, soaring so close to her face, she felt the wisps of their wings sting at her cheeks, wrapping around her legs to try to trip her again. Too little, too late. Dylan had the safe house to gaze upon, and nothing the wraiths could do would tear her eyes away.

Dylan flung herself round the corner of the building and burst through the door. She knew she didn't need to, but she slammed it behind her. Calm descended at once. She stood in the middle of the single room, hauling oxygen into her screaming lungs, shaking all over.

"I made it," she whispered. "I made it."

For a while she burned, heated from within by the panic and adrenaline that was acid in her veins, but in the dim light of the cottage, the air cooled quickly. Soon she was shaking with the chill.

Dylan rubbed her bare arms. It was more than just the cold that was making her tremble. Shadows swirled on the floor of the cottage as the wraiths circled at the window. She tried to ignore them, but it wasn't easy. The sound of their wailing cut right to the center of her brain, and with nothing else but silence in the tiny stone house, there was little to distract her ears.

She dropped down onto one of the chairs and hugged her knees to her chest for warmth. It wasn't enough, though, and soon her teeth were chattering. Dylan heaved herself up and moved stiffly over to the hearth. There were no matches to get a fire going like there had been in the last safe house, but she remembered how the oars had appeared in the boat. Using wood from a little basket to the side, she built a lopsided triangle and stared hard at the center of it.

"Please?" she asked in a small voice. "Please, I need this."

Nothing happened. Dylan shut her eyes and thought her pathetic plea once more, holding her breath and crossing her fingers. There was a snap, swiftly followed by a spitting sound. When she opened her eyes again, there were flames.

"Thank you," she whispered automatically. It was uncomfortable kneeling on the cold stone floor, but she didn't move. The fire was small and gave out little heat. She had to hold her fingers just above the tiny leaping flames to feel their delicious warmth. The light, too, held her there as the shadows thickened outside. She wished there were candles to light.

Slowly, the fire grew, dissolving the shivers that were still racking Dylan's body. She wrinkled her nose as she caught the putrid stench of the lake water rising from her warmed clothes. She felt filthy, and she could only imagine how she looked. Glancing around, she saw the big Belfast sink, the dresser. This was the safe house where she'd managed to wash her clothes before. She'd used all the soap, she knew, but even if she could just rinse them out she'd feel better. Cleaner. And this time there would be no Tristan to see her clothed in the hodge-podge, too-big outfit he'd found stuffed into one of the drawers.

She smiled to herself, remembering how embarrassed she'd been, wandering around half-clothed, her underwear slung over one of the chairs in full view.

Without Tristan's stories, it seemed to take a lot longer to fill the sink, and without the sliver of soap she wasn't sure how much difference she could make to the foul black stains coating her clothes. Still, she pounded the dirt from them as best she could and hung them on the chair backs. She put on the massive clothes from the dresser, then, ignoring the bed where she'd snuggled into Tristan's warmth, she sat on a scrap of faded carpet beside the fire. There was no point lying down anyway. Here, alone, with the endless howling of the wraiths outside, she was never going to sleep.

The night dragged. Dylan tried not to think, but let the flames lull her into a stupor, the way Tristan told her he did when the souls slept. It wasn't easy—every noise made her jump, her head craning round to peer through the windows into the inky dark— but eventually a bloodred dawn roused her. She groaned as she rolled off the rug and stood up. She'd stiffened up overnight, and her muscles were groaning in pain. Awkwardly, trying to move as little as possible, she shimmied out of her borrowed outfit and eased back into her torn, half-rigid clothes. They still looked horribly grubby, but they smelled a little better. She fussed for a while over the lie of her jeans, trying to reinstate her cuffs to stop the sulfurous mud from soaking into them quite so quickly. Then she dealt with her hair, trying to fasten it up into a neat bun.

What she was really doing, she knew, was procrastinating. It was beyond time to step back outside, and she was wasting valuable daylight. But today was going to be hard. She'd crossed the lake, yes, but now she had to try to find the next safe house in an almost featureless and totally alien wasteland with its red earth and blackened shrubs. And she had to journey without looking at any of the other souls, their guiding orbs, or the wraiths that clustered round them. Oh—and somehow do all this whilst looking for her own orb that may or may not look like Tristan.

Impossible. Totally impossible.

She gripped the chair in front of her, seized suddenly by an overwhelming sense of panic, and squeezed her eyes shut against tears. It was no use crying; she'd put herself in this position. Go forward or go back. That was the choice. The boat was still there, now nicely beached against the shore. She could row across the lake, take refuge in the final safe house, and be back across the line tomorrow.

And be totally, utterly, *eternally* alone.

Dylan took one deep breath, held it, and forced herself to exhale slowly. Swallowing hard, she pushed the fear and the uncertainty away. She imagined Tristan's face when he saw her, saw that she'd come back for him. She imagined the feel of his arms around her as he hugged her close to his chest. The smell of him. Holding that image firmly in her mind, she marched across the narrow room and threw open the door.

As soon as she stepped outside the protective confines of the cottage, the waiting wraiths began their cruel dance, circling and diving and trying to make her look at them. She ignored them, keeping her gaze fixed on the horizon, seeing but not looking. Like staring through the windshield of a car whilst a million raindrops were splattering on the glass. It was hard, not allowing her eyes to focus, and it hurt her head, but it was easier than staring straight down all the time. Her glazed eyes swept across the peaks and valleys, trying to pick out something she recognized—a path, a landmark, anything.

Nothing. She was almost positive she had never been in this place before. Terror gripped her once again, and she was very nearly undone, unsettled by a demon whistling close to her ear, hissing menacingly at her. Though she flinched, she managed to fight the urge to turn toward it. *Think,* she told herself. *There must be something.*

But there wasn't. Nothing but the unfriendly jagged rocks and the bleeding ground. That, and the first wisps of souls floating toward her, way out in the distance.

"Where are you coming from?" she wondered aloud.

A safe house. They must have each spent the night at a safe house, of course. And they all seemed to be drifting from the same direction. The only sensible thing to do, she reasoned, was to head for them and hope their trail would lead her at least close to where she needed to be.

Dylan strode forward purposefully. She tried not to think about the fact that she was leaving the only safe house whose location she was certain of. That only let the fear creep back in, and then it was harder to fight the wraiths.

Tristan. She might find Tristan today. That thought she repeated over and over again, a silent mantra. It gave her strength. Strength to plow her way forward when the ground tilted up in front of her, and strength to battle on when the sun reached its zenith, raining fire on her. Strength to ignore the darting shadows in the corner of her eyes.

Soon she began to pass the first of the souls walking wearily in the other direction. They were hard to ignore: many were wailing and weeping, and every flickering being that she glimpsed, whose face was unlined or whose shadow rippled too short across the ground, was a soul lost too soon. A child, not ready to die. They made her think of the little cancer patient that Tristan had ferried, although she had to remind herself that that tragic soul might now be one of the greedy wraiths.

She made herself glance at each one, however. She had to. Because any one of them might be being guided by her orb, her ferryman. None of the pulsing balls of light called to her, though, and as soul after soul after soul passed by, her hopes began to sink. She truly was looking for a needle in a haystack. If she made it all the way back to the train and she still hadn't found him, she didn't know what she was going to do.

It was a shock to Dylan when she came upon the safe house. She hadn't expected to be close yet, or if she was even going in the right direction. The souls were much less frequent now, but the sun was still searing its wrath into her brow. The small stone cottage was almost hidden by the great shadows of two mountainous peaks that towered over it. If Dylan had been paying attention, she would have seen the deep basin beyond and realized where she was. As Tristan had said, the valley was always there.

Dylan cried out with relief when she saw the safe house's crumbling walls, its cracked and rotten windows. She accelerated to a jerky run, despite her aching limbs, to close the final few yards.

Spent, Dylan all but fell into the door and stumbled over to the bed. Resting her elbows on her knees, she propped her chin in her hands and stared around.

As glad as she was to have made it, she didn't like being back here. This was the safe house where she'd spent a day and two nights alone, waiting desperately for Tristan. Just seeing the wrought-iron fireplace, the single chair that she'd sat on for a whole day, watching the true wasteland go by—the first time she'd ever really seen it—brought a flood of memories and emotions rushing back. Panic. Fear. Isolation.

No. She shook herself free of the despair that threatened to strangle her. It was different this time. She was different. She forced herself to her feet, grabbed the chair, and pulled it over toward the door. Swinging it open, she plonked herself down just inside the threshold and stared outside, at the wraiths, at the bloodred valley.

In the morning, she was going to go into the valley and search for Tristan. This time, she swore to herself, she would not be held captive by her fear. This time *she* was going to find *him*.

TWENTY-SEVEN

"WE'RE GOING TO HAVE TO MOVE A LITTLE FASTER."

Tristan made a face as he looked back toward the woman, then up at the darkening sky. They had taken a long time to cross the mud flats. Too long. There wasn't much light left, and they still had the full length of the valley to cross. It wasn't her fault; she'd found it hard, wading through the thick mud, weaving a path around the high grasses. She'd needed help, but Tristan hadn't wanted to touch her.

He wished he had now, though. The air around them was full of howling. They were out of sight still, but they were there. The light was different, too. A thick layer of clouds hovered over them, which meant the daylight would end sooner. He supposed that was only to be expected. It was too much to hope that the woman would retain her calm, contented frame of mind. Not when she knew she was dead.

She hadn't said much about it. There had been tears, but quiet ones. As if she hadn't wanted to bother him. Another thing to be grateful for. This soul really had made things as easy as possible for him. He felt bad that he had been so cold, so aloof toward her. But it had been the only way he could keep going. They wouldn't have made it this far otherwise.

"Please, Marie." Tristan hated using her name. "We need to move."

"I'm sorry," she apologized meekly. "I'm sorry, Tristan."

Tristan winced. Stupidly, he'd given Marie the same name. He had been too suffocated by grief to come up with a new one, and it suited the form he seemed stuck in. He hated it, though. Every time she said it, he heard Dylan's voice.

She started to walk forward with more purpose this time, but one glance at the long shadows pooling ominously in front of them told Tristan it wasn't enough.

He sighed, gritted his teeth. "Come on." He held her elbow as he pushed past, forcing her to go faster until she broke into a choppy jog. He jogged, too, and because it was easier, he dropped her elbow to reach down and grab her hand, pulling her along. The howling intensified and the air stirred as the wraiths started to descend, freed by the encroaching dark, the thickening shadows. The woman heard the change, and her fingers squeezed Tristan's more tightly. He could feel her fear, her total reliance on him. It was painful. He had to fight the urge to drop her hand and run, although not from the wraiths—from her.

"It's not far, Marie," he encouraged. "The safe house is just between these hills. We're going to make it."

She didn't answer, but he heard her footsteps speed up and the strain on his arm slackened as she moved from a jog into a full-out run. Relieved, he pushed himself faster.

"Tristan!" The word was almost snatched away on the wind

before it reached his ears, but he caught the echo of it and snapped his head up. "Tristan!"

Was his mind playing tricks on him? Or was this some new torture the demons had devised, to distract him, to make him lose focus? Because there was no other way that voice could exist in the wasteland. It was gone. *She* was gone.

"Tristan!"

"It's not her, it's not her," he hissed, tightening his grip on the woman. Dylan was gone, and he had a job to do. He had to get the woman to the safe house. Almost there. Almost there. He lifted his head and fixed his eyes on the cottage. The door was open.

"Tristan!"

There was a figure standing in the entryway, waving at him. Just a silhouette, nothing more than that, but he knew who it was. It couldn't be; it couldn't possibly be. But it was.

Astonished, Tristan let go of the woman's hand.

DYLAN CLAPPED HER HAND OVER HER MOUTH, REALIZING, A second too late, what she'd done.

She'd seen him from across the valley. An orb, much brighter than all the rest. It had caught her eye, drawn her attention like a moth to a flame. As she'd focused on it, strange things had happened. The riotous red of the barren landscape, the deep burgundies and purples of dusk, had flickered, the color zapping in and out like a badly tuned television. Blood red turned to the muted greens and browns and mauves of her Scottish wasteland.

Dylan had rocketed out of the chair, thrown herself forward to the door, toes nibbling at the threshold. The wraiths had screamed in anticipation, but she'd stopped just short, staring out.

Tristan. She could see him. *Him.* Not as a pulsing ball of light, but a person, a body, a face. Dylan smiled, gulping in air as if she hadn't breathed since . . . since he'd left her. He was running, pulling at something as the picture cleared. The landscape stopped flickering and solidified into the heather-clad wilderness she'd known before. The other souls disappeared, the wraiths dimming to shadows. Only their hissing and crowing stopped her from running out to meet him.

As she watched, she realized he was towing another soul. She couldn't see who it was. They were distorted, not quite as transparent as the other souls, but still not quite real. Half in, half out. A woman. She was running, too. Dylan felt a stab of jealousy when she saw they were holding hands.

That's when she'd shouted out, shouted his name. She'd had to do it one, two, three times to be sure he'd heard her, but at last he'd looked up toward the safe house. She'd waved, delighted and frantic—and he'd seen her. She'd seen it in his face. Shock. Horror. Joy. All at the same time.

And he'd dropped the woman's hand.

It was instantaneous. The twisting, writhing shadows that hovered above them, like their own personal thundercloud, descended on the woman in a thrashing swarm. She panicked, clawing at empty air. Dylan watched, her hand still wrapped over her mouth, as they took hold. It was more horrific, more solid, more real than watching the soul being taken into the depths of the lake.

And it was all her fault.

They grabbed the woman's hair, her arms, attacked her torso, all in the blink of an eye. Tristan turned almost at once, saw what was happening, and Dylan watched as he tried to save her. He reached up, seemed to be trying to pull at the air, but nothing happened; the demons continued their assault on the woman. He waded in, hauling wraith after wraith off her, but they simply circled back and came again from another angle.

Dylan stood in the doorway, her hand reaching out in sympathy, and gazed as the soul was dragged down beneath the surface.

Guilt tumbled over her, crushing her with its weight. She'd killed the woman. Whoever she was, Dylan had killed her. Did she have a partner? Children? Had she counted on seeing them again? A flash of Eliza, waiting endlessly for someone who was never going to come, screamed in her brain. All because she had shouted out. She clapped her hand over her mouth to stop herself from calling for him again. It was too late. The woman was dead.

What had she done?

Tristan didn't turn to look at her, but stared down at the spot in the long grass where the soul had disappeared. He didn't seem to notice the remaining wraiths, who were circling him like sharks, teeth bared, ready to rip into their prey.

He still didn't react when one swooped down, tearing at his shoulder. Or the next, which smashed into his face. Dylan gaped. Was that blood, running down his cheek? Why wasn't he moving? Why wasn't he doing anything to defend himself?

Why wasn't he running for the safe house? For her?

Another wraith went for him, and another. Then more. They seemed delighted at his apathetic stance. Without realizing it, Dylan threw herself from the doorway and was pounding down the path before her brain caught up with her actions. It was very dark now. The fire burning in the cottage behind her glowed much more brightly than the dying light of day. If he didn't move, if she didn't reach him . . .

"Tristan!" she gasped, flying toward him. "Tristan, what are you doing?"

Wraiths were whipping round her face, but it had never been easier to ignore their darting movements.

"Tristan!"

At last he seemed to come awake. He turned, still besieged by the smoking black shadows, and his face, blank at first, seemed to come alive, like waking from a trance. He reached for her just as she barreled into him.

"Dylan," he whispered. Then he took control. "Move!"

Whatever had frozen him before was gone now. Wrapping one hand around her lower arm and squeezing so tightly it hurt, he bolted back the way she had come. A step at a time, Tristan pushed and fought against their grabbing talons and biting teeth. Head down, jaw clenched, hand firmly wrapped around Dylan's wrist, he drove them toward the safe house.

"What the hell are you doing here?" He rounded on her the instant they were inside. The clamor from the wraiths faded into the background, and the cottage was quiet and tranquil but for the anger that seemed to emanate from Tristan's every pore.

"What?" Dylan looked at him, confused. Wasn't he pleased to see her?

The icy fire in his eyes said no. They glowed as they stared at her. Not a trick of the light; it was frightening.

"What are you doing here, Dylan?"

"I . . ." Dylan opened and closed her mouth, but no sound

came out. This wasn't how she had imagined their reunion going.

"You shouldn't be here," Tristan continued. He started to pace in an agitated manner, running a hand through his hair and then gripping a handful. "I took you across, right to the line. You weren't supposed to come back."

A strange feeling crept over Dylan. Her cheeks grew hot, and her stomach squirmed. Her heart was thumping at erratic intervals in her chest, hurting her. She dropped her eyes before Tristan could see the fat droplets that were trickling toward her chin.

"I'm sorry," she whispered to the flagstoned floor. "I made a mistake."

She could see that now. The words he had said had been nothing more than lies to get her safely across. He hadn't meant any of it. She thought of the soul he'd just been ferrying, the woman she'd accidentally killed with nothing more than her own carelessness; thought about the way they'd been holding hands as they'd run from danger. Had that woman swallowed Tristan's lies as easily as Dylan had? Her gaze burning into the ground, she suddenly felt childish, selfish.

"Dylan." Tristan said her name again, but much more gently. The change in his tone gave her just enough courage to look up. He'd stopped pacing, was scrutinizing her with much softer eyes. Embarrassed, she scrubbed at her cheeks, sniffed back the tears that still lingered. She tried to look away as he approached, but he walked right up to her until he was close enough to rest his forehead against hers. "What are you doing here?"

The same words, but this time a murmured question, not an accusation. This one was easier to answer, if she closed her eyes, if she didn't have to look at him.

"I came back."

He sighed. "You weren't supposed to do that." Pause. "Why did you come back, Dylan?"

Dylan swallowed, confused. Now that his anger was gone, now that he was touching her, she was back to being muddled. There was only one way to discover the truth. She took a deep breath.

"For you." She waited for a reaction, but there wasn't one. At least not that she could hear. She kept her eyes shut. "Did you mean it? Any of it?"

Another sigh. But that could be frustration, embarrassment, regret. Dylan trembled, waiting. Something warm pressed to her cheek. A hand?

"I didn't lie to you, Dylan. Not about that."

Her breathing spiked as she processed his words. He'd meant it. He did feel what she felt. Dylan curled her lips up into a timid smile, but she held a tight rein on the warmth building in her chest. She wasn't sure she could trust it, not quite yet.

"Open your eyes."

Suddenly shy, Dylan hesitated for a moment, then with a deep breath, she looked up until she met his gaze. He was close enough for their breath to mingle. Still holding her cheek, he drew her face forward until their lips pressed together, blue eyes still boring into hers. He held her there for a moment, then pulled away and curled her into his chest.

"I didn't lie to you, Dylan," he whispered into her ear, "but you shouldn't be here."

Dylan stiffened, tried to pull away, but he held on tightly, refusing to let her move.

"Nothing's changed. I still can't go on with you, and you can't stay here. You saw what happened to that woman. Sooner or later, that would happen to you. It's too dangerous."

Dylan's breath caught in her lungs as she processed his words. She felt another avalanche of guilt smash down on her.

"I killed that woman," she mouthed into his shoulder. There was no volume in the words, but Tristan somehow heard her.

"No." He shook his head, the motion rubbing his lips against her neck. The skin there tingled. "I killed her. I let go of her hand."

"Because of me—"

"No, Dylan." Tristan cut her off, firmer now. "She was my responsibility; I lost her." He took a deep breath, and his arms tightened around her. "That's what this place is. It's a hellhole. You can't stay here."

"I want to stay with you," Dylan implored.

Tristan shook his head at her gently. "Not here."

"Then come back with me," she begged.

"I told you, I can't. I can't ever go beyond, I . . ." Tristan made a frustrated noise, his teeth snapping together.

"What about the other side, then?" Dylan pulled back again, fighting against his grip when he tried to hold on to her. "My world. Come back across the wasteland with me, back to the train. We could . . ."

Tristan stared at her, his eyebrows drawn together in aggrava-tion. He shook his head slowly, placing a finger on her lips.

"I can't do that, either."

"Have you ever tried?"

"No, but—"

"Then you don't know. The soul I spoke to said—"

"Who did you speak to?" Tristan's eyes narrowed.

"An old woman, Eliza. She's the one who told me how to get back here. She said we might be able to, if we—"

"*Might*," Tristan echoed dubiously. "Dylan, there's no going back."

"Do you *know* that?"

Tristan hesitated. He didn't know, she realized. He believed. That wasn't the same thing.

"Isn't it worth a try?" Dylan chewed on her lip anxiously. If he really, truly had meant what he'd said before, if he honestly loved her, wouldn't he want to try?

Tristan turned his head from side to side, his expression forlorn, somber. "It's too big a gamble," he told her. "You believe this woman because she's told you what you want to hear, Dylan. The only thing I know is that you're not safe here. If you stay in the wasteland, your soul won't survive. Tomorrow I'm taking you back."

Dylan shuddered at more than just the thought of crossing the dark water of the lake again. She took a step back, folded her arms across her chest. Her face set in a stubborn mask.

"I am not going back there. Not alone. I'm going back to the train. Come with me. Please?" She made the last word a plea. It was. Going back to the train was completely pointless without him. This whole thing, everything she had risked, it had all been about being with Tristan. She hadn't known she could find him, not for sure, but she'd still done it. Wasn't he willing to take a chance, too? A chance for her?

She watched Tristan lick his lips, swallow; saw the hesitation in his face. He was wavering. What could she say to tip him over the edge, to make him give in?

"Please, Tristan. Can we just try? If it doesn't work . . ." If it didn't work, the wraiths could have her. She wasn't going back across the line alone. Better not to mention that, though. "If it doesn't work, you can bring me back. But can we just try?"

He screwed up his face, torn. "I don't know if I can," he said. "I don't choose . . . I mean, I don't have free choice, Dylan. My feet, they're not mine. Sometimes they make me go where I have to. Like . . ." He hung his head. "Like when they made me walk away from you."

Dylan considered him. "You're still my ferryman. If I ran from you, if you couldn't make me come with you and I ran, would you have to follow?"

"Yes," he said, drawing out the word, not seeing where she was going.

Dylan smiled at him. "Then I'll lead."

Dylan knew she had not entirely convinced Tristan, but he didn't try to talk her out of it. Instead they sat close together on the single bed, and he listened to her describe everything that had happened to her since he'd left her at the line. He was fascinated by every detail, never having seen any of the things she'd experienced—never having known what happened to the souls he ferried successfully across. He smiled when she told him about Jonas, although his eyes darkened when she confessed that he was the one who had helped her back to the wasteland. Caeli interested him greatly, too, and his eyes widened in surprise when Dylan explained about the books in the records room.

"You saw a book of my souls?" he asked.

Dylan nodded. "That's how I found Jonas."

Tristan considered that for a moment. "Were there many empty pages left?"

Dylan stared at him, baffled by the question. "I'm not sure," she hedged. "It was about two-thirds full maybe."

Tristan nodded, then caught her confused expression. "I just wondered whether . . . if I filled my book, whether I'd be done."

Dylan didn't know what to say to that, to his words or the painfully sad look that came into his eyes when he said them.

"It's strange," he said, after a long moment of silence. "I can't even decide if I'd like to see it. If I had the chance, I mean. How would I feel, looking at all those names?"

"Proud," Dylan said. "You should feel proud. All those souls, all those people, they're alive because of you. You know what I mean," she said, elbowing Tristan gently in the ribs when he shot her an amused look at her choice of words. If they were still thinking and feeling, then they were alive, surely?

"I guess I ferried more souls than I lost, when you weigh it up."

Dylan's breath caught in her throat, thinking of the crossed-out records.

"I saw names with a line through them," she said quietly.

He nodded. "I suppose they are the lost souls. Souls taken by the wraiths. I'm glad they're recorded somewhere, and it is only fair that their names are kept close to the one responsible for losing them."

A small sob worked its way from Dylan's lips, but she strangled it quickly. Tristan turned his head to look at her, his eyes concerned, curious, and she had to confess her thoughts.

"There should be a book for me, then," she whispered.

"Why?" Tristan looked puzzled, not understanding what had painted the anguish across her face.

"Today," she croaked. "That was my fault. That woman's soul should go against my name."

"No." Tristan shifted round on the bed, took her face in both his hands. "No, I told you. That was *my* fault."

Fat, hot tears slipped down Dylan's cheeks and coated his fingers as she shook her head in denial. *"My fault,"* she mouthed.

He wiped her face clean with his thumbs, gently pulling her around until their faces rested together, forehead to forehead. Guilt still churned in Dylan's stomach, but suddenly it didn't seem so overwhelming. Not when she couldn't breathe, not when her skin was tingling everywhere that he was touching her, her blood boiling and racing around her body.

"Shh," Tristan crooned, mistaking her ragged breathing for crying. He half smiled at her, and then closed the final millimeters between them. Gently, slowly, he prized her mouth open, his lips brushing softly against hers. Against her will, he pulled away for an instant, gazing at her with cobalt fire, before pushing her back against the wall as he sought deeper, hungrier kisses.

~~~~~

When the dawn broke, the sky was clear and blue. Dylan stood on the threshold of the cottage and looked up at it. This wasteland must have been a thousand times better than the desert furnace she'd endured before. Tristan, too, gave a wry smile when he emerged and saw the weather.

"Sun," he commented, staring up at the glittering sky.

Dylan smiled at him. Her eyes were a green much more vibrant, much more beautiful than the hues of the wasteland.

Tristan couldn't help but smile back at her, despite the lead in the pit of his stomach.

This wasn't going to work. But Dylan simply refused to believe that. He was afraid of her crushing disappointment, the disappointment he knew in his very bones was coming, so for now he tried to put it out of his mind. She was here, for the moment she was safe, and he should try to enjoy the extra time he got to spend with her. This was more than he'd ever dared to imagine.

He just hoped it wouldn't end with a quill delicately obliterating her name from a page in his book.

"Let's go," Dylan said, striding down the path away from him. The valley looked wide and inviting, bathed in early morning light, but Tristan lingered in the doorway, watching her go.

She walked maybe a hundred yards before she seemed to realize there was no crunch of gravel echoing her own footsteps. He saw her stop, head half-cocked, listening for him. After a second she whirled around. Alarm widened her eyes before she caught sight of him, right where she'd left him.

"Come on," she called, smiling encouragingly.

He pressed his lips together in a thin line. "I don't know if I can," he shouted back. "It goes against everything, every rule."

"Try," Dylan coaxed.

Tristan sighed, aggravated. He had promised her he would try. Closing his eyes for a moment, he concentrated on his feet. *Move,* he thought. He expected nothing to happen—expected to remain glued to the ground, an unyielding pressure holding him in place.

Instead he stepped easily onto the path.

Instantly Tristan halted. He hardly dared breathe, waiting for a bolt of lightning, a slash of pain. Something to punish him for disobeying his unspoken orders. Nothing happened. Incredulous and suspicious, he continued down toward Dylan.

"This feels weird," he confessed in a low voice once he reached her side. "I keep waiting for something to stop me."

"But nothing yet?"

"Nothing yet."

"Good." Dylan wound her fingers around his. She started walking, and after a gentle tug, Tristan followed.

~~~~~

The valley gave them no difficulties. In fact, it was almost pleasant. They could have been any young couple, striding hand in hand through the countryside. There was no sight or sound of the wraiths. It unsettled Dylan to know they were there, hovering at her shoulder, hoping she'd lose focus, look away from her orb. She wanted to ask Tristan what he saw right now—whether it was the lush grass and heather-covered hills that she could see, or the wasteland as it truly was. But something held her tongue. She was nervous that, if she talked about it, if she drew attention to it, the mirage would disintegrate and they'd be back under the burning red sun. That landscape, she knew, would be much harder to traverse. No—ignorance was bliss.

Beyond the valley lay the wide expanse of marsh. The clement weather had done nothing to soak up the stagnant pools of water or dry out the squelching mud. Dylan eyed it distastefully, remembering the way it had grasped at her ankles. After the tranquility of the valley, it was a stark reminder that she was in the wasteland, that danger still hung around her neck.

Beside her Tristan sighed dramatically. She looked at him,

confused at the sound, and saw his eyes were amused. He flashed her an indulgent smirk.

"Piggyback?" he suggested.

"You're wonderful," she told him.

He rolled his eyes, but turned so that she could scramble up onto his back.

"Thanks," she murmured into his ear when he had her in position.

"Uh-huh," he replied sourly, but she could see his cheeks lift in a smile.

She felt heavy on his back, her arms soon tiring of holding herself in position, but Tristan didn't complain, picking his way through the worst of the mud. Even with her extra weight, he didn't seem to sink into the sludgy mire. Soon the marsh was no more than a distant memory, and Dylan's gaze was filled with the sheer slant of a giant hill, waiting patiently for her. She wrinkled her nose and huffed, disgruntled; she doubted she was going to be able to convince Tristan to carry her up that.

"What are you thinking?" he asked.

Dylan didn't want to admit to her schemes. Instead she asked something that had been quietly preying on her mind.

"I was wondering . . . where did you go? After you left me."

She'd told every piece of her story last night, but she'd purposely avoided asking this. She hadn't wanted to bring up what he'd done, how he'd tricked her. Betrayed her.

Tristan heard the real question.

"I'm sorry," he said. "I'm sorry I had to do that."

Dylan sniffed quietly, determined not to get upset. She didn't want him to feel guilty, didn't want him to know how much his betrayal had hurt. At least he hadn't been there to see her break down.

"It's OK," she whispered, squeezing his shoulders.

"It's not," he disagreed. "I lied to you, and I'm sorry. But I thought . . . I thought that was the right thing for you." The final few words were stilted, and despite herself, Dylan felt her throat tightening. "When I saw you crying, when I heard you screaming for me . . ." His voice faltered. "It hurt more than anything the wraiths could ever have done to me."

Dylan's voice was very small. "You could see me?"

He nodded. "Just for a minute or so." He gave a short, sour laugh. "Usually that's my favorite part. A whole minute where I am responsible for no one but me. And I get to see a quick glimpse of beyond. Just a flash. Wherever it is that the soul called home."

Dylan stiffened on his back. She remembered Jonas saying he'd instantly been transported back home, back to Stuttgart.

"That didn't happen for me," she said slowly. "I didn't leave the wasteland."

"I know," he said, sighing.

"Why not?" she wondered. "Why didn't I go anywhere?"

She counted three of Tristan's long, confident strides before he answered her.

"I don't know," he mumbled, but his words lacked the ring of truth.

Tristan set her down as soon as the ground began to firm up beneath his feet. At first Dylan pouted, missing the warmth of being nestled up close to him—and the luxury of being carried—but he took her hand again and smiled down at her. She returned the gesture, but the smile fell from her face as she eyed the steep incline before them.

"You know, I really hate going uphill," she said flatly.

Tristan squeezed her fingers comfortingly, but the look he gave her was wistful. "We could always go back." He indicated across the bog.

"We'd never make it," Dylan replied. The sun, shining brightly in the cloudless sky, had already rolled over the height of its arc.

"No," Tristan agreed softly. "We wouldn't."

"And there is nothing for me that way," she finished. "I'm not going back if I can't go with you."

Tristan made a face, but he didn't attempt to argue. "Come on, then," he said, starting forward and tugging at her hand.

Trudge, trudge, trudge. Up, up, up. Dylan's calves were soon burning, her breathing ragged. The higher they climbed, the more the wind crept up, and as the afternoon waned, thick tufts of gray began to form above their heads. Despite the chill of the changing weather, Dylan was sweating and she had to yank her hand from Tristan's grasp, embarrassed at her moist palms. Even though the morning had been warm and bright, she felt the familiar creeping discomfort as cold dew seeped up the legs of her jeans.

"Can we slow down?" she panted. "Maybe rest for a bit?"

"No." Tristan's reply was curt, but when Dylan looked round at him, surprised, she saw he was eyeing the sky, not her. His face was screwed up with unease. "It'll be evening soon. I don't want you stuck out here."

"Just for a minute," Dylan begged. "We can't even hear them yet."

But even as the words left her mouth, the rustling noise of the wind changed. A second melody was added, this one shriller, keener. Wailing and shrieking. The wraiths.

Tristan heard it, too. "Come on, Dylan," he ordered, and, ignoring her when she tried to pull away, he took a firm grasp on her hand and continued to stride up the hill.

TWENTY-EIGHT

TRISTAN KNEW DYLAN WAS TIRED. HE COULD HEAR IT IN HER heavy tread, her labored breathing; he could feel it in her lagging arm, tugging back on him with every stride. He knew it, and he felt bad, but if they were caught on this hill when the shadows descended, the wraiths would offer no quarter. Dylan almost seemed to have lost her fear of them—or perhaps it was just that she thought he could protect her from their hunger—but she was a fool to flirt with danger. She couldn't sense it, he realized, but the wraiths were furious. Not only had they failed to take her on her way across the wasteland, but she'd come back. And she'd beaten them. Alone. Without a ferryman to stand between her and their grappling claws.

They were determined to make her pay for her arrogance.

Tristan thought of the assurances he'd once given her—that he would never lose her, that he would never let the wraiths get her. He'd been absolutely confident; now he wasn't so sure. Thanks to Dylan, the game had changed, he'd changed, and he didn't know the rules of this new engagement. He was beginning to have an inkling, though, and that did nothing to allay his doubts.

Cresting the top of the hill, he paused for the briefest moment, letting Dylan catch her breath. This wasn't the highest peak they'd scale if Dylan got her way and they ventured all the way back to the train, but it was tall enough for Tristan to take in the sweeping landscape, undulating for miles and miles in every direction.

Rolling toward him, down sloping gradients and up winding vales, were the pulsing hearts of other ferrymen, urging their souls on to safety, just as he was. It was odd; he didn't usually notice them. But now he felt like a pebble in the ocean, pushing against the tide. His every instinct told him to turn, to join their pilgrimage back toward the line, but he fought against it.

With night approaching, that way was death for Dylan.

"Come on." He started forward again. "Almost there, Dylan. The safe house is at the bottom of this hill."

"I know," she said quietly, her breathing back under control.

Of course she did; she'd been here before. Tristan smiled grimly to himself, then pushed on, his feet finding a safe route down the graveled hillside.

~~~~~

Despite Tristan's misgivings, they made good time slithering down the final peak. He was able to close the door on the frustrated howls of the wraiths before the day grew late enough for them to appear to Dylan. He sighed with relief, leaning his head against the warped wooden entryway for a moment, before moving to light a fire. Dylan stood by the window, staring out. She didn't move, not even when he came up behind her and wrapped his arms around her waist.

"What are you looking at?" he murmured into her ear.

"Nothing," she said softly, frowning. "But that's not right, is it? They must be there. Can you see them?"

"The wraiths?"

"No." Dylan shook her head. "The other souls, the other ferrymen."

Tristan was quiet for a long moment before he finally spoke. "I can see them."

Dylan gave a somber nod, digesting this. Tristan's head resting on her shoulder, he could just see the downturn of her mouth in the corner of his eye.

"It's late," she said.

"It is," he agreed. He squeezed her to him. "But we're safe in here."

His words didn't take the worried look from Dylan's face.

"They can't come in, Dylan. The wraiths. You know that. We're absolutely safe, I promise you."

"I know."

"Then what's wrong?"

"How many souls are still out there?" She turned to face him, her eyes flickering, reflecting the light from the fire.

Tristan stared at her for a moment, then looked to the window, eyes scanning the countryside beyond.

"Not many," he said. "Most of them are already in their safe house."

Her gaze went back to the window. One hand reached up and slowly pressed against the pane. Hissing erupted from outside, and Tristan was tempted to pull her arm away. He didn't want the wraiths to think she was taunting them.

"Can you help me to see them, too?" she asked suddenly. "The way I saw them before, when I was on my own?"

"Why do you want to?"

She shrugged. "I'd just like to see."

It seemed a harmless enough request, but Tristan was alarmed by the strange look that still creased her brow and set her lips. He sighed, then pulled her closer, resting his temple against hers. Concentrating on the window, he forced his mind to strip back the grassy veneer, revealing the hell below. Dylan gasped quietly, and he knew it had worked.

"I can see them!" she squeaked. "It's just like before!" There was a pause. "What are they doing?"

Tristan's voice was grim. "Running."

They had only been in the safe house a few minutes, not even long enough for the fire to properly catch, but in that time the afternoon had melted into evening and light had dissolved into darkness. There were only three souls still visible, and they were bobbing and weaving furiously as their ferrymen tried to exhort them along the final stretch. Tristan's mouth tightened into a grimace; they weren't all going to make it.

Abruptly he pulled away from Dylan, pulling the red wasteland with him.

"Hey, no!" She whirled to face him. "Bring it back!"

"No."

"Tristan, bring it back!"

"You don't want to see, Dylan. I promise you."

She paled. He watched her swallow as she processed his words. "Who's out there?" she croaked.

He pressed his lips together, reluctant.

She took a step forward, toward him, and repeated her question. "Who's out there, Tristan?"

He sighed, his eyes going back outside—where he could still clearly see the three stragglers—rather than witness her reaction.

"An old man, a woman, and . . ." His voice trailed off.

"And?"

"A toddler. A little girl."

Dylan threw her hand over her mouth and darted back to the window, pressing her face against the glass.

"Where is she?" she demanded. "Is she still out there? I want to see it, Tristan! Bring it back!"

He shook his head, and she caught his expression in the reflection of the window.

"Tristan!"

"No, Dylan." He folded his arms across his chest, resolute. It was bad enough that he could see it. He wouldn't make Dylan witness the horror. The woman had disappeared, safely where she should be. The old man, though, had already sunk beneath; just two or three lingering wraiths marked the spot where they'd claimed him.

Only the toddler remained, somehow still there, but surely not for much longer.

"What's happening?" She slammed her hand against the window, making Tristan jump. The glass rippled against the force of the blow but held firm. "Let me see, Tristan!"

What was happening? The girl was so surrounded by wraiths, Tristan could barely see her—just her outline, tucked up tight in her ferryman's arms. And though she was far away, he could see her frightened expression, mouth wide and screaming, eyes screwed up with tears. Her terrified face burned itself into his brain, another memory he knew he'd never lose.

"Tristan!" Dylan's shrill yelp dragged his attention back to her. "What's going on?"

"They're surrounded," he murmured softly.

She chewed down on her lip, her face a mask of despair, and pressed harder against the glass as if she could reach out to them. Suddenly she spun round, stared at him. Tristan held up both hands, took two paces back. He knew what she was going to say.

"You have to help them!"

He shook his head at her. "I can't."

"Why not?"

"I just can't. Each ferryman is responsible for the soul they are ferrying. No others."

Dylan glowered at him incredulously. "But that's ridiculous!"

"It's how it is," he said heatedly.

She turned her back on him, and he felt a stab of hurt at her judgment. It wasn't his fault; he didn't make the rules.

"Have they got far to go?" she asked quietly.

Tristan looked out of the window again. They were still there.

"No," he told her. "But they won't make it. There are too many wraiths."

TOO MANY. DYLAN SHUT HER EYES, THE COLD GLASS NUMB-ing her forehead. She remembered the feel of the wraiths: pulling, scratching, biting. Punching through her and leaving ice and dread behind. She thought of the poor child going through that, and her eyes welled up. It wasn't fair. It wasn't right!

How could Tristan let this happen?

Suddenly she was seized by a wild idea. Not far, Tristan had said. So they wouldn't need long. Just a minute or so. Maybe even a few seconds. All they needed was something to distract the wraiths . . .

She wheeled back and launched herself at the door, her body flooded with adrenaline. A few seconds' distraction; that was all they needed. She could give them that.

"Dylan!" Tristan screamed her name, and she heard him moving, felt his fingers scrape down her back as he reached for her, but he was too slow. She was already out the door.

She didn't know where she was going, or where the struggling soul was, so she settled for plummeting straight out in a direct path away from the safe house. Heavy footsteps thumped behind her as Tristan gave chase. She could still hear him calling her name, his voice a mixture of panic and anger. A millisecond later, every sound was blocked out as her ears were filled with growling and hissing. The air around her was thick with movement, and Dylan felt as if she'd been submerged in icy water. Goose bumps erupted down her arms. She kept running, though. If the wraiths were on her, it meant it was working.

Out of the blue, something grabbed her, held her in a pincer, but this grip was much more substantial than anything she'd ever felt from the wraiths. It was warm, too. Dylan realized what it was a second before she heard Tristan yelling furiously in her ear.

"What the hell are you doing, Dylan?"

She ignored him, fighting when he tried to wrestle her backward. Instead her eyes scanned the dark uselessly.

"Are they still here? Can you see them?"

"Dylan!" Tristan was much too strong for her. He forced her

back a step at a time as she continued to struggle against him. "Dylan, stop it!"

It was hard to distinguish what was coming from the wraiths and what was Tristan, but Dylan felt as if she was being attacked from all sides. Her face stung, clumps of her hair were being ripped from her scalp, and she couldn't breathe, as Tristan's arms were painfully tight around her middle. She stumbled, one foot catching on Tristan's leg, and felt her weight dropping down to the ground. The wraiths cackled in delight, and for the first time Dylan realized what she was doing, what she was risking.

Her life. Her time with Tristan.

How long had she been out here? A minute? Maybe a few seconds more? That would have to be enough. Abruptly she allowed Tristan to drag her back toward the safe house and the burning light of the fire.

FOR THE SECOND TIME, TRISTAN SLAMMED THE DOOR CLOSED. He leaned back against its weight, gasping, trying to quell the panic that was sending his pulse out of control. Dylan had stumbled to the middle of the room, and he could feel her eyes on him. He kept his gaze straight ahead, trying to rein in his anger.

"Did they make it?" she asked quietly.

"What?" He whipped his head round and glared at her.

"The toddler and her ferryman. Did they make it? I thought . . . I thought if I created a distraction . . ."

Tristan gaped at her. "Is *that* what you were doing? Sacrificing yourself for a complete stranger?" His voice rose in pitch and volume. "Dylan!" Words seemed to fail him, and he lapsed into silence.

"Did they make it?" she repeated, her soft tone a gentle rebuke.

"Yes," he hissed through clenched teeth.

A timid smile crossed Dylan's lips. The gesture only aggravated Tristan further. Their survival would be justification to her—proof that she had done the right thing. He gritted his teeth.

"Never, ever do anything like that again!" he ordered. "Do you realize how close you were to being taken?"

Dylan hung her head, finally repentant. "I'm sorry," she whispered, shaking now, more afraid of his anger than she'd been of ceasing to exist. "I just had to do something. I couldn't let someone else be taken, too."

Her eyes blurred with tears before she could see Tristan's expression soften.

TWENTY-NINE

IT SEEMED TO DYLAN THAT TRISTAN'S ANGER WAS SLOW TO fade. He sat in one of the hard-backed chairs in the cottage, his arms folded across his chest, his gaze firmly directed at the fireplace. The one or two tentative stabs she'd made at conversation had been closed down before they could begin, and she'd retreated to the narrow, uncomfortable bed. She lay on her side, her arm the only pillow, and stared at his silhouette.

She wasn't sorry. Some of the guilt she'd been carrying around since she'd caused the poor woman's loss had lifted. She could never bring that soul back, she knew, but at least her presence here had done *something* good. And she hadn't been hurt, hadn't been taken. *So really, Tristan has nothing to be angry about,* she thought.

BUT TRISTAN WASN'T ANGRY. STARING INTO THE PIT OF THE hearth, he couldn't feel the heat of fury, just the cold lead of doubt and uncertainty. He was worried. They were halfway back to the train, had already overcome the most dangerous obstacles, and it hadn't been enough to convince Dylan to stop, to return to the safety of her new life beyond the line. He wondered why he wasn't arguing with her, why he was letting her drag him farther and farther away from where she was supposed to be. The answer was obvious, and it aggravated him even more.

He wanted her to be right.

Weakness, that's what it was. He was weak, giving in to her, letting himself hope that at the end of this journey, they just might get to be together. Weakness. And tonight it had almost gotten her killed. But looking over his shoulder, taking in the way she stared at him, her eyes wide and defiant, her whole body crying out for comfort, he knew he didn't have it in him to tell her no. To take control and force her to follow him. He *could*, he knew. He'd done it before in those early days.

He could—but he wouldn't.

Tristan sighed and stood, shoving the chair aside with his foot. "Is there room on that thing for two?" he asked, wandering over to her and pointing to the rickety bed.

Dylan smiled at him, her expression saturated with relief, before she scooted back to the wall, making just enough space for him to spread out. When he lay down beside her, their bodies touched from head to toe, and he had to grip her waist or risk toppling off. She didn't seem to mind. Her smile widened, and a blush tinged her cheeks.

"I really am sorry about before," she whispered. Then she grimaced slightly and rephrased. "I'm sorry for making you worry."

Tristan smirked. That wasn't the same thing at all. It was probably the only apology he was going to get, though.

"And I won't do it again," she added. "I promise."

"Good," he grunted, and pressed his lips gently against her forehead. "Rest," he murmured. "We've got a long way to go tomorrow."

HE SHIFTED ON THE BED, TURNING TO LIE ON HIS BACK, AND pulled Dylan onto his chest. She nestled her head into his shoulder, smiling to herself. What would Katie say if she saw her now? She wouldn't believe her. If she and Tristan did make it back, that was going to be one hell of a chat. Then after that, at school. She tried to imagine Tristan sitting beside her in class, writing an essay, watching the paper airplanes fly overhead. What would he think about the students at Kaithshall? Dylan could picture his horrified face. She laughed quietly but refused to explain to Tristan when he lifted his head to eye her curiously.

~~~~~

In the morning, a thin veil of mist hovered over the wasteland, hiding the highest of the peaks from view. Tristan didn't comment on it but pulled the long sleeves of his sweatshirt down to cover his arms. Then he looked at Dylan. Her T-shirt and blue top were thin and ripped in places. They wouldn't offer much protection against the bite of the cold morning air.

"Here," he said, sliding his arms out of the sleeves. "Wear this."

"Are you sure?" Dylan asked, but she was already reaching for it. Gratefully, she yanked the heavy fabric over her head, pulling the arms down until they covered her hands entirely. "Ooh, that's better," she said, shivering a little as she felt the warmth from his body heat against her skin.

Tristan grinned at her, his eyes raking up and down her body. She smiled back impishly, knowing she probably looked like she was swimming in the sweatshirt. It was ridiculously big for her, but it was cozy, and as she dipped her chin down to warm her nose against the collar, she realized it smelled of Tristan.

"Ready?" he asked.

Dylan eyed the nearest hill, its top still hidden by the low-slung clouds, and nodded morosely.

They walked at a steady pace, climbing throughout the morning. Though the swirling fog retreated farther up into the sky, it didn't completely dissipate, and so the day stayed cold. Despite Dylan telling Tristan she would take the lead, he forged a path for them. He had to—Dylan had no idea which way to go. She tried to remember making this journey the first time, marching in the opposite direction. Had she known yet that she was dead?

She was surprised when her eyes picked out something familiar, something she *did* recognize.

"Oh!" she exclaimed, stopping suddenly.

Tristan walked on two more paces, then halted, looking back at her curiously. "What?"

"I know this place," she said. "I remember."

A meadow. Filled with lush green grass and dotted with wildflowers in purples, yellows, and reds. A thin dirt path wound elegantly through the heart of it.

"We're nearly at the safe house," she said. And sure enough, as soon as the words were out of her mouth, she lifted her head and there, just beyond the pasture, was the cabin. The little wooden cabin where she'd learned why she had been the only one to crawl her way out of the train carriage.

Though the sun was hidden, the light was still strong, and for once they didn't have to rush. Instead Tristan seemed content to amble along, his fingers wrapped tightly around Dylan's. The path was really too narrow for two people to walk abreast, but as their legs gently brushed against the wildflowers, delicate scents bloomed up to perfume the air. It was picture-perfect, like a dream.

That thought nudged something at the back of Dylan's memory. Another dream, walking hand in hand with a handsome stranger. The last dream she'd had before she died. The setting was wrong: the heavy dampness of the forest replaced by the tranquil beauty of the meadow, but the feeling, the sense of happiness, of completeness, was the same. And though the man in the dream had never really had a face, Dylan knew instinctively that it had been Tristan. Had her mind had some inkling that all of this was going to unfold? That it was meant to be? Destiny? It seemed impossible, but still . . .

"You know, I have a theory," she said quietly, not wanting to disturb the peace of the moment.

"Go on," Tristan encouraged, just a hint of wariness in his tone.

"About what happened when I crossed the line."

"Uh-huh," he prompted.

"Well, I think . . ." She clasped Tristan's hand a little tighter. "I think I stayed in the wasteland because that's where I was meant to be."

"You're not meant to be here," he replied very quickly.

"No, I know that." She smiled at him, refusing to be put off by the frown on his face. "But I think I was meant to be with you."

Silence.

Dylan didn't look at Tristan again to gauge his reaction, but stared around her, drinking in the beauty of the scene. She was right; she knew it. And with that certainty came an inner peace, a contentedness. She suddenly felt at home here, a place where she had no right to be.

"You know, it'll be funny," she mused, speaking to cover Tristan's continued silence, not wanting to hear him tell her she was wrong.

"What will?" he murmured. He dropped her hand but lifted an arm to wrap it round her shoulders, fingers playing with a rogue lock of her hair.

Dylan found it hard to concentrate over the chills that ran across her skin and raised the hairs on the back of her neck, but Tristan turned his face to hers, waiting for an answer.

"Being normal again," she said. "You know, eating and drinking and sleeping. Talking to people. Going back to my old life, pretending this never happened." Then a thought occurred to her. "I . . . I will remember, won't I?"

Tristan took a moment to answer, then she felt him shrug.

"I don't know," he admitted. "You're trying to do something no one's ever managed before. I don't know what will happen, Dylan."

"*We're* trying to do something no one's ever managed," she corrected.

He didn't say anything, but she saw his lips twitch, a hint of a frown about his brow.

Dylan sighed. Maybe it would be better if she didn't remember. It would be much easier to go back to being a pupil at Kaithshall, a girl who fought with her mother, who had to rub shoulders with the world's worst neighbors. She couldn't imagine herself doing any of those things now.

Maybe it would be better.

Then she realized that there was one thing she needed to remember. She turned her head and caught Tristan watching her. His expression made her wonder if he could read her mind.

"No matter what happens, I will remember you," she whispered. She wasn't sure if she was reassuring him or herself.

Tristan gave her a sad smile. "Hope so," he replied. Then he kissed her, lowering his head and brushing his lips against hers. As he pulled away, she realized he had something in his hand, cupped gently between his thumb and forefinger. A flower, its delicate stem almost bowed with the weight of the vibrant purple petals. "Here." He slipped it into the thick folds of her hair. "It brings out the color of your eyes."

He trailed his fingers down her face as he dropped his hand, and Dylan blushed furiously, her cheeks scarlet. Tristan laughed and grabbed her hand again. With gentle pressure, he urged her a little faster toward the cabin. Just in case.

That night passed far too quickly as far as Dylan was concerned, and yet, at the same time, not quickly enough. She wanted to savor every second with Tristan, but she worried that every time they stopped like this, he would try to find other ways, other arguments, to convince her to turn around. He seemed to be in a good mood, however, laughing and joking, and though Dylan wasn't entirely sure it was genuine, she couldn't help but be swept along. He even convinced her to dance with him, singing a tune—just slightly out of key—since there was no music, barring the distant whistling and wailing of the wraiths.

She was surprised when the light began to change outside, but she immediately started to harass Tristan, eager to get going. He took his time, stamping out the last glowing embers in the grate, brushing up rogue piles of ash with his shoe. Then, even though there was no more reason to delay, he refused outright to let Dylan sweep open the door before the sun peeked over the first of the hills, far out to the east.

"Can we go *now?*" Dylan moaned when at last rays of light poured through the cabin's windows.

"All right, all right!" Tristan replied, but he was smiling at her indulgently, shaking his head at her eagerness. "Used to be I couldn't get *you* moving in the morning. I had to just about drag you out the door."

Dylan grinned at him, remembering how she'd pouted, whined, complained. "I must have made your life a bit of a misery at first."

He laughed. "Misery is too strong a word. Nightmare, per-haps . . ." He winked at her.

"Nightmare!" Dylan left her post by the door to shove jokingly at his arm. "I'm not a nightmare!" Then she turned and looked outside, at the unending hills of the wasteland that waited for her. "It feels easier going this way. Like going downhill." She shrugged, then went back to mock-glower at Tristan. "So get moving!"

Dylan's enthusiasm lasted until about halfway up the first hill. Then the burn set into her calves, and a stitch erupted deep in her left side, stabbing with each gasping breath. Now it was Tristan's turn to push on, and he pretended to not hear her complaints and constant pleas for a break.

"Remember how long it took us to get to the cabin last time?" he barked when her moaning broke through the final layer of his patience. "The wraiths caught us and I almost lost you. We have a long way to go, and this was your idea," he reminded her.

Dylan made a face at the broad width of his shoulders, sticking her tongue out. She wasn't really looking forward to the final safe house, either, because it was a total wreck: no roof, and only one wall still standing tall. It was also the last real obstacle between them and the tunnel, and Dylan knew, she just knew, that Tristan was going to use this as a last chance to talk her out of it.

She wasn't wrong. As soon as they were safely ensconced in the safe "house," the wraiths no more than whispers chasing on their heels, and the fire crackling merrily away, he sat down opposite her and fixed her with a very serious look.

Dylan sighed inwardly but kept the emotion off her face.

"Dylan . . ." Tristan hesitated, chewed on the inside of his cheek. "Dylan, there's something wrong."

She pursed her lips, repressed a growl. "Look, we've already gone through this. You promised you'd give it a go. Tristan, we've come all this way. We can't go back now, not without—"

He held up a hand to halt her in her tracks. "I don't mean that."

"What, then?"

"There's something wrong . . . with me."

"What do you mean?" She stared at him, eyes wide and suddenly nervous. "What's wrong with you?"

"I don't know." He let out a slightly shaky breath.

"Do you feel sick? Are you ill?"

"No . . ."

But he was hesitant, unsure. Ice solidified in Dylan's stomach. "Tristan, I don't understand."

"Look at this," he said softly. He lifted his T-shirt, revealing his abdomen.

At first Dylan was distracted by a thin trail of soft golden hair running downward from his belly button, but she quickly saw what he was talking about.

"When did you get that?" she whispered.

He had a raw red gash running in a jagged line down his right-hand side. The skin around the wound was puffy and inflamed and surrounded by shallower gashes.

"The other day, when the wraiths were attacking you."

Dylan gaped at him silently. She hadn't thought her actions might hurt Tristan, but seeing him wince as he shifted on the seat, he was clearly in pain. How had he managed to hide this from her for a whole two days? Was she so self-absorbed that she hadn't noticed? She felt sick at herself.

"I'm sorry," she murmured. "That's my fault."

He lowered his shirt, hiding the injury from her. "No." He shook his head. "That's not what I'm talking about, Dylan. It's the wound."

She stared at him, not comprehending.

"It's not healing," he explained. "It should have disappeared by now. Even when I was attacked before, it healed within a few days. But now . . . it's like I'm . . . I'm . . ." He grimaced.

Dylan continued to look at him, astonished. Had he been about to say *human*?

"And that's not all," he went on. "When I . . . left you," he said, tripping over the phrase. "When I went to the next soul, to Marie, I didn't change."

"*What?*" Dylan mouthed, but no sound came out.

"I stayed like this, this shape exactly." He paused. "That's never happened before."

For several long moments, there was quiet as Dylan considered his words. "What do you think it means?"

"I don't know," he murmured, keeping a lid firmly on the hope he felt, hope he didn't like admitting to, even to himself. He laughed. "I shouldn't even be here."

"Why not?" Dylan's brow wrinkled with confusion.

He shrugged, like it was obvious. "When I lost Marie, I should have been pulled away, taken to the next soul."

"But . . . but I was there."

"I know." He nodded. "And at first I thought maybe that was why I didn't go, that I had to stay until you were safely delivered again. But maybe that's not right. Maybe I'm . . ." He hesitated, searching for the word. "Maybe I'm broken or something." He grinned at her briefly. "I mean, I really shouldn't be able to go backward like this. It's not right, Dylan."

"Maybe you're not broken," she said slowly. "Maybe you're fixed. Maybe, like you said, maybe when you've done enough, ferried enough souls, you'll be finished."

"That's an awful lot of maybes." He smiled gently at her. "I don't know. I don't know what it means."

Dylan didn't seem to share his uncertainty, his caution. She sat up straighter, her mouth widening into a grin, eyes bright. "Well . . . well, apart from that . . ." She nodded toward Tristan's side, which, she now realized, he was protecting with his right arm. "Everything seems to be working in our favor. Maybe we should just go with it."

"Maybe," he said, but his eyes were doubtful.

THERE WAS A NIGGLING WORRY IN THE BACK OF TRISTAN'S mind. The farther they went back across the wasteland, the worse his injuries seemed to get. Dylan thought she was fighting her way back to life. Tristan couldn't help but wonder if there was something different in store for him.

THIRTY

DESPITE HER ASSURANCES TO TRISTAN, DYLAN WAS NERVOUS about returning to the train tunnel, about trying to climb back into her body. She thought about what Jonas had said, how he'd warned her it'd be exactly as it was when she died. She wished it hadn't been quite so dark in the train carriage. She had no idea how badly she'd been injured, what it was that had ripped her soul from its physical shell. She had no idea how much it was going to hurt when she woke back up.

And finally—worst of all—she was scared that she'd wake up alone. That she'd make it back to the world, to life, only to discover that Tristan had been right: that he couldn't come with her. She didn't know what she'd do if that happened. She could only hope, pray even, that fate would not be so cruel.

It was a big gamble, and her stomach writhed with nausea every time she thought about it, but there was no other choice, no other option. Tristan was absolutely adamant that he couldn't— physically couldn't—go past the line, and he wouldn't let her stay here. Where else was there to go?

Nowhere.

It was a lot to worry about, yet somehow, despite all this, the sun stayed high in the sky through their final day's march, the clouds nowhere in sight. Dylan could think of no other reason for it except that she was with Tristan. Whatever happened, so long as she stayed with him, she could survive; she could cope.

Dylan expected to recognize the end of the journey, to be able to pick out landmarks that would tell her they were almost there, allow the excitement and nerves to percolate. But the last hill was just the same as the one before it, and the one before that, yet suddenly they were standing at its peak, looking down on a set of rusting train tracks.

This was it. This was the place where she'd died. She stared down at the railway line, waiting to feel something. Loss or sadness—pain, even. Instead she just felt the creeping sickness of fear and anxiety, the same nerves she'd been fighting all day. She swallowed it back; she'd already made her decision.

Her hand slid into the pocket of her jeans, fingers stroking the satin-soft petals of the wildflower Tristan had given her. It had wilted since he'd picked it, but she'd refused to throw it away, holding on to it like a talisman. Something to bind her to the wasteland; something to bind her to Tristan. Dylan only hoped it would be enough to keep them together.

She took a deep, steadying breath. "We're here."

She knew she didn't need to say it. Tristan couldn't possibly have missed the train tracks; they were the only thing to look at in the barren landscape.

"We're here," he agreed.

He didn't sound nervous, like she was. Or eager. He sounded

sad. Like he was convinced this wasn't going to work. She didn't let his cynicism faze her; she had enough trouble silencing her own doubts.

"So we just follow the tracks?" she asked.

Tristan nodded.

"OK." She swung her arms back and forth a couple of times, dithering. "OK, let's do it."

Tristan didn't move, and she realized he was waiting for her to take the lead. She took one deep breath, then another. Her feet didn't seem right. They felt leaden, too heavy to lift from the dew-soaked grass. Was that just fear, or was it the wasteland, reluctant to let her go?

"It's going to work," she muttered to the air, too low for Tristan to hear. "We will make it back."

Setting her mouth into a determined line, she trudged forward. One hand gripped Tristan's tightly and, step by step, she dragged him along behind her. He was limping now, one hand permanently fixed to his side. But he'd be all right. If she could just get him through this last little bit—get him back to her world—he'd be all right. She made herself believe it.

They walked down the hill until Dylan was able to step up onto the ties. Then she turned—after locking eyes with Tristan—and began to follow the line. The track curved through the country-side, so at first she couldn't see the tunnel mouth, but then, out of nowhere, there it was. A giant hill stood immovable in their path. The tracks seemed to wind toward it, then disappear: a road to nowhere. The closer they got, though, the larger the dark arch at the base of the hill seemed to grow, until Dylan could clearly see where the train had entered the mountain. Entered, but never left.

A black hole. Gaping and wide, it seemed to call to her. She shivered, the hairs standing up at the back of her neck. *What if, what if, what if?* Doubts whispered ferociously at the back of her head, but she tried to ignore them. She set her chin high in the air and marched forward.

"Dylan." Tristan pulled her to a stop, spun her to face him. "Dylan, this isn't going to work."

"It will—"

"No, it won't. I can't go to your world. I don't belong. I don't belong anywhere but here." He seemed to be pleading with her— half-angry, half-desperate.

Dylan caught her tongue between her teeth, stared at him. For the first time he looked like a sixteen-year-old boy, small and uncertain. Rather than frighten her, however, his uncertainty gave her courage.

"Why did you come, then?" she challenged.

Tristan lifted one shoulder in a half shrug, looking for all the world like an awkward teenager.

"Tristan? Why did you come?"

"Because . . . because . . ." He blew out an exasperated breath. "Because I love you." He dropped his eyes to the ground as he said it, missing the shock and joy that rippled across Dylan's face. A heartbeat later, he pulled his gaze back up. "I want you to be right, Dylan. But you're not."

"You promised me you'd try," she reminded him. "Have faith."

He huffed out a dark laugh at that. "Do you?"

"I have hope." She blushed. "And love." Dylan gazed at him, green eyes scorching. "Trust me."

She had come a long, long way for this chance, and she wasn't going back now. Not without at least trying. Besides, they couldn't stay here. Tristan was hurt. Whatever had happened to him, the wasteland was *hurting* him now. This wasn't where he belonged. He needed to get out. Dylan told herself that and tried not to listen to the whispering voice at the back of her head that said his injuries, his agonies, were happening because she was trying to *make* him leave the wasteland. Squaring her shoulders, she headed into the dark. Tristan had no choice but to follow; she refused to let go of his hand.

The lack of light was disorienting at first, and their footsteps echoed off the closed-in walls. The air smelled of damp. Dylan shivered.

"Are there wraiths in here?" she whispered. The air was silent, but surely they would lurk in such a damp, desolate place.

"No," Tristan replied. "They don't usually come this close to your world. We're safe."

That was small comfort, but it wasn't enough to chase away the chill that was raising goose bumps on Dylan's arms and making her teeth chatter.

"Can you see anything?" she asked, not liking the silence. "Are we nearly at the train?"

"Almost," Tristan said. "It's dead ahead. Just a few yards."

Dylan slowed. It was so dark that she could barely see her hand in front of her face, and she didn't want to bang into the bumper at the front of the train.

"Stop," Tristan barked. She complied at once. "Reach out. You're there."

Dylan felt with her fingertips. Just before she reached full stretch, her hand came into contact with something cold and hard. The train.

"Help me find the door," she ordered.

Tristan gripped her by the elbow and guided her along several feet.

"Here," he said, taking her hand and placing it in midair, just at the height of her shoulder. Dylan scrabbled around and felt the texture of dirt and rubber under her fingers. The tread on the floor of the open door. It was high up, she realized. They were going to have to climb.

"Ready?" she asked. There was no response, but she could still feel his hand on her arm. "Tristan?"

"Ready," he whispered back.

Dylan moved closer, preparing to clamber up. Her fingers peeled Tristan's hand from her elbow and curled it into her palm. She was taking no chances; she wasn't letting go of him. It didn't matter how awkward it was. She was not going to be tricked again.

"Wait." He tugged at her, pulled with enough pressure to turn her to face him. Tristan's other arm snaked round her waist, and he drew her closer. The tunnel floor was uneven and so, for once, his face was level with hers. She felt his breath tickling her cheek. "Look, I . . ." he started, and then fell quiet. She heard him take a deep breath, then another. He gripped her chin, lifted it a fraction. "Just in case," he whispered.

Tristan kissed her like he was saying goodbye. His mouth pressed hungrily against hers, and he squeezed her so tight it was hard to breathe. Letting go of her face, he slid his fingers into her hair, pulling her closer still. Dylan screwed her eyes shut and tried to fight the tears that sprang forth.

It wasn't goodbye; it wasn't. This was not going to be the last time she felt the heat of his embrace, smelled him, held on to him. It wasn't.

They were going to share a million other kisses just like this.

"Ready?" she asked again, breathlessly this time.

"No," Tristan whispered back in the dark. His voice was husky; he sounded almost frightened.

Dylan felt her stomach twist. "Me neither." She tried to grin, but her mouth wouldn't work. She reached blindly for his hand again. She wasn't going to lose him.

Still holding on, she hoisted herself through the half-open doorway and then shuffled round to help Tristan up. It was difficult, and she smacked her hand against the buckled door, making her knuckles throb, but eventually they were standing together in the carriage, breathless.

"Dylan," Tristan murmured, his voice just beside her ear. "I hope you're right."

Dylan smiled into nothingness. She hoped she was, too.

"I don't know how we do this," she said quietly. "I think we have to find me. I was somewhere in the middle."

Cautiously, she edged forward. The carriage was silent, but her pulse was roaring in her ears, so loud she could barely hear the sound of Tristan breathing just a step behind her. Her stomach was squirming. What if this didn't work? What if her body was battered and broken beyond repair?

And what was lying on the ground between her soul and her

body? What were they going to have to crawl over? Blood? Body parts? That awful woman's bags? Dylan laughed at that, a tense bark. She turned to share the joke with Tristan and felt her sneaker swivel much too easily. Something was slick under her shoe. And it wasn't spilled juice, she was sure of that. Disgusted, she tried to yank her foot up, but something caught her heel. Off-balance, she shuffled with her other foot, but there was something in the way. Her weight tilted back, leaning precariously, then tipping just a bit too far.

Dylan had time for just one, quick intake of breath, then she was falling. She reached out, desperate to stop herself from tumbling down to the graveyard floor. Reached out with two hands. Two empty hands.

THIRTY-ONE

SCREAMING.

There should be silence. Tranquil, deathly, solemn silence.

But there was only screaming.

Dylan opened her eyes and was instantly blinded. Brilliant white light pierced her brain. She tried to twist away, but the light followed her, moving a fraction of a second later, then eclipsing the darkness behind. She gaped at it, stunned.

Just as suddenly as it had come, the brightness disappeared. Dylan was left staggered, blinking away dancing spots of color. She started as a face dropped into her vision. Filled it. It was pale, coated in a sheen of sweat and smeared with inky red. A man, stubble bristling around his mouth, his lips moving urgently. Dylan tried to focus on what he was saying, but there was a high-pitched ringing in her ears, and she could hear nothing else.

She shook her head, forced her mind to concentrate on the man's lips. Slowly she grasped that he was repeating the same phrase, over and over.

"Can you hear me? Look at me. Can you hear me? Can you hear me?"

Now that she knew what he was saying, Dylan realized that she *could* hear him. In fact, he was shouting, his voice hoarse and strained. How had she not heard him before?

"Yes," she mumbled, spitting through a mouth filled with liquid too hot, too thick to be saliva. She swallowed, tasting metal on her tongue.

The man looked relieved. He flashed the little penlight across her face again for a moment, causing her to screw up her eyes against the assault of white, then ran it down the length of her body. Dylan watched him train it on her legs, his expression anxious. He looked back up at her.

"Can you move your arms and legs? Can you feel that?"

Dylan concentrated. What could she feel?

Red fire. Pain. Agony. Torture. She stopped breathing, frightened even of the tiny movement of her rising chest. What was wrong with her?

Everything hurt. Just . . . everything. Her head was throbbing, her ribs clasped in a grip of iron that was squeezing far too tight. Where her stomach should be was a pool of molten lava, burning like acid. And below that? She shut her eyes, tried to feel her legs. Were they there? Maybe she just couldn't feel them because of the waves of excruciating pain coming from everywhere else. Panicking, she felt her heart start to pound, and every ache around her body throbbed with its furious beats. She tried to move her feet, to shift position; she was so uncomfortable.

"Mww!" It was somewhere between a gasp and a whimper.

She'd only moved her legs a tiny bit, an inch maybe, but the explosion of agony that jolted through her had been enough to take her breath away.

"OK, OK, love?" The man was frowning, the penlight clenched between his teeth, hands moving somewhere below Dylan's waist. He stopped whatever he was doing and wiped his hand on his jacket.

Was that blood? Blood from where he'd been touching her legs? Ragged gasps started hissing between her lips, each breath stabbing at her lungs.

"Love?" The man was gripping her shoulder, shaking it. Dylan made herself look at him, tried to think through the terror. "What's your name?"

"Dylan," she whimpered.

"Dylan, I have to go away. Just for a minute. But I'll be right back, I promise."

He smiled at her, then stood up and began to jink his way down the carriage. As Dylan watched him go, she realized the thin coach was crowded with men and women in jackets: firefighters, police, paramedics. Most of them were hunkered over seats or in new-made gaps, talking, treating, comforting—their faces grim.

Only Dylan seemed to be alone.

"Wait," she croaked, far too late. She raised her hand, reaching in the direction he had disappeared, but the small effort exhausted her. She let her arm fold in half, dropping her hand to her face. It was wet. Drawing her hand back, she stared at it, glistening in the artificial brightness of flashlights and emergency lighting.

What had happened? Where was Tristan?

She remembered falling—bracing herself, arms stretched out—her only thought not tumbling down to lie with the bodies on the ground.

She'd let go of him. She'd let go of him to save herself, to keep her face out of the blood, the debris of death.

She'd let go of him.

Dylan's lungs were aching, but she couldn't stop herself from gasping and retching. Her eyes stung and her throat constricted painfully. Whatever injuries she had dulled mercifully into the background, and tears coursed down her face.

She'd let go of him.

"No," she hissed through chapped lips. "No, no, no."

Frantically, she shuffled position on the floor and thrust her hand into her pocket, ignoring the searing pain every movement triggered, her fingers desperately searching. Her heart stopped for a painful moment.

It was there. The flower. If that had made it through . . . where was he? Why wasn't he lying beside her?

Had she lost him when she'd let go of his hand?

"Right, this is her. Dylan?" Her name distracted her for a moment. "Dylan, we're going to slide you onto this board, love. All right? We need to get you to an ambulance. We'll give you something for the pain. Can you understand me? Dylan, nod if you can understand me, sweetheart."

She nodded obediently. She understood. An ambulance. Painkillers would be good—they'd help put out the fire burning in her belly. But they wouldn't do anything for the gaping hole in her chest, the agony of being so empty. What had she done?

It took the men a while to get her loaded onto the ugly yellow stretcher. A high plastic collar was fixed round her neck, forcing her to stare up at the ceiling. The men were gentle, reassuring her constantly, worried about hurting her further. Dylan hardly heard them. It was all she could do to answer their questions, to squeeze yes and no through her lips. She was glad when they started to lift her, when she didn't have to listen and didn't have to talk anymore.

Getting her out of the carriage seemed to take a long time, but once she heard their feet crunching against the stones of the tunnel floor, she felt them moving along at a brisk walk. They seemed eager to get her outside as quickly as possible. Dylan couldn't quite find it within herself to be alarmed by this fact.

The air changed as she was bumped and jostled headfirst along the tunnel. Wisps of breeze broke through the stagnant dampness, and a fine mist of raindrops caught in her tangled bangs, cooled the fiery heat of her forehead. Dylan tried to look behind, to see how close she was to the tunnel mouth, but the neck brace and the straps around her shoulders meant she couldn't move much at all, and rolling her eyes up and back sent stabbing pains shooting around her skull. Still, she glimpsed a blurry halo of natural brightness before she had to collapse back down onto the bed of the stretcher, panting from the tiny exertion. She was almost out.

Shuffling backward, a careful step at a time, the two men eased Dylan into the murky gray of an autumn evening. She watched the stone archway, cut elegantly into the side of the hill, spit her out and then slowly recede, the gaping chasm reduced to quiet black. About ten yards away from the tunnel entrance, they turned her and began the lurching journey up the steep embankment. That was when she saw him.

He was sitting to the left of the tunnel entrance, his hands wrapped around his knees, and he was staring at her. From this far away, all that she could tell was that he was a boy, probably a teenager, with sandy hair that was being tossed around by the wind and whipping all around his face.

"Tristan," she whispered. Relief and joy swelled in her chest. She drank in the sight of him, here, in her world.

He'd made it.

Someone stepped in between them, cutting him off from her. A firefighter. Dylan watched as he stooped down and wrapped a blanket around Tristan's shoulders. He said something to him, a question. She watched Tristan shake his head. Slowly, slightly awkwardly, he levered himself up from the grass. Saying a final word to the firefighter, he started shuffling in her direction. Just before he reached her side, he smiled.

"Hi," he murmured, stretching out a hand to gently stroke the blanket that covered her. Trailing his fingers down her side, he grasped her hand.

"Hi," she murmured back. Her lips twitched, a trembling smile. "You're here."

"I'm here."

ACKNOWLEDGMENTS

A huge and heartfelt thank-you to the following people who have made *Ferryman* come to life:

To my husband, Chris, for believing in me and being my official "critic." I love you. I am eternally grateful to Clare and Ruth for reading everything so quickly and for telling me that you loved it! Love and thanks to my parents, Cate and John, for supporting me and teaching me to love stories.

To Ben Illis, my agent, for holding my hand and shouting my praises. Thanks also to Helen Boyle and all at Templar for having faith in *Ferryman* and helping me mold it into something so much more than I could have ever achieved alone.

If you're from the 'Gow and you're reading this—hello, and I miss you. Be good (and don't forget to tuck your chairs in!). Thank you for teaching me how to take others into the world of make-believe.

And finally, thanks to Dylan and Tristan for appearing in my head and insisting that I write them down.

READ AN EXCERPT FROM

TRESPASSERS

BOOK 2 IN THE FERRYMAN SERIES

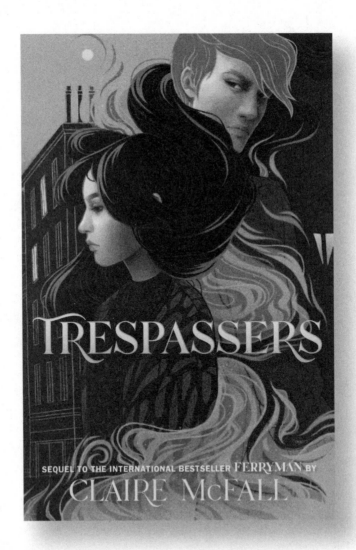

PROLOGUE

HE JUST . . . HE JUST VANISHED.

Susanna sat on the damp grass on the side of the hill and contemplated the tunnel mouth where the ferryman who called himself Tristan had disappeared. She had no right to be there, she knew, lingering, holding off her next soul—but she'd seen him going the wrong way.

Toward the world of the living—him and his soul. And vanishing.

There was only one possible explanation, but that was the thing: it was impossible. She'd sat here for a long time—though time was all relative in the wasteland—and hadn't been able to come up with any other answer except the one that sent equal bolts of fear and excitement coursing through her veins.

Somehow, Tristan had found a door to the world of the living.

Somehow, he'd gone through it.

He was a ferryman just like her, and he'd left his post. The pull of Susanna's next soul, her next job, scraped painfully against her every nerve ending, but she couldn't make herself move from the spot. She couldn't stop seeing Tristan's broad shoulders, his mop of sandy hair, being swallowed up by the darkness as he walked right out of the wasteland.

ONE

DYLAN FLOATED IN A WARM HAZE. EYES CLOSED, SHE LAY FLAT on her back, thick cushioning underneath her and soft covers tucked up almost to her chin. She was comfortable, she was cozy, and she wanted to stay that way.

Unfortunately, there were several voices nearby intruding on her peace, and one of them, at least, wasn't going to be ignored for long.

"Who, exactly, are you, young man?" Joan's words were frosted with ice. Dylan knew that tone, knew it intimately. She'd been on the receiving end of it more times than she could count. What she'd never noticed before, though, was the undertone of anxiety and fear that sharpened its edge.

"I'm with Dylan."

At the second voice, Dylan's eyes snapped open. She couldn't help it. She'd crossed the wasteland for that rich timbre, faced beings more deadly and terrifying than anything she could have imagined in the world of the living. There was nothing she wouldn't do . . .

Although there was one thing she *couldn't* do. With her neck trapped by an unyielding plastic collar, she wasn't able to twist and see Tristan, check with her own eyes that he was really there. She tried, though, letting the hard material dig into her collarbone and rolling her eyes so far upward that her temples throbbed. But he remained frustratingly just out of sight.

"Are you, indeed?" A pause heavy with suspicion that made Dylan wince. "Funny how I've never heard of you. Doctor, why have you allowed this young man access to my daughter?" Rising volume, rising anger. "She's lying unconscious. He could have done anything!"

Dylan had heard enough. Mortified, she tried to yell, but all that came out was a croaky "Mum!"

Unable to see anything except an ugly white strip light above her head and the circular curtain rail that typically surrounded a hospital bed, she had to wait a couple of seconds for Joan's face to rush into her field of vision.

"Dylan! Are you all right?"

Joan looked like she'd aged a hundred years. Her eyes were bloodshot, and the bags beneath them were streaked with mascara. The tight bun she always kept her hair in was bedraggled, wisps hanging limply round her face. She was wearing her nurse's uniform under a baggy cardigan, and it struck Dylan suddenly that she'd been wearing that when they'd said goodbye—no, when they'd fought instead of saying goodbye—just that morning.

And yet it had been days ago for Dylan. Days of struggling through the wasteland. Without warning, Dylan's eyes filled with tears that spilled hot and fast across her cheeks, disappearing into her hair.

"Mum!" she repeated. Her face scrunched up against the stinging in her eyes, her nose, and her throat.

"It's all right, sweetheart. I'm here." Fingers curled around her right hand, and even though Joan's grip was icy, Dylan felt comforted.

Dylan sniffed and tried to lift her left hand to wipe her cheeks dry, but a tug followed by a sharp pain brought her up short. She flinched, drew in a startled breath, and tried to raise her head, but along with the neck brace, someone had run a strap across her shoulders. She couldn't lift herself more than an inch—and even that hurt.

"Just hold still, baby," Joan crooned. "You're in the hospital. You've had a bad accident and you need to stay very still." She squeezed Dylan's right hand very gently. "You've got an IV drip in your other hand. It's best if you just"—a choked breath—"if you just stay as still as you can, all right?"

No, it isn't all right, Dylan thought. She felt helpless lying there flat on her back. And she couldn't see Tristan.

"That's right, Dylan, just stay flat for now," another voice cut in smoothly. A doctor, stethoscope dangling around his neck, leaned into Dylan's vision on the opposite side of the bed from Joan. He looked as tired as she did, but he smiled. "We need to examine the extent of your injuries before we start letting you move around. You may have a spinal injury, so we have to be very careful."

Sudden panic as a memory from the train flooded Dylan's mind.

"My legs?" she whispered.

She remembered the agony of lying buried under the debris from the crash, the feeling of fire that had ripped through her legs with every breath, every shift of her weight. Now there was . . . nothing. A sea of numbness. She tried to wiggle her toes, but it was impossible to tell if they were moving.

"They're still there." The doctor held up both hands in a calming gesture, that same smile fixed on his face. Dylan wondered if he looked like that even when he was giving really bad news. Suddenly it wasn't comforting anymore.

He dropped one hand down, resting it on the covers. Dylan couldn't tell if he was touching her or not; if he was, she couldn't feel it.

"I don't . . . I can't . . ."

"Relax, Dylan." An impossible order to follow. "There's no reason for alarm. You're on a high dose of painkillers, and we had to heavily bandage you because you have some deep lacerations. That's why you don't have much feeling, all right?"

Dylan stared at the doctor for a moment, weighing the truth of his words, then allowed herself to breathe.

"I'll come back in a few minutes when you're taken for X-rays," the doctor added. He smiled and backed out of their curtained section.

"Mum." Dylan swallowed and then coughed a bit. Her throat felt like sandpaper.

"Here." Joan thrust a plastic cup in her direction, the straw just an inch from her lips. Greedily Dylan sucked down the water, although Joan took it away before she was anywhere near satisfied. "That's enough for now."

"Mum," she repeated, a little more strongly. She tried once more, unsuccessfully, to raise her head. "Where's Tristan?"

Joan's lips thinned. She turned her head away slightly, as if she were turning her nose up at some unpleasant smell, and panic coiled heavy and cold in Dylan's chest.

"I thought I heard—" Dylan struggled against the confines of the bed, did her best to wrestle with the restraints holding her down. "Where—"

"I'm here." Better than just his voice, Tristan's face slid into view on the other side of the bed, as far as possible from Joan— which was a good choice because she was glowering at him with unconcealed suspicion and anger.

Tristan. Relief and joy flowed through Dylan like a river. He was here. He'd made it.

They both had.

Tristan went to reach for Dylan's hand, the one with the IV needle thrust uncomfortably into her vein, but a sharp noise from Joan stopped him short. Needing his touch, Dylan ignored the discomfort that tugged repulsively every time she shifted her hand and covered the remaining distance, wrapping her fingers around his.

He squeezed tight and it hurt, but Dylan smiled at him.

"You're here," she whispered.

Then it slammed into her—the memory of saying those exact same words, lying flat on a gurney as two paramedics carried her from the wreckage of the train. The feeling of seeing him there, in the world, alive and solid and real, after thinking that she'd lost him. After thinking that she'd let go of his hand and left him behind. Fresh tears fell down her face.

"You see! You see!" Joan reached across and tried to slap Tristan's hand away, but the waist-high railings and the width of the bed prevented her. "You're upsetting her! Let her go!"

"No! Mum." Dylan tightened her grip on Tristan and used her free hand to bat Joan's arm away. "Stop it."

"Clearly you've bewitched her," Joan spat. "And now here you are, confusing her when she's vulnerable and doesn't know which way is up!"

"Mum!"

Joan totally ignored Dylan, her focus fixed on Tristan.

"I want you to leave," she said firmly. Then she shifted her gaze to beyond the curtain. "Doctor? I want him out. He isn't family, he has no right to be here."

"Nurse McKenzie," the doctor began, leaning in through the curtain, but Joan ranted right over the top of him.

"No. I know the rules. I've worked here for eight years. I don't know who let that young man in, but—"

"Don't go." Dylan was only concentrating on Tristan. He, too, was ignoring her mum, his hand still folded tightly around hers, his piercing blue gaze fixed on her face like he was trying to memorize her features. "Don't leave me."

He squeezed a hair's breadth tighter, causing a jolt of pain to streak across the top of Dylan's hand, and shook his head imperceptibly.

"I'm not going anywhere," he promised.

Joan was still raving at the doctor, but with Tristan gazing down at her, Dylan tuned her mum out completely.

"I still can't believe you're here," she told him.

"Where else would I be?" He gave her a crooked smile, a puzzled line forming between his eyes.

"You know what I mean." Each time Dylan blinked, she expected Tristan to disappear. To be pulled back into the wasteland, called back to his never-ending duty. It didn't seem real that he could've broken his bond of servitude so easily.

"We're meant to be together," Tristan told her, sliding even closer. "Wherever you are, that's where I'll be."

"Good." Dylan smiled at him, hoping against hope that it would somehow be as easy as he said. She looked over to where Joan stood, hands on hips, face screwed up in anger.

"Mum."

No response from Joan.

"Mum!"

Still no reaction.

"Joan!"

That did it.

Joan turned on her, ready for battle as usual. "Dylan—"

"I want Tristan to stay." Dylan wasn't as stupid as the doctor—she had no intention of letting Joan get started on her. "If he can't be here, then I don't want you to be, either."

Joan reared back as if she'd slapped her. "I am your mother, Dylan."

"I don't care." Not the truth: Joan's hurt expression brought a hard lump to Dylan's throat, but she pushed on regardless. "I want Tristan."

"Well." For once Joan seemed to be at a loss for words. She blinked furiously, and Dylan was horrified to realize she was near tears. She'd never seen her mum cry, not ever. Seeing it now made snakes writhe in her belly. She fought hard not to back down.

At that moment two orderlies trundled in, oblivious to the tense scene.

"One for the X-ray Department?"

There was a moment's pause before the doctor seemed to come back to himself.

"That's right," he said, now looking thankful for the timely reprieve. "Dylan here." He waved unnecessarily in Dylan's direction.

The orderlies shuffled around, unlocked her hospital bed's brakes, and wheeled her out, IV pole and all.

It was both a worry and a relief leaving Tristan and Joan behind. What would Joan say without Dylan there to act as a buffer? Would she have Tristan thrown out of the hospital? Arrested? One of the orderlies noticed her worried glance and attempted to reassure her.

"Not going far, love, the X-ray Department is just round the corner here."

It wasn't enough to calm her. The farther she went from him, the more sick and sore she felt. What if he wasn't there when she got back?

No. He wouldn't leave her. He'd promised.

~~~~~

Time passed slowly. She was X-rayed. The technician was brusque and efficient, and the radiographer didn't even speak to her. Dylan didn't mind, as she was focusing all her energy on not throwing up. The pain in her legs was excruciating—she couldn't wait to get some more painkillers when she was back in her room.

Bizarrely, the trip back through the corridors actually helped, and both her legs and her stomach felt better when the orderlies settled her back in place.

Joan was there, pacing like a tiger, and much to Dylan's relief,

Tristan was, too. He was slumped in a metal chair, looking strangely pale. Joan must have given him hell in her absence. Their eyes met. and Tristan held hers with an intensity that revealed his concern.

At least Joan hadn't managed to drive him away.

"Are you all right? Did the doctor say anything?" Joan went straight over to the side of the bed, crowding in on Dylan before Tristan could get up from his chair.

"I didn't speak to a doctor," Dylan answered. "It was the radiographer, but he didn't tell me anything."

"Of course." Joan shook her head at her own foolishness. This was her hospital, Dylan thought. She must know how things were run. "Maybe I'll . . ." Joan craned her neck, her eyes fixed beyond the door of the room, and Dylan could tell she was thinking about going to find the doctor, harassing him until he put Dylan at the top of his list. But then Joan's eyes drifted back to Tristan. "We'll just wait, shall we? Won't be long."

Dylan tried to keep the disappointment from her face. She wanted to know what was wrong with her legs, but mostly she wanted Joan out of the room for a few minutes so that she could speak to Tristan. Privately. It still didn't feel real to see him here, in a hospital room, rather than striding confidently through the meadows and mountains of the wasteland.

Nobody said much as they waited. Joan fussed over Dylan's water, plumped her pillows, and tried to detangle her hair until Dylan snapped at her to leave her be. It felt like a lifetime before the doctor finally, *finally* made an appearance. It was the same one from earlier, looking haggard and harassed.

Joan got straight to the point. "Do you have the results, Dr. Hammond?"

He grimaced before smoothing his face back into a professional, reassuring mask. "Well, I've spoken to the radiologist and it's as we thought," he said. "The right leg's broken."

"Is it a clean break?" Joan asked.

There was an ugly pause. Dylan felt a curl of dread in her stomach—that obviously meant no.

"There are multiple breaks, Nurse McKenzie. We're going to have to pin it and insert a brace while it heals."

"An operation," Joan whispered, the blood seeping out of her cheeks.

"Mum?" Dylan whimpered, panic forming at Joan's reaction.

"It's all right." Joan was back at Dylan's bedside in a heartbeat, a smile on her face, though it was strained. "It's only a small one."

"A very routine procedure, Dylan," the doctor continued. "You'll be fine. Although there are further complications . . ."

"Doctor?" Joan prodded.

"There's also a very fine fracture on your left leg, Dylan. It's not significant enough to need a cast, but you're going to have to keep your weight off it while it heals, too."

"Both legs!" Dylan said, a shudder going through her at the thought.

"It'll be fine." Joan squeezed her shoulder in reassurance. "I'll be there to help you."

"Tristan," Dylan said. At the edge of her vision she saw him stand, but her focus stayed on Joan. "Tristan will help me, too. He can stay with us."

"No!" Joan's response was a bark.

Dr. Hammond cleared his throat, clearly keen to extract himself from this discussion. "I'll pop back in a while, once I know when we can slot you in for the operation." He slid out as Joan rounded her attention back on Dylan.

"I'm not having *him* in our house. He's—" Dylan narrowed her eyes as Joan visibly collected herself. "We don't need him," she finished with deliberate calm.

Tristan approached the bed but stood on the opposite side from Joan. "I would like to help," he said evenly. His calm tone and relaxed posture were belied by his white-knuckled grip on the bed railings. Dylan reached out and tugged one hand free, folding her fingers around his.

"No," Joan repeated. "The two of us will be just fine. I'll take some time off work and—"

"Dylan's recovery is going to take weeks, Ms. McKenzie," Tristan interjected quietly. "Likely months."

A tense moment passed as Joan clenched her teeth, and Dylan fought to keep the victorious expression from her face. There was no way Joan would be able to take that much time off. Even if the hospital allowed the absence, she knew they couldn't afford to lose Joan's wages.

"Plus, Mum, we live on the second floor of an apartment building. You're not exactly strong enough to carry me up and down two flights of stairs!" Dylan squeezed Tristan's hand, sensing the inevitable.

After several long, angry seconds of silence, Joan turned to Tristan and spat her words out: "You sleep on the couch. Understand?"

ABOUT THE AUTHOR

CLAIRE McFALL is a former English teacher. *Ferryman*, her debut novel, won the Scottish Children's Book Award and was long-listed for both the Branford Boase Award and the Carnegie Medal. She is also the author of *Black Cairn Point*, published in the US as *The Last Witness*, which won the inaugural Scottish Teenage Book Prize. Claire McFall is from Scotland and now lives in Colorado.